The Blueb

THE BLUEBEARD CLUB

THE BLUEBEARD CLUB

JACK MURRAY

Books by Jack Murray

Kit Aston Series
The Affair of the Christmas Card Killer
The Chess Board Murders
The Phantom
The Frisco Falcon
The Medium Murders
The Bluebeard Club
The French Diplomat Affair (novella)
Haymaker's Last Fight (novelette)

Agatha Aston Series
Black-Eyed Nick
The Witchfinder General Murders

DI Nick Jellicoe Series
A Time to Kill
The Bus Stop

Jackmurray99@hotmail.com

ISBN: 9798479052545
Imprint: Independently published

Cover by Jack Murray after J.C. Leyendecker

For Monica, Lavinia, Anne, and Baby Edward

Prologue

Paris, France: Sept 1888

It could have been anywhere in the world. A sunny afternoon: two young people, sitting on a wall, watching the world go by. Like young people the world over, all their senses were directed, focused, and heightened by the prospect, the sight, and the smell of romance in the air. Real life theatre and they had front row seats.

One of them, a young man nearly out of his teens, smiled pleasantly and nodded as the women passed by. Gallantly, he distributed this attention to all that passed. Many young women smiled back. Even some of the older ones, pleasantly surprised, perhaps, that someone should be so bold. Others were less enamoured. A scowl followed by a quickened step. This made the young man laugh. It was as if he gained as much pleasure from these failures as his successes. He didn't care. It was a beautiful day; he was in the most beautiful and romantic city in the world. Life was, by any standard applied, rather good.

The other was younger and more timid; happy to sit in the shadows wanting to stop the torrent of shameless 'bonjours'. Yet to say something would only have brought a certain shame. Nothing was said. As usual.

'I don't know how you do it, Henri.'

Henri turned to his friend and grinned. However, there was pity in the smile and the other looked away, unable to bear the unwanted sympathy.

'What do you mean?' asked Henri, gesturing towards the street.

'I think you know.'

Henri laughed. It was a pleasant laugh, warm like a blanket. Then he shrugged. They were silent for a few moments then Henri spoke.

'You should smile more. You have good teeth. You are very good-looking you know, Pipsqueak.'

Pipsqueak. Unsure of whether to laugh or be angry, the other elected for silence; as ever, caught between what to do, what to think and how to act. Age would bring the wisdom and savoir fair that Henri had. This was the attraction of Henri Landru. Henri was by no means handsome. His teeth were irregular. There was just a hint, even at such a young age, that his hair was beginning to recede. His eyebrows seemed like they were trying to compensate for this. They were dark, forest-like and hung heavy over dark eyes that, when the light caught him in a certain way, made his face look like a cadaver.

Yet women loved him. Well, perhaps loved was putting it too strongly. There was no doubting the attraction, however. Or was it repulsion that compelled them? The prospect of this was too much for Pipsqueak to consider. Perhaps such naivety was a good thing. One could retain a sense of morality.

Henri had no morals. He was more akin to an alley cat than a man. This was not to say he boasted of his success. Far from it. Yet it was clear for all to see. There was a smugness in his smile, a knowingness in his look, a lack of fear in his social contact. Henri's dark eyes were hypnotic. Compelling. They were penetrating and dark; hooded eyes that were transparent in their thoughts. Perhaps this was his secret. The shamelessness with which he looked at women.

'Do you disapprove?' asked Henri, a half-smile traced across his lips.

'You know I don't,' lied Pipsqueak, face reddening. Henri's smile widened. He recognised a lie the way most people recognise a friend. The disingenuous response was dismissed but Henri was, if nothing else, sensitive to his friend's inhibited nature.

'Do you want to know a secret?' asked Henri.

This could mean anything, so Pipsqueak shrugged.

'Women like confidence in men. Men like confidence in women, but not too much. Remember that. You can be funny with them. You can be serious with them. You can be honest with them or lie like an adulterer: it's all the same in the end. You can be as brazen as you wish, or you can even be quiet. But you must do all with confidence. This is the secret to gaining attention. What happens then is still in the hands of the gods of course. But never, on any account, be diffident. You will be dismissed as quickly as a beggar by a rich man. Or worse, you will be pitied. Overcome your fear, my friend, and all the world, not just its beautiful inhabitants, will be yours.'

Henri patted his friend gently on the back. They had been friends since Pipsqueak had been a toddler. Henri was five years senior. An older brother. He was genuinely interested in helping his friend. But he was not beyond using Pipsqueak for his own ends. Yes, he felt no remorse at using his friend in this way. But he wanted to help, too.

'Watch this,' said Henri. Two young women are coming.

'What are you going to do?' asked Pipsqueak, heart sinking.

'I will look at the plainer of the two women in the eye and smile.'

'What?' exclaimed Pipsqueak, unsure whether to laugh or be appalled at such cynicism.

'I mean it. Look, they're almost upon us.'

For some reason, colour flooded Pipsqueak's face. Oh, to be anywhere but here. The two women were but a few yards away. Henri was smiling now, looking away from the women.

Then he looked up.

He fixed his eyes on the shorter of the two women. She looked at him. He smiled.

She ignored him.

Pipsqueak turned away unable to look at Henri's humiliation. But rather than being crushed, Henri laughed. He laughed loudly enough for the woman that had just ignored him to turn around. If looks could have killed at that moment, Henri Landru would have been a dead young man.

'Look. Two more,' said Henri, enjoying himself immensely. At least one of them was.

Neither of the two women was particularly young, but this did not seem to trouble Henri. Pipsqueak was horrified by the look in Henri's eye. Horrified and something else. This did not bear thinking about. Rather than tell him off, another tactic was called for.

'You're not going to try that again, are you?'

'Why not? The whole point of the exercise is to keep doing it. The only way for you to lose your fear of the opposite sex is if you lose your fear of being rejected by them. And, my friend, this means you will have to face the odd snub, or disapproval occasionally and, very rarely, outright rudeness.'

This was hardly the reassurance a frightened soul needed. But Henri was nothing if not completely convinced.

'Perhaps you can try smiling at those two young men,' said Henri, a twinkle in his eye.

Pipsqueak was about to fire off a riposte to this when Henri spotted a woman walking alone. As she drew closer, he could see she was in in her late thirties. Another generation from Henri but not unattractive. A teenage boy appeared from nowhere and joined the woman. He was about Pipsqueak's age and was, quite simply, the most beautiful looking boy Pipsqueak had ever seen.

Henri started laughing. Pipsqueak knew what was coming. The sun beat down on Pipsqueak's back. It was hot now. The air seemed to evaporate around them. They were being sucked into a vacuum. Beads of sweat formed on Pipsqueak's forehead and began to drip remorselessly down.

'Smile,' whispered Henri, from behind the hand covering his mouth before looking away to the square.

Then the women said something to the boy. She became aware of Henri. True to form, Henri smiled at her. She blushed but she smiled back. The boy looked at Pipsqueak. Then he looked away as he met Pipsqueak's steady gaze. A wave of triumph coursed through Pipsqueak's small body. It worked! It really worked. This was a moment Pipsqueak would never forget. And the boy was beautiful.

Perhaps Henri Landru was right after all.

1

West Coast of Scotland: 5th February 1921

Kit Aston opened his eyes. Slowly. His breathing was laboured. The room was revolving around him. He lay on the floor and knew that death was imminent. He was dimly aware of a bird outside the window, fluttering its wings in an unnecessarily raucous manner. Elsewhere, a worm was excavating in the garden at an hour when most civilised beasts would still be in bed. It was just after ten in the morning.

Kit could still taste the poison in his mouth. The least stiff part of his body was the prosthetic limb that, following the War, made up the lower part of his leg. He didn't know who or what had beaten him up, but they'd made a thoroughly decent job of it.

There was a crash nearby. With an enormous effort of will he moved his eyeballs in the direction the deafening sound had come from. His eyes could just about make out a figure in front of him. Perhaps they were coming to finish off the job. The man was weaving towards him as if on a ship in the middle of storm. He stopped and clutched at a table.

'Kill me,' croaked Kit. His voice had disappeared along with, apparently, his will to live.

The man got down on his knees. In fact, the thump with which he hit the ground suggested that he had fallen. Heavily.

'I mean it,' mumbled Kit. 'Kill me. Use your gun.'

'No bullets,' whispered Charles 'Chubby' Chadderton, his lips pressed against the cold stone of the floor. The effort of replying proved too much, and he promptly lost consciousness.

'Bash me over the head, then. It might distract me from the pain,' breathed Kit, unaware that his friend was no longer capable of listening, never mind undertaking the commission.

Kit's head was thumping like a toddler with a brand-new toy drum. He shut his eyes in the hope that it might, at least, stop him seeing his pain. This ingenious plan was doomed to failure. He wrenched his eyes open once more to find Aldric 'Spunky' Stevens, or what was left of him, half standing, half crumpled against the table. He was looking distinctly green about the gills.

'I need a doctor,' said Kit, pitifully.

Spunky arched his back and turned dramatically in the direction of the faint whisper he'd just heard. For a few moments it was touch and go but his one good eye fixed on the prone figure of his friend.

'Doctor?' asked Spunky in a manner that suggested his brain had momentarily forgotten what the word meant.

'Yes,' repeated Kit with more spirit. 'I need a doctor.'

Spunky turned slowly and Kit followed the direction of his gaze. On the bed, lying inert, was Doctor Richard Bright.

'I think the doctor needs a doctor,' was not the reassuring reply Kit sought from Spunky just then.

Kit shut his eyes and groaned. The events of the previous evening began to replay in his head. It was no comfort to the desolation he was feeling that they brought no credit to either him or his chums. In his one score and ten years, he could not remember drinking so much nor feeling so catastrophically ill afterwards. Even that one occasion in

Russia a week before the Revolution, with Boris and Ludmilla. Or was it, Tatyana?

Through the fog of drink and self-pity a thought was beginning to nag him like an early morning alarm clock. His whisky-addled brain could not fix on what the problem was. An image of a man playing a fiddle swam past him. Then another of the crowded Scottish inn where they had spent several hours in the company of Scottish fishermen drinking like the end of the world was nigh. He wished that it were. The sound of the Scottish ceilidh music filled his mind. The drinking races with the locals. The malted laughter of revelry. He saw it all: Chubby dancing the Gay Gordon. Spunky successfully negotiating a yard of ale. Richard Bright singing 'Garryowen' and finally, making eyes at the landlord's daughter; that young, romantic fool Reggie Pilbream…

Kit sat bolt upright and shouted, 'Reggie!'

-

At that moment, as Kit had correctly surmised, Reggie was not with the rest of the revellers. Reggie was one of those young people for whom life is a perpetual cycle of falling in love, rejection, and accidents. Yet through these travails his optimism never wavered; rather like a spirited Labrador, he kept going undeterred or better informed for the next occasion he faced similar difficulty. Perhaps the only difference with this noble animal was that Reggie was distinctly less intelligent but no less loved for being so.

On the last occasion in which your chronicler had cause to include Reggie in these humble histories, the intrepid archaeologist had fallen into a pit in the bowels of a fortress belonging to Military Order of St John on Malta.

He escaped.

Now his situation was every bit as perilous. At that moment the normally irrepressible Reggie was feeling distinctly unchuffed. Fifty or sixty feet below where he was standing, waves crashed against the rocks with a viciousness that seemed to shake the walls of the cliff. A chill descended on Reggie like a curtain. In fact, the chill may have had something to do with the wind lashing the side of the cliff where he was so precariously perched. The wind ripping into Reggie's face just then had started out as a low-pressure system somewhere in the less charitable areas of the North Sea. It had started blowing on the eastern coast of Scotland a few hours earlier, coinciding with Reggie's own unscheduled arrival at the cliff face. No inkling had been apparent the night before when Reggie, after an epic evening of drinking with his pals, had mentioned in passing an urgent need to relieve another type of high pressure located somewhere in the region of his bladder.

Reggie Pilbream is as heedless of risk as any chap has a right to be. Vertigo was not a word in his limited lexicon. As he stood by the side of the cliff emptying what he had accrued over the course of the evening, he sensed nothing of the potential danger that his greatly diminished sense of balance might bring to such a task.

To give Reggie his due, it was not the effects of the alcohol that brought, quite literally, his downfall. Rather, the spot where he'd chosen to relieve himself was structurally unsound. One moment he was congratulating himself on a job well done; the next his feet, swiftly followed by his body, was sliding arse-over-tit down the side of the cliff towards certain death.

Despite his persistently accident-prone nature, the good Lord had, in perhaps a moment of conscience, provided Reggie with an unusually large number of cat lives. This may have been as much for the entertainment of the residents of Paradise as anything else for it meant that whatever scrape Reggie found himself in, some form of help was always at hand. In this case he managed to grab a piece of scrub which interrupted his progress as he hurtled calamitously towards the rocks fifty feet below. This was, of course, good news. The downside of this serendipitous escape was that he was now trapped on the side of a cliff and, if he was not mistaken, his friends, or to be more precise, his drunken friends, were already on their way back to the cottage they had rented for the weekend.

All of which had occurred some hours ago. At some point he must have passed out because he could see that it was daylight now. This gave him a better view of his situation. And it was grim. Yes, he was well and truly stuck. His head was thumping like a kettle drum, his ankle hurt damnably, and his foot appeared to be wedged under a large rock that had accompanied him on the way down. He wasn't sure if he should touch this rock lest he inadvertently engineer another rock fall.

In short, he concluded, his options were limited, and chances of survival were, even by his high standards, catastrophically lower than usual. Help did not appear to be at hand. However, the spirit of the Pilbreams was not to be discounted so easily. Had not his forefathers fought, and invariably died, at the side of English Kings since the days of Henry V? Like them, he would go down fighting. He glanced down at the waves violently assaulting the innocent rocks below and gulped. Perhaps going down fighting was not such an apt metaphor in this instance. Then inspiration struck. Despite his raging hangover, he needed to alert people to his situation. He would shout for help. There was no dishonour in this. The survival of the Pilbream line was at stake.

Reggie took a deep breath. There was little point in keeping it a secret. He would give his cries the full Pilbream treatment. Lungs suitably filled and ready to give passionate vent to the extent of his peril, he looked up.

And immediately wished he hadn't.

-

'I say,' said Spunky, 'You know Kit has a point. Where is Reggie?'

Just at that moment Richard Bright awoke from the deepest of deep slumbers and said, 'Cliff.' Then he promptly returned to the state of happy catalepsy from which he had briefly emerged.

'Good Lord,' cried Spunky, 'He's not wrong you know.'

Kit's brain was slowly emerging from the swamp of self-pity and torpor. His scrambled senses began to re-assemble at a sluggish pace. Then the full import of Bright's revelation became plain.

'He went to the cliff to…'

'Yes, I remember now,' replied Spunky. 'You don't think he fell?' This last point was added in a tone which suggested disbelief that any accident could have befallen him despite his being utterly pie-eyed.

Kit rose gingerly and, it must be reported, reluctantly to his feet. He gave Chubby a gentle kick but decided against trying to wake Bright. He had suffered particularly badly the previous night during some of the drinking games.

'I don't feel well,' said Chubby, rising to his feet in a matter of minutes. Chubby had the look of a man who was several furlongs behind the leading riders. He gripped the edge of the table for dear life as Kit and Spunky outlined their plan. They were to retrace their footsteps back to the inn, along the cliff overlooking the North Sea.

The plan was faultless in conception. Where else could their unfortunate friend be? The practical execution, however, proved to be an unforeseen challenge. The phrase 'blind leading the blind' could easily have been modified to become, 'the blind drunk leading the blind drunk'.

The three men picked their way up the hill towards the headland where they had last seen their young friend relieving himself of a great weight. The sound of the wind was rising to something like a scream. Its ferocity was not quite at a peak, but it was more than enough to make walking in a straight line particularly tricky given the delicate physical condition they were in and the pummelling they had given their senses over the previous ten hours.

'I don't feel well,' repeated Chubby at various intervals. Paradoxically this suggested he was in better nick than his companions who had not the energy to even admit this. Instead, they focused what was left of their will power on moving one foot on front of the other. The Irish Sea was in sight at last. This was accompanied by the first inkling that the wind would not be their friend.

Spunky reached the edge of the cliff first. He put his hand to his head and staggered back.

'Any sign?' asked Kit hopefully.

'Give me a moment,' replied Spunky before peering over the edge. Kit held him around the waist. How much use this would have been had push come to shove, so to speak, was doubtful. Kit would have been defeated in an arm-wrestling challenge by a kitten just at that moment.

'I don't feel well,' repeated Spunky, approaching blindly the edge of the cliff. He stopped just in time, bent over and promptly offered up a sacrifice to Bacchus.

It was at this moment he heard an anguished, 'I say' from somewhere below. Chubby was approaching six feet five and had all the balance and dexterity of a three-legged giraffe. Thankfully, even in this somewhat diminished state, Chubby was aware of his limitations. He lay down on the ground and peered over the edge. There, twenty feet below him, was Reggie.

'Chaps,' shouted Chubby weakly. 'I've found him.'

Kit and Spunky weaved their way over towards Chubby. They lay on the ground, inched forward to the edge, and peered over. There was no question about it. Reggie was alive if not quite safe and sound. He also appeared to be covered in scraps of food and something semi-liquid.

'I say, Reggie, what on earth is that all over your blazer?' asked Chubby.

And face if Reggie's attempts with a handkerchief were anything to go by.

'Some blasted bird, I think,' said Reggie mournfully.

'More like a Pterodactyl,' remarked Kit. Neither saw Spunky looking away sheepishly.

At this point a conference took place between the four still drunk and heavily hungover men on how to expedite Reggie's rescue. The plan agreed upon called upon them to tie together their overcoats and have Reggie abseil up the side of the cliff. Agreement was not quite unanimous, however.

'I say chaps, are you sure?' appealed Reggie. 'Can't you go and get some help?'

'Nonsense, Reggie,' replied Spunky dismissively. 'Where's your pluck?'

To be fair to Reggie, his doubts were not unreasonable. Even three fully fit, healthy, and sober men would have found this a serious test. However, although Reggie would have fought to his final breath the notion that his friends were anything less than stout, it couldn't be ignored that they were all somewhat the worse for wear; the three of them were, in addition, missing an assortment of limbs and, in Spunky's case, an eye, thanks to the war.

The decision made and the three men took the strain at one end while Reggie prepared to make his ascent. There was just the matter of the large rock his foot was wedged under.

'One moment, chaps. I'm stuck. I need to get my foot from under this boulder.'

No point in downplaying his predicament, thought Reggie. One hand on the arm of the coat-rope that had been thrown, the other on the rock, Reggie bent down to push it away. This is when he lost his balance and began to fall backwards.

'Oh bugg…'

2

Highgate Cemetery, London: 6th February 1921

Mary Cavendish and Lady Agatha stood either side of their friend Betty Simpson. Each put a consoling hand on their friend's arm. Betty, meanwhile, sobbed quietly. She rarely cried. Betty was one of life's optimists. Big-hearted, loyal to a fault and generous of spirit as well as, these days, girth, her irrepressible good nature had made her a friend to many and a sister in all but name to Agatha. It broke Agatha's heart to see her friend so forlorn.

The three women stood before a large, white gravestone. It read:

The Honourable James Barclay Simpson. Born 1848 – Died February 6th, 1914

Beneath his name was a large space that Betty knew, one day, would see hers written. On days such as these she wished for nothing more than to re-join her beloved James. They had been married thirty-seven years with not one cross word uttered between them in all that time. As Agatha often said, they were two peas in a pod. In truth, Agatha did not always mean this as a compliment but nor was it meant to be unkind. She, too, had adored James and recognised from the first day that she'd met him how wonderful a match he and Betty were. Just as 'Useless' had been for her. Eustace 'Useless' Frost. The man she had married; the man she had lost just a couple of years before Betty had lost James. A wave of sadness engulfed her. However, this was Betty's moment. James's anniversary.

After a few minutes. Mary and Agatha left Betty alone with James. They walked away slowly knowing Betty would catch them up in her own good time.

'What was he like?' asked Mary.

'James?' replied Agatha. 'Just like Betty really.'

Agatha added nothing to this, nor did she need to. Mary took her arm and they walked towards the exit. They walked in silence initially. Mary sensed the sadness within Agatha as only women can.

'Will you go to Eustace's grave this year?' she asked after a few minutes.

'Yes. Yes, I think so. It's been too long.'

'You weren't in Monte Carlo last year,' said Mary. It was a statement more than a question.

Agatha looked more of her own self as she turned shrewdly to Mary.

'No, I had guests, if you remember. I certainly wasn't going to leave them on their own.'

'Ahh,' remarked Mary. 'Couldn't be trusted, could they?' She smiled at the memory of when she had first moved in with Kit's aunt. She acted as a chaperone to Mary and her sister, Esther. The first and last defence against any attempt by the men in their lives to take advantage of them before they were married. It was a role that Agatha had taken to with a zeal that would have impressed a Mother Superior.

'Ahh indeed and no, I'd would have trusted a dog with a joint of meat sooner,' said Agatha but there was a twinkle in her eye. 'Anyway, next week you'll be Kit's problem.' There was a faint catch in her voice as she said this. She recovered quickly, though. 'Are you nervous yet?'

Mary seemed surprised by the question and turned to Agatha with a grin, 'No, I can't wait. Were you nervous before you married Eustace?'

They were far enough away from Betty now for Agatha's emotions to become more apparent. Her eyes welled-up but she smiled, nonetheless.

'No. I couldn't wait either. As independent as I was. Am, even. I couldn't wait. He knew me, you see.' Then she stopped herself. Agatha was not a woman to spend much time wallowing in sentiment. She'd always lived in the present, yet even here, Eustace could outflank her defences as he always had. Agatha turned to Mary. 'It pains me to think that nearly fifty years have passed since I was your age, yet young women can still not forge their own path in the world except through marriage.' She shook her head sadly.

'I know,' agreed Mary. Between them lay the unspoken acknowledgement of the paradox of both their lives. Each was limited by the flip of the coin that determined their gender and thus set in stone, to a great degree, their future. Yet, both women had met another who would never stand in their way. Instead, they would march in step by their side.

'I would never say this to his face, of course,' said Agatha, 'But Christopher is exceptional. I say this not because I'm his aunt. Infuriating in his own way, of course. They all are.'

Agatha left the rest unsaid. She felt a squeeze on her arm. Mary understood all too well. They sat down and waited for Betty to join them at the exit gates. A comfortable silence fell between them. Mary thought about Kit once more and the wedding just over a week away. Her stomach felt light. The crisp, fresh February air made her face tingle and she felt she could hear every sound in the cemetery. In fact, the most apparent noise was the crunch of

Betty's footsteps over the gravel path as she marched with purpose, as she usually did, towards them. The smile had returned to her lips once more.

'Where to?' asked Betty.

In such circumstances, when an Englishwoman is feeling particularly sensitive to the slings, arrows, and delights of fate, there really is only one answer.

'Tea?' suggested Mary.

They found a tearoom near the cemetery. Agatha and Betty spent a convivial hour with Mary advising her on the organisation of the upcoming nuptials. They hinted at husband management, too, but that seemed to be a conversation for another time, if Agatha's eyes at Betty were any indication. To Mary's ears it sounded very much that the word husband could have been replaced by the word dog. Training was all important. They had to know who was boss. The part around rewards sounded interesting but Agatha quickly closed off conversation on this topic. There was no mistaking the widening of Betty's smile and a certain faraway look in her eyes.

Agatha and Mary parted with Betty at this point. She was to visit James's family before making her way up to Little Gloston for the wedding. Meanwhile, Mary and Agatha had an appointment with a former employee at Agatha's Grosvenor Square house.

'I must say, I've been rather looking forward to seeing Alfred again,' said Mary. Agatha rolled her eyes a little at this. Mary grinned, 'Oh come now, Aunt Agatha. Admit it. You are a tiny bit curious about moving pictures surely?'

Agatha shrugged nonchalantly. She couldn't wait, either.

-

Alfred Hitchcock viewed the arrival of Mary and Agatha in much the same way as a lion tamer might feel when he steps into the ring to face a fearsome beast accompanied by his beautiful young assistant: a mixture of terror, power, and something altogether more exquisite. He'd spent a few months the previous year in the employ of Agatha as a part-time chauffeur to earn extra money to support his embryonic film career. This had coincided with an adventure where Agatha, Mary and Kit had been involved with the notorious 'Phantom', a famous jewel thief.

'Yes, I want the light to shine particularly brightly through the French window,' ordered Alfred authoritatively, emboldened as he was by the arrival of a fresh bacon sandwich.

It was midday and he could hear his guests arriving. His ears picked up the sound of Agatha ordering an assistant cameraman out of her way. Alfred took a deep breath.

He looked around him and felt his chest swell in pride. Before him, sitting on a table, was the slate used to identify the film stock, the film, scene, and production information. The name of the film was '*Dangerous Lies*'. Although he was only the title designer, the director Paul Powell clearly recognised talent when he saw it. He'd entrusted him with shooting a couple of scenes using stand in actors while the main cast went to Cornwall for two days to shoot exterior scenes for the film.

Alfred liked Powell and not just because he'd been given this opportunity. The American was very experienced; there was much Alfred could learn much from such a man. Powell worked with Mary Pickford on his last film, '*Pollyanna*'. It had been a tremendous success. Yes, this was a chance to learn the trade from a master. Just then he saw his guests appear on the set which, in this case, was the bedroom of a country house. He stood up and smiled nervously. Agatha terrified him but Lady Mary…

'Ah there you are, Alfred,' said Agatha by way of greeting.

Alfred bowed nobly to the two ladies as they approached. This allowed him to swallow the last of the bacon sandwich and give his mouth a surreptitious wipe. He rose and smiled a greeting. His confidence that had been fairly fizzing not five minutes earlier was slowly dissolving along with his bowels when confronted by the old warhorse herself and the delightful Lady Mary.

'Well, Alfred,' began Agatha looking around her, 'This is quite something.'

What 'something' meant in this situation was anybody's guess but the three seemed to be in accord. The film set was rather like a stage, noted Mary. The bedroom furniture was somewhat threadbare, and the back walls were made with thin board which had hideous green wallpaper. The fake walls were around seven feet high which clearly marked the point at which they went beyond the eye of the camera. Signs indicated on the wall behind Alfred indicated the name of the production company: *Famous Players – Lasky*.

Alfred noticed Lady Mary looking up at the name. This was an opportunity to explain who his employers were. 'Famous Players are an American motion picture company.'

'Not British?' remarked Agatha with just enough huff in her voice to suggest disapproval.

'No, Lady Frost. Motion pictures are still in their infancy here. The film director, Mr Powell, is an American gentleman. He made '*Pollyanna*' with Mary Pickford.'

'I haven't seen it,' said Agatha. The subject matter of a young girl who has a sunny and optimistic outlook on life was altogether too twee for someone whose tastes in literature ran to murder.

'I gather Mary Pickford was rather good,' said Mary in tone meant to conciliate Alfred and censure Agatha. If this was the intention, then it succeeded brilliantly. Alfred grinned delightedly and Agatha half-smiled, half nodded her acknowledgment of Mary's true meaning. She liked Mary very much, never more so than when she unsheathed her intelligence and, gently, challenged her to a duel. Kit was a very lucky man.

'Who are the players?' asked Agatha in an attempt to show interest although, in truth, the set was hardly humming with activity.

'We are making a motion picture called '*Dangerous Lies*'. This seemed more to Agatha's liking and her ears pricked up at this. 'Mary Glynne plays a young woman who marries a bounder.'

'Sounds like my brother Lancelot,' said Agatha.

'Let's hope it doesn't run in the family,' added Mary with a wide smile.

'If I may say, Lord Aston is nothing like the character David Powell plays. The bounder, it transpires, has faked his death to avoid creditors. Mary Glynne's character, unaware of this, has since gone to London and married another,' said Alfred.

'A trifle precipitous,' commented Agatha.

'What is?' said a woman's voice behind Agatha and Mary. The two women turned around to find a short bespectacled lady of American tendencies standing in a rather aggressive pose. She was in her fifties and was clearly not someone to be trifled with.

'And you are?' asked Agatha in a tone of voice that was likely to bring out the Paul Revere in any American worthy of the name.

'Mary O'Connor. I wrote this picture. Who, might I ask, are you?'

For Mary and Agatha, the combination of aggression and the highly admirable fact that she had played such a prominent role in the creation of this motion picture was, temporarily, enough to stun them into silence.

Alfred stepped manfully into the breach, showing a remarkable degree of fortitude, or naivety, when faced with the terrifying prospect of two female war elephants' moments away from going at it hammer and tongs.

'Lady Frost, Lady Mary, may I present Mary O'Connor. She is a screenwriter for this picture.'

Agatha was nothing if not logical. In fact, it was her greatest fault as well as a decided accomplishment that if something did not make sense to her, she would not remain silent until either the source of the illogicality was made to understand that they made no sense or, at least, they could explain themselves better. She chose the latter course with the uncompromising-looking American.

'But I thought the picture was silent. Are we able to hear the players now?'

This stopped Mary O'Connor in her tracks, and she studied Agatha a little bit more closely now. Then she became aware of Mary. Her manner softened.

'No, motion pictures do not have any sound aside from the accompanying music. Alfred here is helping put dialogue on screen using intertitles. The audience can see what the character is saying. The acting does the rest of the job.'

'I see,' said Agatha. 'Well, you're to be congratulated on having such a position in this enterprise.' She made a point of looking around the set. 'Sadly, there do not seem to be many women employed in the making of this motion picture.'

Mary O'Connor's view of Agatha was now coming full circle. There was something about the old woman that she liked. The young woman, on the other hand, had star potential. Her limited exposure to young women in the country had led her to taking a rather negative view of the Englishwoman. Too demure, too white, and too, well, English. The young woman before her was all these things yet it was clear she could light up a screen like a firework.

Even the old woman had a belligerent charisma about her. She turned to Mary and regarded her unabashedly.

'You know, Lady Mary, it's a pity Paul Powell isn't here today to meet you. He'd sign you up like that.' She snapped her fingers to emphasise her point. Then she turned to Agatha and said, 'How would you feel about your daughter becoming a Hollywood star?'

This startled Agatha for a moment. 'Mary is not my daughter,' said Agatha but there was an unmistakable catch in her voice. Mary looked away. It was too painful to bear. She gripped Agatha's hand tightly. None of this was seen, of course, by Alfred. Mary O'Connor saw it all.

Agatha regained her composure and continued, 'Mary will marry my nephew Christopher next week.'

Mary O'Connor looked Mary up and down and said, 'Pity.'

Mary smiled, 'It's for the best. You should see my husband to be.'

'Good looking?' asked the American screenwriter, cocking her head to one side.

'Very.' All eyes turned to Alfred Hitchcock, who'd said this.

'Very,' agreed Mary, proudly.

But Mary O'Connor was not so easily dissuaded. A frown creased her brow then she turned to Alfred with eyes narrowing. There was an unmistakable look of suspicion on her face. The young Englishman seemed to recoil under the intensity of the questions it posed. He knew what was coming. Thankfully he'd prepared for such a moment.

'Why exactly did you bring these good people here?'

3

Mary and Agatha sat side by side in front of a large mirror lit by small bulbs. The younger of the two ladies was enjoying the experience immensely. It would be fair to say Agatha, less so. However, this was Mary's last week of freedom. Not that the life ahead was likely to be one of serfdom either, but she seemed quite enthused by the acting idea, so Agatha had felt duty bound to go along with her.

'Not too much makeup for me,' ordered Agatha to the young lady whose job, it seemed, was to cake faces with brown clay. "And this young lady hardly requires any.'

'The lights require a certain amount of makeup otherwise you'll look like a ghost, Aunt Agatha,' pointed out Mary.

'As I understand it, our appearance will be fleeting at best, and I suspect that both men and women in the audience will be looking at you.'

Mary turned to Agatha and giggled affectionately. Agatha shook her head grumpily although, in truth, she was rather looking forward to the whole thing. But she had a reputation to maintain.

'Lady Mary, will you come with me to the changing room,' asked the young woman who had been applying the makeup.

'Oh,' said Mary. 'Am I not just wearing this?'

'No, Mr Hitchcock had something else in mind. I also need to fit the blonde wig. You'll be standing in for Miss Glynne, you see.'

It was Agatha's turn to laugh now. This surprised Mary which only made Agatha laugh even more. There was more than a 'I-told-you-so' in Agatha's merriment. Even Mary couldn't resist a smile when she'd left the room.

The blonde wig turned out to be the least of Mary's surprises. Her costume was, if anything, an even greater source of wonder.

'It's her nightdress,' explained the young woman. She left the changing room to allow Mary to don what there was of her costume. Mary appeared a few minutes later.

'Are you sure?' she asked.

'Mr Hitchcock was most insistent.'

Mary was given a dressing gown and led onto the set. Awaiting her was Agatha who was sitting with a cup of tea. Mary O'Connor was nowhere to be seen but Alfred was busily directing the crew on placement of props while the cameraman fixed a film spool onto the camera. Mary joined Agatha and waited for a few minutes while the crew made ready to begin shooting the scene.

Finally, all seemed ready, and Alfred strolled over to the two ladies. He'd not really had much to say to the technicians. Rather, he'd wanted to extend the amount of time he could surreptitiously look at the blonde bewigged Mary. His forehead was beaded with sweat, and a lake had formed under his arms. This was not entirely due to the heat of the lights.

'Thank you once more. I cannot tell you how grateful I am for this. Now, let me tell you about your scene.'

Mary and Agatha both leaned forward. The two ladies were by now fully engaged in the film-making process and had agreed that a trip to see a motion picture would need to be made before they took the train to Little Gloston the next day.

'Lady Mary, you are filling in for Miss Glynne. She plays the young woman Joan Farrant who is now remarried to someone she loves. Lady Frost, you will play her mother. This part is being played by Minna Grey. You, Lady Frost, will come into the room and break the news to Lady Mary, or Joan, that her first husband is still alive.'

The two ladies nodded. This seemed straightforward enough.

'How should I react, Alfred?' asked Mary.

'In motion pictures, we rely on a more physical reaction,' replied Alfred. 'I believe Mr Powell prefers a hand perhaps covering the mouth.' Alfred proceeded to demonstrate this particular trope. Then he walked over to the bed. 'Perhaps we could rehearse the scene a little. Lady Mary if you could remove your dressing gown and step into bed.' Alfred's voice seemed a little tight at this point.

'Does Aunt Agatha wake me?'

'No, you shall wake yourself. The room will be in darkness. We shall see you step out of the bed and go to the French windows. You will throw open the curtains. At this point, Lady Frost will knock on the door. You say, "Who is it?". Then Lady Frost enters the room and breaks the news. Lady Agatha, we will film you saying, "Eli is still alive", to Lady Mary.'

'Certainly direct,' commented Agatha huffily.

Alfred's smiled enigmatically and he replied, 'Your character is very strong-willed and not a little volatile.'

'That will really stretch you, Aunt Agatha,' said Mary, a grin on her face.

Agatha raised an eyebrow and said sardonically, 'Yes, dealing with a young romantic fool of a daughter will require much imagination on my part.'

Mary climbed into the bed and waited for the instruction from Alfred.

'And action,' said Alfred from his, or rather Paul Powell's, director's chair.

Mary rolled a few times in the bed and then threw the bedclothes away. She rose and padded over to the French windows, yawned daintily and then pulled the curtains aside. She didn't have to act being blinded by the light. The lights behind the windows were the brightest she'd ever seen. Moments later, there was a knock and Agatha entered from behind a rather flimsy set door and said her line.

Alfred ended the rehearsal by saying, 'And cut' although no actual filming had taken place. In truth he'd barely been able to speak, such was the loveliness of the vision that he beheld. There really was something about blue-eyed blonde ladies that would have made him weak at the knees had he not already been sitting. He could've happily spent the day gazing at Mary by the brightly lit window.

Alfred requested several more rehearsals before shooting commenced. By now he was satisfied that Mary had the scene under control. He'd all but melted into the chair too. Alfred wasn't the only one enjoying the scene. Several of the older technicians were palpitating badly. The scene was finally completed to Alfred's and, it must be said, the crew's satisfaction a few minutes later.

Mary and Agatha had both enjoyed their acting stint. Each had played major parts in school plays over the years and the smell of the greasepaint never truly leaves you. Mary donned her dressing gown and walked over to Alfred with Agatha.

'Well, that was fun,' said Mary brightly.

Alfred couldn't have agreed more. He was a little overcome at that moment and could do nothing else but nod.

'Tell me, Alfred,' asked Agatha. 'I noticed that the crew were all standing behind you while they filmed us. Is this standard practice?'

Alfred's eyes widened and, from the corner of his eye, he saw several crew members disappear like poachers when the farmer comes.

'Well, Lady Frost,' started Alfred, praying feverishly for inspiration, then it struck, 'it is useful to have more than one pair of eyes looking at a scene. Filming is a very collaborative enterprise.'

'Ahh,' said Agatha nodding. 'That does make sense. Will that be all then?'

'Yes, thank you. Lady Frost, Lady Mary. I cannot begin to tell you how grateful I am for your help today. I'm so glad you enjoyed yourselves.'

Alfred's smiled unctuously.

'We did,' said Mary.

'Yes,' said Agatha before adding as an afterthought, 'Almost as much as your colleagues.' She fixed her eyes on Alfred for a moment and then swept off towards the dressing rooms followed by a mystified Mary.

4

Cavendish Hall, February 12th, 1921

Mary looked up at Kit and smiled. She felt him grip her hand a little more strongly. Then they turned their attention to the large car approaching. The Irish chauffeur, Devlin, was in the driver's seat. Beside him was a small woman wearing a purple cloche hat.

The car pulled up and Curtis, the butler at Cavendish Hall, marshalled his troops into position. Devlin hopped out from the driver's seat and quickly opened the door for the passenger in the back.

A man of around sixty stepped out. He took off his hat to reveal a head that was once a veritable forest of light brown hair. None of it remained aside from a few stragglers that had not received the message to pull out.

'Uncle Alastair,' said Kit and Mary in unison.

Alastair Aston stopped and surveyed the front of Cavendish Hall. He removed the panatela cigar from his mouth and a wide grin exploded across his face. The grin turned into a chuckle and his shoulders began to shake. Mary skipped down the steps and planted a kiss on his cheek. She took his arm and said, 'I told you it was hideous.'

'My dear,' responded Alastair in delight, 'Nothing could have prepared me for this. It's…' he searched for the right words. 'Extraordinary. Tell me, did your forefathers insist on blind architects?'

He stood back and took in the full glory of Cavendish Hall, a glory that encompassed, with no great success, a blend of Tudor, Baroque and Gothic architecture to which was added just a hint of Palladian for good measure.

'It is perfectly ghastly, isn't it?' giggled Mary.

'And yet…wonderful,' agreed Alastair. He looked up and saw his nephew, Kit. He grasped him firmly by the hand.

'So good to see you again, Uncle Alastair. And you, Ella-Mae.'

Alastair did a double take as he realised his housekeeper was standing beside him.

'I do you wish you wouldn't sneak up on me like that,' snapped Alastair.

'I know, you're going to put a bell on me. You've been threatening that for decades.'

Alastair shook his head resentfully and informed Kit that you couldn't get the staff these days. Both Kit and Mary greeted the tiny housekeeper like a friend. She had been Alastair's housekeeper and sparring partner for almost three decades.

Alastair was introduced to Curtis, the head butler at Cavendish Hall. Curtis took over matters and introduced the new arrival to the rest of the staff. First to meet him was Miss Buchan followed by Elsie, the cook. She, in turn, introduced Polly, who helped in the kitchen and acted as a maid.

'And this,' said Curtis proudly, 'Is my wife, Mrs Curtis. She was governess to Lady Mary, Lady Esther and Lord Henry, or Lord Cavendish, I should say.'

'Pleased to meet you all,' said Alastair, a warm smile on his face.

Alastair was led inside by Mary to meet the rest of the Cavendish family. He leant down to Mary's ear and whispered, 'And how are things between the two aunts?'

There seemed to be just a hint of anticipation in his voice. Like any man worth his salt, he enjoyed having a ringside seat as two women of a certain age engaged in territorial warfare at a wedding. Sadly, it appeared this would be denied to him.

'Remarkably peaceful so far. Both are on their best behaviour. I think they reached some sort of accommodation at Esther's wedding. Aunt Emily seems to have accepted that my living in London has not resulted in the good name of the Cavendish family becoming muddied by association with fast-living young men like Kit.'

'Pity,' said Alastair before realising that this was not quite the answer expected under the circumstances. Mary chuckled at Alastair's momentary discomfort at revealing his true thoughts on this matter. Then he laughed too. Her reaction suggested she understood all too well the enjoyment to be had from watching the foibles and eccentricities of other people made manifest. It was all the more reason to congratulate Kit on his choice of partner for life.

The first person he met from the family was a tall, aristocratic young man accompanied by a young woman with astonishing green eyes.

'This is my cousin Henry and his…' Mary paused for a moment before deciding on, 'future Lady Cavendish, Jane.'

This introduction brought a smile to the two young people. Alastair was then introduced to Esther Bright, Mary's recently married sister and her husband, Richard.

'My word,' said Alastair, 'So much beauty in one place, and that's just the gentlemen.'

After a few minutes' conversation with the newly-weds, Alastair was led into the drawing room. Aunt Agatha and Aunt Emily were engaged deeply in a conversation over tea. Agatha looked up as she saw her brother enter.

'Ahh there you are.'

'Delighted to see you, too, Agatha,' replied Alastair in a tone that managed to be both sardonic and warmly sincere in equal measure. It bespoke an undying affection and an underlying amusement towards the woman who had been and always would be, his elder sister.

Aunt Emily proved to be less fearsome in real life than Alastair had been led to believe by Kit and Mary. Perhaps growing up with Agatha had inured him to strong-willed women.

'Are we all looking forward to the wedding?' asked Alastair of the two women at one point.

'Yes, Christopher is a wonderful match for Mary,' replied Emily. Alastair couldn't decide if by 'match' Emily meant Mary's equal in intellect and interest or was it more feudal in connotation. He certainly was not about to ask and, instead, settled back to bask in the presence of Emily's unalloyed conviction in the importance of rank.

Agatha did not reply, and he sensed a sadness in his sister. He'd only known Mary a short time and had fallen under her spell. It wasn't difficult to imagine that Mary leaving Agatha's Grosvenor Square home after a year would be a wrench. The brief look they exchanged merely confirmed this suspicion. He smiled affectionately towards her and squeezed her hand.

Moments later some tea arrived beside Alastair. He looked around to see by what magic it had appeared then heard Agatha say, 'How are you, Ella-Mae?'

Alastair glared up at his housekeeper. She glared back at him while replying to Agatha, 'Very well, your ladyship,' before adding witheringly, 'for the most part, anyway.'

Kit and Mary joined them moments later followed by Esther and Bright. Agatha glanced at Aunt Emily when Henry came into the room with Jane Edmunds. The smile on Emily's face seemed like an effort of will. Ordinarily this would have amused Agatha but for once she had sympathy for a mother gazing at her son and the woman, he was likely to wed one day. This sympathy was not based on any misguided loyalty to the idea of marrying within rank. Agatha was too practical not to appreciate the benefits of such an arrangement but, in this case, she was woman enough to be moved by the romance. Rather, she understood the sense of loss that Emily would feel when her son left her to become a husband and, one day, a father.

Alastair's voice interrupted her thoughts. He was chatting with Kit when a thought seemed to strike him.

'Do you know, my boy, I haven't met the young man who saved your life.'

'Yes, where is Harry?' asked Mary.

-

Harry Miller gazed across the valley at Cavendish House. He was sitting in a small wood with Sammy, Kit's pet Jack Russell. Over the last year, the notoriously ill-tempered canine had grown closer to Miller. Each, in their own way, had seen their position change with the arrival of Mary. They both adored her but there was no question things would never be the same following the wedding.

Miller had long-known this moment would come but had tried to avoid thinking of it. He enjoyed his life with Kit but only the kindest of imaginations would ever describe him as being a manservant. As much a figure of fun as Curtis, the butler at Cavendish Hall, could seem, there was no doubting that he was born to play such a role. Harry, on the other hand, had come into his role by way of cracking safes before a certain disagreement with Germany had resulted in him saving the life of Kit one wintry night at Cambrai.

He did not doubt for one moment that Kit and Mary would wish him to stay. The question looming for Harry was whether he wanted to or not. The answer was not as clear cut as he would have liked. On the one hand he enjoyed the life of privilege he led. Who could not enjoy living in Belgrave Square, driving a Rolls Royce, and enduring servant duties that barely required him to make the breakfast? And this was before one considered his role in the various adventures over the last year and half that had taken him to jail, to India, to Paris and to a number of activities that called upon the old skills developed over many years when he and his family were burglars.

No, he had a great life, yet the thought that it would soon end persisted; it plagued him like a wasp at a picnic. Sammy, despite his sometime capricious nature, sensed the turmoil with Harry and put his head on his lap. A few minutes later Harry slowly rose to his feet and made his way down to the Hall carrying Sammy. He passed the cottage of Bill Edmunds, the groundskeeper, whose daughter was likely to marry young Henry. He remembered the haunted eyes of the mother and father who, like so many households, were still in mourning for the loss of their son during the war. The thought of their loss and the friends who had died stiffened his back. Miller became, just for a few moments, Corporal Harry Miller. His steps became quicker, and his eyes took on more purpose. Whatever the future held, he would meet it as he'd met everything fate had thrown at him: head on.

Miller arrived at the back door which led into the kitchen of Cavendish Hall. Elsie didn't look up from the pot. She held a finger up as she sensed Miller's approach. Miller stopped immediately. Elsie ruled the kitchen like a benevolent dictator. Her word was law, her temper, violent, and the food was heavenly. She inhaled the aroma rising from whatever was in the pot. Miller guessed soup. Then she took a ladle, thereby confirming Miller's suspicion, and collected some of it.

'Need a taster, Els?' asked Miller.

'Just in time as ever, Harry,' replied Elsie putting the ladle up to his lip.

The cauliflower soup was piping hot, just the way Miller liked it. After three years at the front, his throat was made of leather. The soup was thick and tasted so good he felt like grabbing the pot and running away.

'I'll save some for you, Harry,' smiled Elsie, sensing, as ever, that her creation had won the approval of the Kit Aston's manservant.

Curtis appeared in the kitchen just then.

'Mr Miller,' said Curtis, who always insisted on such formality. 'I believe you are wanted in the drawing room.'

Miller's heart sank at this news. Yet, he'd expected it. Kit had warned him that his Uncle Alastair would want to meet the man who'd saved his nephew's life. He'd hoped the introduction might happen in private. And be brief. Miller felt uncomfortable when confronted by praise. He knew what he'd done in saving Kit Aston's life. His lordship knew what he'd done, what he'd risked. That was enough for him. Even his lordship's gratitude rarely extended beyond calling him a 'bloody fool'. On the face of it, this seemed ungrateful. For Miller, there was no better acclaim nor greater truth. Under orders or not, he had been a bloody fool. He smiled as he climbed the stairs up to the entrance hall. It lasted until he reached the door of the drawing room and heard the chatter of the upper classes inside. Then he felt his heart leap up into his mouth and he felt like running away.

He knocked, then opened the door.

The room was crowded, and he searched for Kit. When he saw the smiles erupt around the room, he realised he was still carrying Sammy. The little Jack Russell began to bark, and Miller set him down gently on the floor. He ran to Esther Cavendish. The little lovestruck so-and-so, thought Miller. The room was laughing at Sammy's antics. All except one man. He was as tall as Kit Aston, but his head was bald. The clear blue eyes were the same. The man approached Miller; hand outstretched. As he drew nearer, Miller could see there was something close to tears in his eyes. Just behind the man, Miller spied Lady Mary and Aunt Agatha. They, too, were feeling the emotion of the moment.

'Thank you, Harry, for saving my nephew.'

Miller remembered the rather casual first meeting with Lord Lancelot Aston., Kit's father The man was a rake, yet Miller rather liked him. He and Kit had a troubled relationship due to his treatment of Kit's late mother. The comparison with Alastair Aston could not have been starker. Fear, gratitude, and sadness filled the older man's eyes. At that moment, Miller knew with utmost certainty that these were the eyes of a father.

5

Cavendish Hall, February 14th, 1921

Agatha stepped forward nervously and knocked on the bedroom door. For all the veneer of an old war elephant, and this was more than skin deep now, there were moments when emotions that she kept under severe restraint would surface. The thought of Eustace was often enough for her to seek a quiet place and be alone. Now the thought of losing Mary, after only a year sharing their house in Grosvenor Square was proving more difficult to manage in public than she had previously imagined. She would miss Mary. Yet she knew the time had come for a long-delayed decision to be made. She would address this, but only after the wedding, when they were away.

Something else was on her mind as she waited at the door. Her family had been at war with itself for decades. Now, perhaps, the time had come for peace. For the two sides to lay down their arms and embrace.

Like brothers.

The door opened and Alastair appeared. For once he did not greet his sister with a smile. His eyes betrayed the nervousness he felt. Agatha said nothing; she merely nodded. Alastair nodded back and took a deep breath. He came out of the room and walked alongside Agatha down the stairs. Curtis and Mrs Buchan were milling around the entrance hallway. He heard a laugh coming from one of the rooms. A woman. He didn't have to ask who it was.

'The games room,' said Agatha, pointing at a closed door.

Alastair stopped and seemed not to understand. Then he asked in a surprised voice, 'Aren't you coming?'

Agatha shook her head.

Alastair was a little put out at this but realised it was for the best. He nodded once more and took slow, heavy steps towards the games room door. His heart was now beating at a rate of knots that probably wasn't healthy in a man nearing his mid-sixties. He put his hand up to knock and then thought better of it. He opened the door and walked in.

A man was sitting on a brown Chesterfield sofa. He looked up and stared at Alastair for a moment. He leapt to his feet. Alastair could barely move his.

'Hello, Alastair,' said the man. There was no welcome in his voice but nor was there animosity. Only curiosity.

'Hello, Lancelot,' said Alastair, finding his voice.

The two men had not seen one another in over thirty years. Lancelot looked up at the bald pate of his brother. His own hair was silver and luxuriant. He spied Alastair gazing at it with some envy and smiled.

'You take after the Melcroft side, I see.'

Alastair tapped his head and smiled sheepishly, 'Yes, just a little.'

'How's Algy? He's a nice boy, I thought,' said Lancelot, thinking of the Alastair's son who he'd met briefly just after the end of the war. He'd served with the American troops.

'You heard what happened to him?' asked Alastair. Lancelot nodded. Alastair's shoulders slumped a little. Then he straightened up and a wistful smile appeared on his face. He said, 'Takes after his mother.'

Lancelot smiled at this, 'Probably for the best. Kit is his mother's son.'

Alastair smiled, 'Yes. He always will be.'

The two brothers stepped forward at this moment, their hands outstretched. Thirty years of resentment, anger and silence vanished in a handshake.

-

'I must admit, Mary, I never thought I'd be giving away the bride at the age of eighteen. To do it for the second time in as many months beggars' belief,' said Henry Cavendish looking affectionately at his cousin.

'Thanks, Henry,' said Mary. There was a catch in her voice, a moment of recognition that both her father and Henry's could not be here because of the Great War. Henry squeezed her hand.

'Shall we?' asked Henry. He glanced towards the entrance of the church, just in time to see Harry Miller rush inside, no doubt to communicate to the bridegroom that his fate was approaching in a beautiful, flowing white dress with a dropped waist and beaded front.

They stepped out of the car that had taken them the short distance from the Hall. Outside the church the whole of the village craned their necks to have a first look at the bride. Mary smiled and waved to the crowd. Applause broke out as Mary made her way through the entrance of the church.

She nodded briefly to an attractive young woman who was pregnant and, it seemed, minutes away from giving birth.

'Not long now, Kate,' said Mary with a grin and swift glance towards the young woman's stomach. Kate was one of the villagers. She was married to the blacksmith, Stan Shaw.

'It'll be your turn soon,' said Kate. She took Mary's hand briefly. Mary could see she was crying. Beside her a young boy looked up at the two young women, utterly baffled by what was going on. They both laughed at his expression then Mary swept into the church.

-

'Sir, the car has just pulled up. Lady Mary will be here in a minute,' said Harry Miller, popping his head through the door of the presbytery.

There were four men in the room: Kit, Spunky Stevens, Chubby Chadderton and Richard Bright. They all leapt to their feet and rushed for the door. Soft organ music piped around the church. At the altar, Reverend Simmons, the former soldier, and boxer, broke into a wide grin of welcome. Spunky said something to him about Egypt and Kit answered absently.

'Just in time,' said Simmons.

Kit rolled his eyes and then he heard the silent hum of the organ transform into something louder and all together scarier for any prospective young man standing at an altar, no matter how love-struck he is. And Kit was certainly love-struck. He spun around and saw Mary walking up the aisle. He caught his breath. This was a moment that he wanted to remember forever. Any nervousness he felt evaporated to be replaced by a sense of humility followed by relief and then utter happiness.

Mary arrived at the altar beside him. Kit glanced momentarily at Henry Cavendish. The young man nodded to him and then stepped away. He took Mary's hand, resisted the urge to kiss her and then they both turned to face the grizzled chaplain. He smiled at them both and then began to speak.

'Dearly beloved, we are gathered here today in the sight of God to join this man and this woman in holy matrimony. Not to be entered into lightly, holy matrimony should be entered into with solemnity, with reverence and with honour. If any person here can show cause why these two people should not be joined in holy matrimony, speak now or forever hold your peace.'

'Marriage is a sacred union between husband and wife. It shall remain unbroken. It is the basis of a stable and loving relationship and is a joining of two hearts, bodies and souls. The husband and wife are there to support one another and provide love and care in sickness and in health.'

'We are all here today to witness the joining in wedded bliss of Christopher Alastair Aston and Mary Katherine Cavendish.'

Alastair's heart plummeted and rebounded when he heard Kit's full name. He realised with some shock he'd never heard the full name before. Kit had always been Kit, except to Penny Aston, Kit's mother, and Agatha. Both referred to him as Christopher. Just for a few moments he found it difficult to breathe. He turned to Lancelot, who was beside him. It took a moment for Lancelot to understand and then a slow smile appeared on his face.

'You never knew?' whispered Lancelot.

Alastair shook his head mutely. Then he smiled and arched an eyebrow, 'Penny?'

The smile faded from Lancelot's face for a moment then it reappeared but there was ruefulness that gave Alastair a tinge of regret. Then Lancelot whispered back, 'No, old thing. I chose it.'

6

5 weeks later

Monte Carlo, Monaco: early April 1921

The taxi swept along Avenue Des Beaux Arts. There were two passengers inside. Kit and Mary Aston held hands and stared out of the window as they arrived in Place du Casino. The square was virtually empty but would soon become more crowded. It was after six in the evening. This was a time between afternoon tea and evening cocktails. Even the wealthy needed a break from eating and drinking.

The taxi, at Kit's request, drove past the gardens, towards the majestic fountain at the centre of Place du Casino. Behind it lay a large three storey building. Mary giggled delightedly at its extravagance. Despite having seen the Pyramids, the Acropolis and Coliseum over the last five weeks of her honeymoon, this was the first time Kit had heard Mary laugh at the sight of a building. The other locations had been visited with a sense of reverence and humility. Not Monte Carlo. It made Kit love her all the more that she understood this was a place not to take too seriously. It was a playground for rich people. More pertinently for Kit and Mary, it was the final stop on their honeymoon before they returned to England. Here they would re-join Aunt Agatha, Uncle Alastair, Betty Simpson and Harry Miller.

'That's the casino,' said Kit pointing towards the large building that had amused Mary so much. It was modestly extravagant. Not in any Baroque sense, though. Rather, it seemed to go out of its way to wear its careless elegance, its echo of a past when well-dressed, old-rich counts, Russian Grand Dukes, English lords, and maharajahs regularly stayed, played, and sashayed with French actresses. It thrilled, appalled, and saddened Kit in equal measure.

The thrill always came from being on the Riviera. Its beauty had beguiled him every bit as much as it had artists. The naked display of wealth made him more uncomfortable though, especially following the war. He could not change what he was, yet he had changed profoundly in the mud of Flanders. There, men of all ranks and upbringing were mown down in a murderously democratic fashion by the deadly tools of an industrial era that laid waste to the age of elegance. The knowledge of this saddened Kit in ways that he could not bring himself to examine. When this mood descended on him, he recalled something he had read in Proust: *Remembrance of things past is not necessarily the remembrance of things as they were.*

He did not want to return to his youth because the last five weeks had been, quite simply, the happiest of his life. Any demons remaining from the war had now surely been cast off for good. The recurring dream of Robert Cavendish's death and his own rescue had died the day he'd uncovered the man who'd killed him. The survivor's guilt, however, would never leave him. It would not be shared with Mary. This would be his and his alone. Its presence would be felt most when he was with other men who had been through the horror of Ypres, Passchendaele, Cambrai, and the Somme. This cemented the bond he felt with Harry Miller. He hoped, as did Mary, that the man who saved his life would always be by his side.

Mary's eyes lit up at seeing the casino. The large entrance was framed by two turrets. Mary's eyes swept along the elegant balustrade running along the top, interrupted by bronze sprites carrying torches, and figures which represented spring, summer, autumn, and winter.

'It's so decadent. I love it,' said Mary. Kit knew that she was joking. Like his Uncle Alastair, Mary had a wicked sense of humour that positively delighted in unnecessary ostentation or superfluous embellishment in architecture. 'Can we go in?'

'Now?' queried Kit in surprise.

'Why not? We're a little early.'

Kit thought for a moment. They were a little early; two hours, in fact. They had taken a boat from Genoa which stopped at Nice rather than going directly to Marseilles. Perhaps a quick trip into the gaming rooms to show Mary wouldn't do any harm. He nodded to Mary and requested the taxi driver to stop outside the casino and wait for them.

Kit climbed out of the car first and took Mary's hand as she stepped down. It was not quite dark yet. The sky had an orange tinge and slanting shadows split the ground like long daggers. Hand in hand, they walked up the steps of the casino. Mary smiled at the doorman which saw him scurrying to open the door and doff his hat in a well-practiced manoeuvre.

The atrium of the casino lived up to the promise of the exterior. The floor was made from marble with twenty-eight onyx columns surrounding the interior leading them gently towards the gaming rooms where the promise of excitement and riches lay. The columns soared upwards to a mezzanine floor with balustrades running along all four sides. The back wall was decorated with an enormous painted frieze of the coast. As they walked through the atrium, they passed some patrons sitting down by the bar drinking cocktails.

'If you think this is opulent, you should see the gaming rooms,' whispered Kit.

They continued to the *Salle Renaissance*, an antechamber to the gaming rooms and marched straight ahead towards the *Salon Europe*. Mary's grin widened as she entered. Enormous Belle Epoque chandeliers hung from ceilings. Large paintings decorated the walls. Mary chuckled as she gazed up at the *naiads* on the ceiling smoking cigars.

'I hadn't realised that Greek goddesses were so fond of smoking,' commented Mary.

'Yes, an unusual insight of the artist,' agreed Kit.

Despite the hour, the salon was quite crowded already with roulette players and *vingt et un* tables.

'Do you fancy breaking the bank at Monte Carlo?' asked Mary, eyebrows raised.

'I daresay we'll give it a go, but the odds are always stacked against you. I'm afraid it really is just a music hall song.'

'Where do those poor people go who've lost everything?' asked Mary.

Kit smiled at Mary and replied, 'It's not actually in Monte Carlo. The "Suicide leap" is up on the rock in Monaco by the Oceanographic Museum. There's a rather large cliff there that could do no end of damage should you fall off it. I'm not sure anyone has actually made the leap, but it makes for a romantic story.'

'I'll stick with Jane Austen for romance, if it's all the same,' said Mary gazing at the room in wonder. Men and women of all ages were around each of the tables. On closer inspection she revised this opinion. The men tended to be older, and the women were most certainly younger. She saw Kit smiling at her with one eyebrow raised. The smile was returned, and she took his arm in both hands.

'I could be your courtesan,' suggested Mary, a wicked grin sneaking across her lips.

'I'm a happily married man, I'll have you know.'

They strolled around the outer perimeter of the Salon then parked themselves at one of the roulette tables. The croupier was a middle-aged man with an extravagant grey and black moustache. His head appeared to have a grey squirrel perched on it. Kit saw Mary gazing at this impressive thatch. It was swept back off his forehead like he was facing into the teeth of a gale. She glanced up at Kit.

'Don't,' warned Kit.

Mary shrugged innocently and said, 'I was just going to say that I felt like some peanuts.'

'To store in your tree perhaps?' responded Kit. 'Anyway, I'm sure we'll be back here soon. I vote that we return to the taxi and head over to Aunt Agatha's place. I know she's not expecting us quite yet but I'm sure they'll cope.'

Mary looked a little reluctant to leave. There was a fascination to watching the men and women gambling. There seemed to be no young men. Perhaps this was a sad affirmation to the mass cull they'd suffered. The men seemed either middle-aged or elderly, very rich and utterly absorbed in the cards or the spin of the roulette wheel. There could be little doubt about their young and, often, beautiful companions. They were the dubious *demi-mondaines* of the gaming halls. She felt a tug on her arm. Kit smiled at her. She made a face back at him but they both started back in the direction from which they'd come.

Then Kit stopped suddenly.

'What's wrong?' asked Mary

'Good lord,' said Kit simply.

Mary looked up at Kit who was staring at something to his left. She spun around and followed his gaze to one of the tables.

'Oh,' said Mary.

'Indeed,' replied Kit.

Sitting behind the table, in the dealer's chair, was Aunt Agatha. She was dressed, unquestionably, in the same manner as the other dealers. There could be no question as to what her role was in the game being played. Sitting to her side was Betty Simpson. She was one of three other players.

'Do you know,' said Mary in an awestruck tone, 'If this were a novel, I would find this part somewhat stretching one's credibility.'

Kit glanced at her and grinned, 'Darling, if this were a novel then, after the few weeks we've just enjoyed, it would have been impounded by the Lord Chamberlain and the writer imprisoned for indecency and undermining public morality.'

'I do try,' said Mary with a smile that was as wicked as it was innocent. 'So, what shall we do? Go over and let her know we've seen her or…'

In fact, just at that moment Agatha's eyes suddenly fixed on them. Then she turned away and seemed to say something to Betty. Her friend looked up, and around the room, until she caught sight of them. Betty nodded surreptitiously to Agatha, collected her chips, of which there were quite a few, and made her way over to Kit and Mary.

'Look at you two,' beamed Betty. 'The most beautiful couple in Monte Carlo.'

This was a game effort and might have earned Betty some Brownie points, but it was never going to pass muster when a chap has discovered his septuagenarian aunt is moonlighting as a dealer in a gambling den. Betty shrugged. Kit raised his eyebrows. Mary was too genteel to roar with laughter, but it was a jolly close-run thing.

Realising the game wasn't just up but lost with the players trooping off to the bar, Betty smiled because this is what Betty did and said, 'Well, I suppose you want to know what's going on.'

'The thought had crossed my mind,' admitted Kit. He tried to look stern as he said this but was not actor enough to carry it off and, anyway, it merely endeared the two ladies to him all the more.

'Looks like you had a good run of it.'

Betty's face fell a little but only for a second before it resumed its customary good humour.

'I have to return this to the casino. It's their money.'

'I see,' said Kit, who plainly didn't. He turned to Mary to see if Betty's comment had made any more sense to her. Alas, Mary was laughing too much to be of much help.

'Perhaps we should retire to the bar,' suggested Betty, 'and wait for Agatha to finish her shift.'

'Her shift?' chorused Kit and Mary.

Around twenty minutes and one Gin Rickey for Betty later, Agatha appeared, still wearing her dealer's costume which was oddly male. It consisted of a black waistcoat and a white shirt with black bow tie. As she passed a waitress, she ordered a Gin Rickey and then, spotting Betty's empty glass, decided to play safe and order two.

She plumped herself down on the seat and smiled at the newlyweds.

'So, how was the honeymoon?'

Kit turned to Mary; one eyebrow raised. This could have been interpreted in any number of ways from admiration at Agatha's cheek at ignoring the more pressing subject to be discussed or an acknowledgement that much of the honeymoon had been spent enjoying sights and activities that were unlikely to find their way onto any reputable tourist guide.

'It was wonderful, Aunt Agatha. So many exciting and romantic places. Five weeks was hardly long enough,' said Mary looking at Agatha with a winning smile. Then she turned to Kit and gave a nod. This motion of the head, of course, was akin to a relay runner passing the baton on to the chap on the final leg tasked with bringing it safely over the line. Kit gave a 'thank-you-darling' look to Mary and turned to Agatha.

'Doubtless,' chipped in Agatha, anticipating the next subject of conversation, 'you want to know why you see me dressed in this manner and dealing cards in the casino.'

'It was rather unexpected,' suggested Kit, carefully.

'Not just for you, Christopher,' admitted Agatha. 'When I came here two weeks ago, I had no more idea that I would be doing this than you had.'

'And yet, here you are.'

'True. You see, over the years of coming here, and I've been coming here since before I'd even met 'Useless', I have met a great many people. Some of these people I have had occasion to help. When Betty and I arrived, we were soon called upon to assist a friend on a most delicate matter. Hence why you see me dressed in this manner.'

Agatha nodded to Kit and raised her eyebrows in a manner that hoped this brief explanation had covered the matter sufficiently. In truth, her hopes were not too high on this point. The Gin Rickeys arrived for Agatha and Betty and the two ladies politely toasted the newly married couple. But destiny waits for no man or, indeed, aunt who has been caught not only gambling but acting on behalf of the casino's bank at *vingt et un.*

'Perhaps you could begin at the beginning, Aunt Agatha,' prompted Mary. Her eyes were sparkling with a mixture of humour and pride, noted Kit.

'Well, that is actually quite a broad question,' reflected Agatha setting her drink down. Half of it was already gone. Clearly, dealing was thirsty work. She turned to the waitress and motioned for some more. Then, remembering her manners, asked Kit and Mary if they wanted another cocktail. The look on Kit's face merely confirmed that Agatha needed to get on with things.

'As I say, we could begin the story in 1877…'

'Let's stick with 1921,' intreated Kit.

'Ahh, probably best. Very well, on the day after we arrived, we were invited up to the palace to meet our old friend, His Serene Highness, Albert, Prince of Monaco.'

'He fancied your aunt, you know,' piped up Betty, beaming proudly at her friend. The smile was wide, warm and, no doubt, had been aided by a number of Gin Rickeys during her stint in the casino.

'Let's stick to the present day, dear. I'm sure they don't want to hear about all of that.'

In fact, Mary did want to hear about 'all of that' but suspected Kit's patience was wearing thin with Agatha's, unusual, dissembling.

'As I was saying, we went up to the palace soon after arriving…'

7

Two weeks earlier:

Prince's Palace of Monaco: March 1921

'Do you think he wants to rekindle things?' asked Betty with no little relish.

Agatha looked askance at Betty.

'First of all, there was never a romance and secondly, I imagine he's a little bit past such foolish notions, and if he isn't, then I certainly am.'

'He is French,' noted Betty in a manner that suggested her point was axiomatic.

'Monegasque,' replied Agatha pointedly. Agatha reached for her umbrella. The skies had turned a decidedly un-Mediterranean-like grey. Rain was in the air. As soon as her umbrella went up, she could hear the first pitter-pattering.

Harry Miller opened the passenger door of their car and they each accepted Miller's hand as they climbed out.

'I'm not sure how long we're going to be, Harry. I suggest you return to the villa and await our call,' said Agatha.

The two ladies moved forward towards the sand-coloured fortress that had been the home of the Grimaldi family since the end of the thirteenth century. Agatha glanced up at the clock tower added by the person they were going to visit and noted they were a few minutes late. Arriving at the gates, Agatha explained in very precise albeit unusually accented French the purpose of their visit and who had invited them to a young guard who had spent too long in front of a mirror practicing his look of studied disdain. Obviously ambitious thought Agatha as he eventually allowed them to pass into the large courtyard that was hidden by the walls of the fortress. Here the two ladies turned left and made straight for the state apartments.

'Gosh, dear, how long has it been?' asked Betty in wonder.

'I was here with 'Useless' a few times. The last time with you was soon after you married James.'

Betty smiled sadly. Such happy times. But James was gone, and she was, if not alone, then without him. As much as she adored Agatha, nothing would ever fill the emptiness, the unbridgeable void left by James Simpson.

In the courtyard they saw a man standing at the base of the horseshoe stairs leading up to the open Gallery of Honour overlooking the court. He was wearing a dark suit and a grave face. This did not augur well. He attempted a smile of greeting which provided little reassurance and only heightened Agatha's spider senses.

The man introduced himself as Auguste Blanc. He led them up the steps to the Gallery of Hercules then into the Mirror Gallery, a long hall inspired by the Hall of Mirrors at Versailles. As they progressed Blanc talked about the design of the palace, not realising that Agatha and Betty had both been there before.

'It was designed as an enfilade, meaning the state rooms lead onto each other rather than via a corridor.'

Betty smiled and was too good-hearted not to show interest. Agatha did not disguise her disinterest and pressed forward quickly towards the Officer's Room, where guests are greeted by court officials before an audience with the prince in the Throne Room. It was obviously still lunchtime for the officials as it was emptier than a pauper's wallet.

From the Officer's Room the enfilade continued through the Blue Room with its Grimaldi family portraits and chandeliers of Murano glass. Finally, they reached the largest of the largest of the state apartments, the Throne Room. The high ceiling displayed frescoes by Orazio de Ferrari depicting Alexander the Great.

The throne was positioned on a dais surmounted by a gilt crown. The floor was made of marble. It was empty thereby dashing a hope of Agatha's that she might be greeted like a head of state.

Instead, the meeting was to take place in the Mazarin Room, so named after the Machiavellian diplomat who kept the Sun King Louis XIV in women, wine, and power. He was a particular favourite of Useless, Agatha remembered. A gentleman of a similar vintage to Agatha and Betty rose to greet them. He held his arms out expansively and was about to speak when Agatha beat him to it.

'Don't say I haven't changed, Albert,' said Agatha, speaking in French.

'I wasn't going to, Agatha,' laughed His Serene Highness, Albert, Prince of Monaco. 'Although perhaps in some ways you are as lovely as ever. And Betty, it has been too long.'

Albert stepped forward, took both Betty's hands, and kissed her on both cheeks. He did likewise with Agatha. Auguste Blanc was somewhat taken aback at the rather informal greeting but accepted stoically that *anglaises* were different.

Albert was an attractive man without being particularly good-looking. Despite her protestations, Agatha had more than a soft spot for the Prince of Monaco. Intelligence radiated from his eyes and a boyish sense of adventure that, even at seventy-three, felt like a coiled spring within him. Agatha had followed his career with interest and fully intended visiting the Oceanographic Museum inspired by his naval career. Yet there was no mistaking the shadow that lurked over this audience. For Betty's sake they spent a few minutes catching up on the last decade of their lives. Yet Agatha could see he was keen to address the issue of why he had invited her to see him.

'You seem worried, Albert, if I may say.'

Albert sighed and nodded. He gazed out of the window for a second to collect his thoughts and then began to speak.

'For the last year, Agatha, the casino has been losing large amounts of money at different times.'

'How large?' interjected Agatha, unable to stop herself.

'Large, Agatha. Very large. It feels like that ridiculous song; you know the one, "The Man Who Broke the Bank at Monte Carlo." Well, it's happening to us, Agatha. Frequently. Of course, strictly speaking, one person should not be able to win so consistently, yet we are sustaining a run of losses for short periods of time. Then it ceases for many months and then it begins again. Auguste is the head of the casino. He can explain better than I.'

Agatha turned to Blanc. Whatever, scepticism the man had been feeling earlier was beginning to evaporate in the heat of Agatha's gaze.

'Monsieur Blanc, do you feel that the pattern of these losses cannot be explained by probability?'

Betty settled down for what she knew would be a discussion that would travel quite a bit beyond what her interest could sustain, or her intellect absorb. Despite the fact that they were now speaking in English, it may as well have been in an as yet undiscovered Sino-Tibetan language dating from the fifth century. Mathematics was another world, and certainly one she had avoided travelling to when she could help it. Its practical application had only intersected with her life, like a Venn diagram, when considering the angles of a pass on a hockey pitch to Agatha or 'Sausage' Gossage fifty years ago or estimating the distance to the green.

'No, Lady Frost, because they happen in sustained clusters then it stops for a while.'

'Have other casinos on the Riviera had similar experiences?'

Albert sat back in his chair and inhaled. Then, for the first time, the smile that followed seemed genuine rather than forced. He glanced at Blanc who seemed to have turned a colour rather akin to his name.

'I did not think to ask, Lady Frost.'

Auguste Blanc could not look at Albert. If he had, he would have seen a man with his eyebrows raised and a flash of anger in those eyes. Blanc did not need to be told that this was a question that he should really have investigated more thoroughly. The prince's face was, if Betty was not mistaken, her bosom swelling with pride, a picture of admonishment for an official who had doubted the wisdom of bringing in an old woman to solve the casino's woes.

'We must ask this question. From Beaulieu, Cannes over to Portofino; from Paris to Deauville and la Foret at le Touquet, Auguste. We must know.'

Blanc nodded but said nothing. The only sign that he accepted his oversight was in the way he stared at his shoes like an embarrassed boy caught stealing apples in the orchard.

'Have you any idea who might be doing this?' continued Agatha. 'We don't need to understand why. The motivation is abundantly clear.'

'This is the thing, Agatha. The winners on each occasion are different men. And the men that win large amounts on some occasions often return and lose,' replied Albert.

'But they are obviously losing much smaller amounts.'

'Yes. The amounts they lose are negligible; what they win is astronomical.'

Agatha stood up causing Albert and Blanc to jump to their feet, too. She waved her arm in a motion which suggested sit down you silly fools. Albert, Prince of Monaco, did as he was told, a half-smile on his face that combined affection, nostalgia, and no little hope if Betty's intuition was accurate.

'Which game are they winning on? It can't be roulette; it must be one of the card games.'

'Always *vingt et un*, Lady Frost,' replied Blanc, finding his voice again.

'Always?' replied Agatha. She was pacing to and fro. 'It's never baccarat, just blackjack. Interesting.'

Betty gazed in adoration at her friend. Her eyes had taken on the look of a hunter. Intelligence beamed from every wrinkle. Albert, Blanc, and Betty followed Agatha like spectators at a tennis match. Her thumb was up at her mouth as if cocking the trigger to unleash another perceptive question.

'How many different winners did you have on each occasion?'

'Usually one, sometimes two. One of them was a woman.'

Agatha spun around at this news with such speed that Blanc was almost ready to hurl himself in front of His Serene Highness to protect him from an assassin's bullet. Or umbrella in Agatha's case.

'A woman you say. Interesting. I wonder.'

'Wonder?'

Agatha looked at Albert shrewdly and said, 'You have, of course, considered the possibility that they are working in league.'

'Well, of course, yet we can scarcely credit the idea. Don't forget it has been different people on each occasion.'

'How many occasions?'

'Four times in the last year.'

'Are they here now?'

'No, but if the pattern repeats itself, then we expect them in the next month or so.'

Agatha nodded and sat down again. She fixed her eyes on the prince and asked the question uppermost in Betty's mind certainly.

'What is it that you wish me to do?'

'Find out how they are doing this, Agatha. Are they cheating or is it some clever system? Are they the same people? Help me, Agatha.'

This did not seem to satisfy Agatha, however. Something was clearly troubling her and, for once, she appeared unable to articulate her thoughts. Such an affliction was rare for Agatha. Normally she had little trouble voicing her thoughts because her unease at upsetting sensibilities declined in inverse proportion to her advancing years. This is a not uncommon occurrence among those who are no longer in youth's first flush. It takes a lifetime to understand the joy of outrageous honesty.

'But if these gamblers are not cheating, and merely good at playing the game, why should I help your casino when the odds are generally, as I understand it, in your favour?'

Albert sighed and then shrugged.

'I ask as a friend, Agatha. An old friend who is seeing his country brought to its knees by a war it did not start and now by clever men whose success will only push us to the edge of extinction. Remember, we do not collect taxes. The casino is our principal source of income. If we have another big pay out, how long will it be before we must deal with similar attacks. If we keep losing, we will soon become a relic, a museum to vanished kingdoms, a footnote in history like Babylon, like Burgundia, Aragon, Savoy, Piedmont. If you wish to see France assimilate this Principality then, yes, Agatha, you are right: why should you help?'

Agatha had the grace look sheepish. She shrugged it off quickly and resumed her business-like demeanour.

'Very well, I shall try to help you as best as I can.'

'What do you suggest?' asked Albert.

'I propose that when your guests come, you send me a message. Both Betty and I shall observe from a distance initially. It may be advisable that I join your casino as one of your dealers. Let me ponder on that. In the meantime, I should learn a little more about *vingt et un* and perhaps receive some training from your staff. We can use Harry Miller, my nephew Christopher's manservant, to assist us. He has some rather unique skills which we may need to call upon. I won't expand on this if it's all the same to you, Albert. I think the less you know the better. And then there is my nephew, Christopher. He we most certainly can use in this endeavour.'

There was more than a hint of scepticism on the prince's face. However, choices were few. He looked at his old friend. Time had not diminished her vigour nor that razor-sharp intelligence. Her nephew was unknown to him. This made him apprehensive.

'I certainly trust your judgement, Agatha, but do you think your nephew will be willing to help us?'

'You can count on Kit,' chipped in Betty, conscious she'd been too quiet for too long. This was something that, as a rule, she liked to remedy periodically with some comment or other. Sometimes these contributions were even relevant.

Albert smiled patiently. His experience of English nobility had long since left him unconvinced that they were the pinnacle of humankind's intellectual possibilities. In short, he viewed them as boorish in behaviour, bigoted in outlook, particularly toward foreigners and, generally, fat-headed to a man. And that was the best of them. The worst were unspeakable.

'This mission will require a mixture of delicacy and a strong grasp of mathematical probability.'

A faraway look appeared in Agatha's eyes followed by a half-smile. Then she turned to Albert and the hapless Blanc. She fixed her eyes on Albert and said with finality, 'I think you'll find Christopher up to the mark, Albert. Mary, too.'

8

Two weeks later:

Monte Carlo, Monaco: early April 1921

'Thank you for the vote of confidence,' said Kit as they exited the casino. Outside, Harry Miller was waiting in a large Mercedes-Benz. He hopped out of the car and greeted Kit and Mary with a huge smile. He was rewarded by Mary with a kiss on the cheek.

'Good to see you again, Harry,' said Mary.

Kit and Miller shook hands. This greeting was followed by a nod from Miller and a roll of the eyes from Kit. For two Englishmen this was more than sufficient acknowledgement of whatever chaps needed to express. However, the limited display of emotion from the two men had Mary shaking her head in amusement. Her beloved was as good-looking as any man had a right to be. He had intelligence and valour, kindness, and good humour. All in fruitful abundance. Yet, put him with another chap of English disposition, temperament, or origin, and all of this seemed to regress to a level that even Palaeolithic man would have found primitive.

Kit cast his eyes over the Mercedes appreciatively. Miller stood beside him and pointed out some of the features of the car before praising its handling. Betty, meanwhile, climbed into the front seat, marginally resisting the temptation to sit on the driver's side. She wasn't used to driving on the 'wrong' side of the road and this probably swayed matters rather than the fact that she was a little bit squiffy following her afternoon acting as Agatha's eyes in the casino.

'Do they do this deliberately, Aunt Agatha?'

Agatha rolled her eyes and replied, 'I gave up a long time ago trying to understand what goes on in their heads. I'm sure it means something to them.'

Mary shook her head and shrugged at the mystery that was the chap of the species. After Kit and Miller had completed one circuit of the car, he joined his companions. He looked at Mary and Agatha and grinned.

'I suppose you'll be wanting me to tell you all about the car, now.'

'Nooo,' chorused the two ladies.

Miller drove down past the port. White sailing boats were scattered across the Mediterranean like pearls on blue satin. The sky was beginning to dim, and pin pricks of light dotted 'the Rock' of Monaco. Miller took them towards the Corniche Inférieure, one of three corniche roads hugging the cliffs of the coast between Nice and Monaco. This led towards Cap d'Ail and Agatha's villa which was situated just on the edge of Principality. Agatha always claimed she lived in Monaco, however. The journey was less than ten minutes.

Agatha's residence in France was a large, white Art Deco villa which had a view of the Mediterranean from the upper floor. It was set into the hillside and the track leading to it was barely wide enough to fit the enormous Mercedes-Benz. Miller negotiated this part of the journey very carefully.

Mary was delighted by the sight of the villa. Although there was a second floor, the flattened roof gave it the feeling of being low, yet each of the upper floor rooms had a balcony. The romantic possibilities seemed endless for Mary from gazing up at the stars in Kit's arms to, well, gazing up at the stars in Kit's arms.

Kit took Mary's hand and led her round to the front of the villa. There was a large terrace and even a swimming pool. There were chairs and sun awnings along the terrace and poolside was a familiar face.

'Uncle Alastair,' said Kit and Mary in unison. Alastair raised a glass to them. The glass was full and, so it seemed, was Alastair by the angle of the grin on his face. He managed to rise unsteadily to his feet but wisely waited for Mary to come over and reward him with a hug and kiss.

'It looks like you're in the holiday spirit,' said Kit indicating the wine.

'I've managed to find some rather convivial company,' replied Alastair smiling before adding *sotto voce*, 'while your aunt is away, that is.'

'Good show, Uncle Alastair, keeping the British end up I hope.'

'As ever, dear boy, as ever.'

The interior of the house was somewhat at odds with the Art Deco exterior. The English country house was a tried and tested model for any home that could afford it. Few could. Large leather sofas, Persian carpets over parquet, a grand piano, paintings by Munnings and silver-framed photographs of family. The white walls were a rare concession to the Med location; even Agatha acknowledged they gave the interior a light and airy atmosphere and that was welcome after the British winter.

The salon was immense with a large marble fireplace that was more decorative than useful. The dining room was rarely used as Agatha liked eating al fresco even when the Riviera was at its chilliest. This never troubled Betty who was made of equally strong stuff but Alastair, despite living in San Francisco which was hardly a tropical climate, found this unfathomable. There were half a dozen bedrooms upstairs, most of which had a terrace and half of which faced the sea. In a nod to the newlyweds, Betty gave up her bedroom facing the sea so that Kit and Mary could have the view. True to her character, she never said anything about it and forbade Agatha and Alastair from mentioning her sacrifice.

As Kit took Mary on a tour of the house, he couldn't help but notice a large leather book on one of the side tables. He glanced at Mary who had also noticed the book. Such tomes usually indicated that the ladies were collecting newspaper articles related to something criminal. The book looked new. It was one thing to be helping Albert, Prince of Monaco, on a matter related to his casino, although this was already surreal; it was quite another to be fishing for murder cases to become involved with. Even Kit, who had form in this area, drew the line. He was still on honeymoon and, if he could help it, would be for quite some time.

'What's this?' asked Mary to Agatha who was standing with Betty at the glass partition that led to the terrace.

'Ahhh,' said Betty. Agatha echoed this. On the whole it said everything without actually resorting to language.

'Ah?' responded Kit, thereby demonstrating a similar level of fluency. It was accompanied by a raised eyebrow which indicated that he was using the interrogative of this English dialect.

Agatha collected herself in record time and understood immediately, despite the lack of words or, indeed, syllables, Kit's meaning, and mood.

'We are just following a case in France which is something of a cause celebre.'

'Yes,' chipped in Betty. 'Have you heard of this vile man Henri Landru?'

'Is this the Bluebeard?' replied Mary, more excitedly than would have been Kit's preference.

'Yes,' said Betty. 'He married, well, became intimate with these poor women and then killed them. Ghastly.'

Mary turned to Kit then back to Betty and Agatha, 'Best keep it out of reach of Kit. I don't want to give him any ideas.'

The three ladies turned to Kit and looked at him in a manner that suggested that all men were probably the same underneath, and that Kit was guilty of having seen off several previous Mrs Astons. Kit threw his arms out in supplication, followed it up with a shrug and wisely, in the circumstances, said nothing. He was now entering that delightful time in any man's relationship with life's soul mate where anything and everything can and will be used in evidence against him. This is better known as marriage.

Kit's guilt having been firmly established, Mary felt it appropriate to open the leather book and examine the contents. As usual, the two ladies had carefully captured a comprehensive selection of newspaper cuttings, many in French, covering the apprehension of the notorious serial killer.

'Ten women murdered by this beast and one young man,' explained Betty. 'Apparently, he acted alone, but I don't believe it. He murdered his victims, stole everything they had. He had to have had help from his family to prevent them from reporting him to the police.'

Agatha listened and then added, 'He probably is guilty but there are some things that haven't been satisfactorily explained.'

'Such as?' asked Mary.

'Well, the fact that only three of the women were actually rich can't be ignored entirely.'

'How did he manage to avoid capture?' asked Mary.

'There were hundreds of thousands of people dying in France during the war. He just lacked ambition,' answered Agatha in a tone that mixed anger and sadness in equal measure.

Mary looked at the photograph of Landru and felt a chill pass through her body. The heavy eyebrows, the coldness of his hooded eyes were all too clear. She was in no doubt that the man was a killer. She turned to Kit and felt reassured by the arms that encircled her waist.

'Yes, everyone's talking about him. He'll go to trial later in the year,' said Betty in a tone that suggested justice would be done.

'And if he's guilty?' wondered Mary.

Betty mimicked the motion of a guillotine by smashing the side of her hand down on her palm. Although Mary didn't quiz Betty on this, she guessed that her friend was more than convinced of his guilt and the rightness of the punishment.

Supper, later that evening, was a muted affair. Kit and Mary were feeling tired after a few days of travel to France from Egypt. Agatha and Betty were fatigued from their afternoon at the casino observing the clients and re-hydrating themselves through the auspices of Gordon's Gin. All agreed a light supper and an early night would be just the thing.

'The plan for tomorrow,' announced Agatha, 'is to introduce you both to Auguste Blanc. Wasn't sure about him at first. In fact, I'm still not sure. Perhaps we may even have a chance to introduce you to Prince Albert. He's a decent chap, Christopher. Quite serious but with a keen intelligence. He's definitely not the usual variety of mutton-headed minor royalty.'

Kit looked at his aunt affectionately. It appeared that his and Mary's help had already been decided. Only Aunt Agatha could command such sacrifice to duty; a pity that the army hadn't had more positions of command for women like her between fourteen and eighteen.

'So, I'm to be drafted onto your team of spies, Aunt Agatha. And there was me thinking that was all over with.'

Agatha ignored the jesting and pressed on in an Agatha-like manner, 'Not just you, Christopher. Between the four of us, I think we can crack this case. Harry, too. We may need his skills in this matter.' She pursed her lips in admonishment of her immature nephew.

'And what will you do while we are cracking this gambling ring, Uncle Alastair?' asked Kit.

Alastair raised his glass of wine and smiled. This answer was serenely eloquent. Inevitably, it met with disapproval from the usual quarter.

'The very least you could do, Alastair, is throw your shoulder to the wheel or whatever that phrase is.'

'I think that you, Betty and our young friends here will have the matter under control in no time. Then the casino can return to doing what it does best: depriving fools of their inherited or hard-earned riches.'

This jibe found its mark even if Agatha ignored it. In truth, there was no right answer to this question. A royal friend in need was one thing but, as ever, it was the challenge. Her curiosity could never be sated by lying around a pool indolently or drinking with buddies. Knowing her nephew and the young lady he'd married, she suspected they would enjoy their little mission. It would add a little spice to the end of the honeymoon. And anyway, what could possibly go wrong? After all, it was only a case of trying to understand by whom and how the casino was on the wrong end of a rinsing.

Mary turned to Uncle Alastair. Her sparkling blue eyes fixed on him. She placed her elbows on the table and rested her chin on the back of her clasped hands. Kit recognised this pose. This was Mary in full interrogation mode.

'So, Uncle Alastair, you are just going to sit by the pool drinking cocktails?'

It was Agatha who answered.

'He'll be with his new friends.'

'Who are they?' asked Kit.

Alastair chuckled at this, 'Oh just some men of a certain age. Very companionable. They're all either widowers or recently remarried. You should meet them, Kit. You'd like them.'

The harrumph from the other end of the table suggested that at least one person was not in favour of this idea.

'Ask your uncle what they call themselves, Christopher.'

Kit raised his eyebrows by way of prompt to his uncle.

'Their nickname is, perhaps, in questionable taste given the circumstances,' responded Alastair. He paused hoping that he would not have to expand on this rather enigmatic answer. However, by now, the eyes of the table were directed his way, the spotlight was upon him; he was centre stage.

'Yes?' probed Mary.

'They like to call themselves the Bluebeard Club.'

9

The next day was overcast and denied Mary a chance to enjoy the light that had been inspiring artists for half a century. It was rather chilly, too. It was a reminder that her wardrobe of light clothes, so practical in Egypt, was somewhat less useful when the Côte d'Azur was taking on the habits and inclinations of many of its visitors from England: cold, grey, and grumpy.

As they were not due to meet Auguste Blanc until the afternoon, Kit used the time to show Mary around the Principality. Walking around Monaco is only for the young and the foolish. The large number of buildings can sometimes hide the fact that the port, at sea level, is the lowest point but the rest is effectively built into the side of hills. Harry Miller drove the couple around.

They started at the palace. This was situated on 'The Rock', the two hundred feet high monolith upon which the old town of Monaco, Monaco-Ville, is situated. From there Kit and Mary walked a short distance to the Oceanographic Museum. The Jardin de St Martin, to the side of the museum, with its starchy grass and palm trees, offered views across the Mediterranean which would have been more spectacular had the cloud not insisted on obscuring the horizon.

They had lunch at the Yacht Club overlooking the port. Kit's father was a long-standing member. In fact, he would not have been surprised to run into his father and Marge. They rarely spoke and had not done so since the wedding.

At least there had been some form of reconciliation between his father and Alastair. However, his uncle had still elected to come with Agatha to the Riviera rather than stay with his brother. Perhaps Alastair wanted to enjoy a warm winter. Or perhaps it was the idea that being around Marge, the woman that his father had cheated on Kit's mother while she lay ill, was too much. Kit knew that Alastair and his mother had been engaged before Lancelot had moved in and stolen her. The split between the brothers had lasted decades.

Mary gazed at her husband. His eyes were directed towards sea. She sensed a sadness. His fine features drawn. She gripped his hand and did not ask the question that all women seemed to ask except her. What's on your mind? Kit turned to her and smiled. He knew what she was thinking and loved her for not asking.

'I was just thinking about my father. He used to come here quite a lot with mother. They loved sailing. I don't think Marge has quite the sea legs of my mother.'

'Did you sail with them?'

'Yes. And Olly Lake came with us on a few occasions.' Kit went quiet for a moment as he thought of his former friend. 'Seems like a lifetime ago. Spunky and Chubby never fancied the idea of sailing so it was just Olly, me, mama, and papa. I daresay I wouldn't be much use now, clumping around like Long John Silver.'

Mary burst out laughing at this. Far from being cruel it was intoxicating for Kit. She loved him and nothing else mattered at that moment.

'What do you make of Uncle Alastair's new friends? This Bluebeard Club.'

'I can only apologise on behalf of my species. We really are terrible, aren't we? I'm not sure how anyone can make light of what that vile man, Henri Landru, has done.'

'Wait until you've been married twenty or thirty years. Maybe you'll change your tune,' suggested Mary with an impish grin.

'Assuming you last that long,' flapping his napkin as the food arrived.

Mary kicked Kit's wooden leg. It was her usual response to any impertinence.

'How was Aunt Agatha with Useless?', asked Mary. 'It doesn't sound like she made him miserable,'

'Far from it. Eustace had her number all right. He may not have had her brain, but he certainly was cannier. It's what made him such a wonderful diplomat. You wouldn't want to be facing Uncle Eustace across the table. He'd sucker you into thinking he was a fool while picking your proverbial pocket. Some of the stunts he pulled. Someone should write a book about him.'

'Maybe they will.'

'Of course, it might run afoul of the Official Secrets Act and send us into another war,' responded Kit, thinking out loud.

Around two in the afternoon lunch was finished and they walked up the Avenue de Monte Carlo from the Yacht Club and into Place du Casino. Mary paused for a moment to look at the opera house which was to the side of the casino. Then, noting the look on Kit's face, hurried to join him.

'So, what if we're late,' said Mary. 'We're doing him a favour.'

'True, but do you really want to keep Aunt Agatha waiting?'

This was a good point which Mary acknowledged with a chuckle. They proceeded along the side of the building and round to the steps of the casino.

-

Nearby in the square, two men were enjoying a light lunch at a cafe. They were sitting facing outwards onto the street, in the French style. In an equally Gallic manner, the youngest of them drew the other man's attention to Mary. Despite the relative cold, she was clad lightly, and in a manner likely to arouse more than just romantic eloquence in a Frenchman and red-faced stuttering from his wartime ally across the channel.

Having satisfactorily described Mary in adjectives likely to stir the interest of his colleague he pointed out where they should direct their gaze. Instead, of being smitten by Mary, however, he found his attention taken by the man accompanying her.

'*Mon Dieu*,' he said. His young companion was in complete agreement with the sentiment even if it was for an entirely different reason. He turned to the young man and his heart sank. He was virtually pawing the ground in enthusiasm. 'Do you see the man with her?'

'What man?' This prompted a smile in the senior man.

Reluctantly, he moved his eyes away from the vision of loveliness towards Kit. Their first impression was one of disappointment. The man was clearly *Anglais*, probably handsome in a fair-haired, tall sort of way and, sadly, certainly richer than Croesus's rich uncle, Midas the Very Rich Indeed.

'Yes? What of him, sir?'

'Follow him. Do not let him out of your sight. I want to know where he is staying. I want to know who he is meeting. I want to know everything that he does while he is here. If you need help, find it. He goes nowhere without me knowing. Do you understand?'

The young man looked confused and, for a moment, wondered if he'd done something to offend. Unfortunately, this pause was enough to cause the older man to glare at him. The young man jumped off his seat and jogged over towards the casino. He hopped up the steps and through the double doors just in time to see the young woman and his quarry being led away by an older man along a corridor then in through a door which presumably was an office.

He turned to the doorman. He was young, probably young enough to be aggressive with. The young man addressed the doorman.

'That man and woman who just came in. Who were they going to see?'

The doorman stood up to his full height which was a shade over five feet six and thus barely worth the effort. The look on his face was not difficult to read – what is it to you? The young man stepped forward and showed what it was to him. In this case it was a not so much the card he showed him as the sight of the gun inside his jacket.

'They are seeing the head of the casino, Monsieur Blanc.'

The young man nodded a gruff thanks and strode over to a free seat near the bar. This position afforded him a view of the interior and time to wonder who the couple were, and why they were of such interest.

-

Auguste Blanc greeted Kit and Mary in the manner of someone meeting his ex-wife's better looking new husband: a querulous combination of resentment and relief. He was resentful that Prince Albert had called in outside help, *Anglais* no less, to deal with a matter that he felt was within his control. Another part of him felt relief that if it all went wrong then he would not be to blame. They were certainly an inconvenience. His early fencing with Agatha had only confirmed the suspicion fostered at their first meeting that she was not to be underestimated. However, he was of the firm view that English Lords were capable of nothing more sophisticated than setting alight their own vapours or shooting animals indigenous to countries they'd invaded. This was a source of reassurance to him.

This feeling lasted less than the time it took for Kit and Mary to join Agatha and Betty in Blanc's office.

'So, tell me, Monsieur Blanc,' said Kit, sitting down. 'Do you have a description of the men that we are seeking?'

Blanc blanched at this question. His mind quickly turned, as it does for so many of us, towards how to admit that this step had not been taken, in a manner least likely to destroy credibility.

'I can introduce you to the dealers who were playing on the nights that these men won.'

'You are sure that we are talking about different men on each night and across the different occasions that the casino lost so heavily?'

Auguste Blanc shifted uncomfortably in his seat. Lady Frost's nephew appeared to be cut from the same sharp stone. The two dealers in question had never been asked to compare notes on the people they had lost to. With each passing second, Blanc began to suspect that his handling of the crisis would appear inept bordering on negligent. By now his head was spinning and he realised that two choices lay before him: a show of indignation at the discourtesy he was being subjected to or acknowledgement that he needed help. All eyes were now not so much on him as boring into him.

'I need your help, your lordship. The attack on the casino, and we must view it as an attack, is outside of my experience. What do you suggest?'

Agatha smiled inwardly. It made a pleasant change not to be the battle axe. She was under no illusions as to how she was perceived. It had always been so. This was the price one paid for being old and smart. Once upon a time she could call upon some beauty to at least mollify the delicate sensitivities of men. No longer. Not that she cared. Those who knew her loved her for what she was. Those who didn't know or love her soon respected her. She counted this as a victory.

Kit paused for a minute. His assessment of the situation was as Agatha had suggested the previous evening. The casino had spent its existence beating deluded gamblers. Like Goliath going into battle against a young lad carrying a sling, their initial reaction to this new threat was amusement at the impudence and imprudence of their opponent. They were ill prepared for the fight.

'I will need to speak to the men that faced the gamblers in question. I want to understand what they remember of who they faced on each occasion.'

'But, Lord Aston, how can you expect them to remember such men. Perhaps the most recent ones, yes, but the other occasions were before Christmas and even in summer last year.'

'You would be surprised at what people will remember, Monsieur Blanc.' Blanc did not feel in a position to contradict the Englishman who was proving a little less like the usual manifestation of the breed that trooped into the casino every winter. Another thought occurred to him.

'Perhaps, but even if they can recall something of these men, what do we do if they return when these particular dealers are not in the casino? We can't expect them to work all day and every day.'

Kit smiled and even Agatha glanced at her nephew with a frown. This problem had occurred to her when she spoke with the dealers.

'I have some ideas on that subject. For the moment I want to understand what they can remember of the evenings in question. Now, another question for you. My aunt mentioned that you had briefed her on standard *vingt et un* strategy. Can you, or perhaps the dealers in question, verify if the men who were beating the casino so badly were following this approach or another?'

'I think you should meet them, Lord Aston.'

Blanc rose from his seat and left the office to speak to a lady. He returned a few moments later and informed the group that the two dealers were on their way. In the meantime, Blanc outlined the traditional approach to playing the game from a player's point of view.

'I presume you know the rules. A dealer deals you two cards, one face up. The object is to reach twenty-one or as close to it as possible. If you need another card, you tap the table. The dealer will deal you another card face up. Of course, it is possible to bet while you do this. You can even double your bet by splitting your cards if you are dealt two cards of the same value. So far so good; I think you understand. Your opponent is the bank, in the form of the dealer. The dealer also deals two cards for himself.'

Kit nodded as he said this. He glanced at his aunt. Her eyes were narrowed like a sniper sizing up a target.

'Standard strategy for a player is to keep hitting for a new card if the dealer has seventeen or higher. If the dealer has low cards, like a five or a six, then it is best to stick unless you are obviously weak. Remember of course, there are likely to be other players playing against the bank. The dealer will usually keep playing up to sixteen or seventeen.'

'What are the odds?'

Blanc looked a little sheepish at this point and, reluctantly it must be said, admitted to between one and two percent advantage for the house even assuming the player followed basic strategy. Kit concluded it would be much higher if they were playing against a fool. He suspected a lot of fools entered through the doors of the casino.

The two dealers arrived as Blanc was taking Kit through the strategy. Bernard Lloris was a young Corsican with hawk-like features and eyes that suggested he was nobody's fool. The second man was the croupier they had seen the previous day with the extravagant salt and pepper hair.

Patrice Rives had light blue eyes that contrasted sharply with deeply tanned skin that appeared to be made from leather.

Kit spoke with them, as he had with Blanc, in French. Both men could remember distinctly the faces of the men who had won so much on the previous visit. Lloris had not been at the casino the previous autumn, but Blanc claimed that he could remember two of the winners on that occasion. He was quite clear that they had been older although the more recent winners had been middle-aged and, this time, there was a woman.

'Did they know one another?' asked Kit.

Both dealers shook their heads and said that they had not seen them together and that they did not always sit together at the table.

'Did you see the men and the woman, Monsieur Blanc?'

Blanc nodded but added that his memory of them was unlikely to be as vivid as the two dealers'.

'Of course,' said Kit. This seemed to be the end of Kit's questions for the time being. He thanked the two dealers, and they were allowed to return to the tables.

'Do you have all you need?' asked Blanc, hopefully.

'In a manner of speaking,' replied Kit enigmatically. I have some ideas on what we should do next.' He did not add to this and glanced over to Agatha and then back to Blanc. 'At the moment I do not know what we are facing, but have you considered the possibility that there is any risk involved to my aunt?'

Agatha, naturally, dismissed this suggestion with a wave of her hand. Blanc, too, seemed amused that the gamblers represented any risk to anyone bar the casino's finances. Kit looked at Agatha again. He sensed there was something on her mind, though. His confidence in Blanc's glib reaction to danger was none too high. More than this, he felt Blanc was not being completely open with him. It was just a feeling, but it was strong one. He would quiz Agatha about this afterwards.

They parted with Blanc soon after and Kit led the group over to a small telegraph office. He scribbled a note down and handed it to a young woman behind the counter. Then he gave her Agatha's address and asked that the reply be sent there immediately it came.

Outside the telegraph office, Kit turned to Agatha and was about to ask her the question uppermost on his mind when she beat him to the punch.

'What do you think of Blanc? Do you believe him?'

'No, Aunt Agatha, I don't think he's told us everything.'

'Good. I didn't think so either.'

Standing nearby was the young man. He heard the exchange clearly and noted it down. When Kit and the others left the office, he strolled over to the young woman behind the counter. She smiled at him. He smiled back.

-

Around seven hundred miles away in London at Scotland Yard, Chief Inspector Jellicoe stared down at the telegram that had been put on his desk. He shook his head then sat back on his chair. From anyone else he would have considered the request extraordinary, but he knew from experience that Lord Kit Aston was an extraordinary man.

He looked up at the young, uniformed officer in front of him. The young man smiled. The smile faded briefly when he saw the serious features of the chief inspector.

'Did you read it?'

'Of course.'

'I should put you on a charge,' said Jellicoe but the tone of voice was markedly at odds with the content of what had been said. This was unusual for Jellicoe. He was a serious man and rarely joked when in the office.

The young constable smiled once more. It was barely discernible, but Jellicoe's face seemed to lighten momentarily. Then the young constable spoke.

'If you did, sir, then you would have a lot of explaining to do with mother.'

Jellicoe shook his head and handed the telegram to his son.

'I have no objection. Let me know what he decides. He has three days. No more.'

'I will tell him, sir,' said Constable James Jellicoe. This was his third week in the Metropolitan Police Force.

10

Two days later the young man summarised what he'd found out about Kit Aston to his companion. They were taking breakfast at a café in the Place de Casino, beside the Hôtel de Paris. The sun remained resolutely behind the clouds which gave the morning a distinct freshness. The report by the young man was met with head-shaking disbelief. The older man, although he was not yet forty, summarised the findings.

'So, this old woman, Lady Frost, the aunt of Lord Aston, is working with the casino to find out who has been winning large sums over the course of the year. Your intelligence suggests Lord Aston will help her.'

'Yes, sir.'

'Incredible. And Alastair Aston is the uncle of Lord Aston,' said the senior man, which prompted another shake of the head. He wiped his eyes with his fingers as if trying to wake up from a bad dream.

'And you say the telegram went to Scotland Yard?'

'Yes, sir,' replied the young man. He was feeling decidedly chipper about the comprehensiveness of his report. There were some gaps of course. The young woman couldn't show him the telegram but at least he'd found out about the recipient. He couldn't rest on his laurels. Not with this man. He leaned forward and asked, 'What do you want me to do now, sir?'

The senior man felt like shrugging. The situation was spiralling out of control. They had been here barely a few days. What would he tell his superiors? He did not want to return home and admit defeat. Nor did he want to cede the field to the English milord, never mind Scotland Yard. Yet the wind was out of their sails. They were in the doldrums. The trail was going cold.

A thought occurred to the senior man.

'What about the chauffeur?' he asked suddenly. The young man opened his notebook to locate the name. 'Harry Miller,' added the senior man.

'I haven't followed him.'

'Do so for next day. See where he goes. Trust me, he's more than a chauffeur.' Nothing else was added to this tantalising piece of information. They continued their breakfast in silence. Just then a taxi drew up outside the Hôtel de Paris. Invariably the people entering the hotel were rich and often attractive enough to halt consumption of even the tastiest patisserie.

A small man emerged from the taxi. He was uncommon enough to raise a smile in the two men. His hair was longer than the current fashion, he was wearing a black cloak with a vivid red velvet lining. It was as if he'd emerged from a Belle Epoque poster by Toulouse Lautrec. He stopped outside the hotel, looked around him, threw his hair back and walked ahead with purpose, swinging his cane.

The little man was barely through the door when the quiet calm of Place du Casino was shattered by a police siren. The senior man frowned as he saw one, then two other police cars tear past the fountain and draw up outside the casino.

'Let's go,' said the senior man.

-

He saw the two men at the café from the corner of his eye. They were staring at him. People usually did. He looked at the exterior to the Hotel de Paris. This was *his* sort of place. Somewhere that he was born to grace. He threw his cloak back and swept forward past the doorman into the foyer of the hotel. Behind him, the taxi driver struggled to carry his valise up the steps.

People stopped and stared at the little man as he marched forward through the marble-floored lobby to the reception desk. And why wouldn't they stare?

He looked *fabulous.*

The interior was everything he'd imagined it would be. Overhead was an impressive domed ceiling decorated with naiads and Tritons. In the hall was an equestrian statue of Louis XIV standing triumphant just like Marcus Aurelius, the Roman Emperor who inspired the work. Legend said that rubbing the horse's knee would bring luck. From the man's viewpoint, many had tried this for the knee had most of its veneer rubbed away. He stepped forward to the reception desk.

'Bonjour,' he said to the lady behind the desk in an accent that he was certain could have been developed in the Sorbonne.

'Good morning,' replied the lady in English.

He wasn't sure if this was a setback related to the French accent or merely recognition of his distinctive dress and manner.

'Good morning,' he replied in English with a smile. 'I believe a reservation has been made for me by Lord Aston.' The last two words were uttered with some emphasis. He smiled inwardly at his boldness. He wasn't beyond a bit of social-climbing name association. It was part of the game. And he loved the game.

'What is the name, sir? Asked the receptionist.

'Watts. Rufus Watts.'

'Yes, Mr Watts, we have a reservation. Do you have any luggage?'

The doors of the hotel crashed open and in staggered the taxi driver dragging a valise which was around the size of a large wardrobe. He dragged the luggage over towards Rufus Watts and then collapsed in a heap on the ground. Watts took a wallet out from the inside of his jacket and extracted one hundred francs and handed it to the taxi driver before returning his attention to the receptionist. The receptionist viewed the enormous valise and motioned for an attendant to take over from the taxi driver.

'Two nights, sir?'

'Yes, two nights.' He stopped for a second then added, 'No. Make it four nights.'

-

Kit and Mary spent two days being driven along the Cote D'Azur by Miller. Dinner in the Negresco in Nice on one evening was followed by a dinner in the Carlton in Cannes the next. Mary was entranced by the Riviera.

'Next year we should come with Esther and Richard.'

'I doubt we'd see much of Esther,' replied Kit, 'I dare say she'd be painting *en plein air* all of the time.'

'In which case you and Richard would be minus the Cavendish girls because I'd be with her.'

'If I may just point out you are now an Aston,' pointed out Kit with a look of triumph. 'In fact, my wife.'

'Your chattel?'

'That's the spirit.'

Mary made a face and then turned to gaze out at the sea. They were sitting on a bench overlooking the sandy beach at Cannes. It was a beautiful evening. The sea was lit up by the lights of the town and the boats bobbing on its surface.

'So, we meet Mr Watts tomorrow.'

'Yes. I'm afraid the work will begin then.

In fact, Mary was looking forward to helping Aunt Agatha. As much as she enjoyed touring the Riviera, there was something intoxicating about being on a case of sorts.

Miller took the couple along with Agatha and Betty on the short drive into Monte Carlo around eleven the next morning. They drove along the port and then up the hill into Place du Casino. The sight that greeted them was something of a shock. There was a barrier outside the casino and inside were a handful of police cars and an ambulance. Police were stopping well-heeled tourists from entering. Betty spoke for everyone in the car.

'Good Lord.'

There was nowhere to park near the casino, so Miller let his passengers out and went away to find somewhere to put the Mercedes-Benz. Kit led the party over towards the casino. Tempers were somewhat frayed. Casino workers stood alongside casino patrons united, if not in wealth, then certainly in confused anger about what was going on.

Before Kit could ask about what was going on, he heard one of the policemen dismiss an enquiry from an Englishman who promptly responded by shouting, 'Do you know who I am?'

Even if this query had been posed in French, Kit suspected the reaction could not have been more Gallic. The policeman smiled at the angry gentleman and shrugged his shoulders. Oddly, Kit was on the side of the policeman who then began to laugh as his new enemy stalked off with the threat of speaking to the man in charge.

'I can see quite a number of the staff,' said Agatha, looking around at the scene. 'I fear the worst.'

'Yes,' agreed Kit. 'I would love to know what's happened. It doesn't look like anyone is being allowed in.'

Of course, in *roman policiers* or popular theatre, at this moment, something would happen that would allow our hero to find a way into the crime scene: an open window, a policeman distracted by a beautiful woman's attention. Sadly, both thoughts did track through Kit's mind just then. Thankfully, he decided against using Mary as a diversion. Not that he believed it would be doomed to failure. He had the utmost trust in Mary's ability to beguile any man.

Rather, he suspected such a request would be met with disproportionate resistance.

'What shall we do?' asked Mary. Interestingly, her eyes were scanning along the front of the casino, noted Kit. It seemed as if she, too, had been wondering if there was a way of gaining entrance. His hearts swelled at this.

'Nothing, my dear. We won't be trying to climb through an open window if that's what's on your mind.'

Mary shot Kit a glance and grinned. 'As if.' Then she shrugged and replied, 'I thought it worth checking.'

'Let's go over to the hotel. I wonder if Mr Watts has arrived.'

-

Rufus Watts had been riveted by the spectacle in the Place du Casino, it was an uplifting end to a long and tiring journey. The trip to France had encompassed a rush to pack followed by an aeroplane flight from London to Paris. The Handley-Page service had recently recommenced thanks to government support. In the matter of a hours, he'd gone from Scotland Yard to Paris Nord to catch the Blue Train down to Nice. All first class thanks to Lord Aston. And Chief Inspector Jellicoe who, suspected Watts, probably owed Lord Aston a favour or three.

A bath and a change into a light cotton suit more appropriate for the Riviera climate meant he was ready to face the work that lay ahead. He glanced down at a leather suitcase containing his equipment. A final check in the mirror. His trim figure looked well in a suit that had been made in Saville Row. Rufus did not believe in stinting when it came to his appearance. He was ready.

Returning to the window, he saw a large Mercedes-Benz car draw up near the casino. Moments later Kit Aston emerged from the car followed by his wife and two elderly ladies, one of whom he recognised as having been involved in a case the previous year.

'Duty calls,' said Watts. He walked over to his small suitcase and picked it up along with the walking stick that he took everywhere. He skipped down the stairs and arrived in the lobby just in time to see Kit Aston enter with his party.

Introductions were made. The most interesting from Watts's point of view was the aunt. There was shrewdness about her that explained many things about what he'd heard of the 'Medium Murders' case. That said, his eyes widened as Kit explained the situation to him over coffee in the hotel. He glanced at the aunt once more with barely contained admiration. She dismissed the implied praise with a growl and a wave of a hand.

Then there was Lady Mary. Lord Aston was a very lucky man. However, his lovely wife was clearly fascinated. By him. How could she not be? He was in Monte Carlo, and he was here to dazzle.

'Now, tell me, Mr Watts,' said Kit.

'Lord Aston, could I trouble you to call me Rufus?'

Kit smiled and began again, 'Rufus, do you speak French at all?'

'Fluently,' replied Watts, successfully trying not to sound too humble.

'Excellent, Rufus. For the purposes of this task, it is imperative that you do not reveal this. I shall act as your translator.'

Agatha shot a look towards Kit and a half-smile appeared on her lips. Betty looked a little lost, but she smiled anyway. Then the penny appeared to drop.

'I say, Kit, you don't think that someone is working with these scoundrels from the inside?' said Betty. Her eyes were wide with excitement.

'We should be prepared for anything,' replied Agatha on behalf of her nephew. 'Now what is our plan for gaining access to the casino?' Once upon a time such a task would have fallen upon her. These days she was more than happy to hand detailed planning over to Kit. He was eminently capable. He'd learned from her, after all. And from Useless.

'Yes, I saw the commotion. Have we any idea what's happened?' asked Watts.

Kit looked the little police artist in the eye and said, 'We have no idea but judging by the number of police and the ambulance I think we should assume the worst. You will be our entry ticket into the casino.'

At a table nearby, the conversation between Kit and the others was being listened to by the same young man who'd followed them for a couple of days. He watched them rise from the table and head towards the exit of the hotel.

He followed them.

It was clear they were heading towards the casino. The young man overtook them and jogged over to the front of the casino. The same policeman was standing in front of the makeshift barricade at the front. There were pressmen there, too. The atmosphere was electric. The noise levels had increased considerably in the half hour they'd been in the hotel. Meanwhile, casino patrons and pressmen were united in their curiosity and desire to gain admittance. And being mostly of a French persuasion, this desire was unlikely to find its outlet through the agency of silent protest. Instead, they were jolly well going to let the world know by shouting at the poor policeman standing guard.

'Are you sure, Kit?' asked Mary as they approached the crowd.

'Not really,' admitted Kit in a low voice, 'but you know, fortune favours the shameless, as they say.'

Mary frowned and narrowed her eyes at Kit then broke out into a grin. Kit saw the young man in the suit who'd obviously been listening to their conversation in the hotel café. He walked up to the policeman and said a few words. Moments later he was allowed through. Both Agatha and Mary grabbed Kit's arms simultaneously. A policeman. He had to be a policeman This was becoming more interesting by the second.

'Did you see that?' exclaimed Agatha.

'He was in the café with us,' replied Mary. She turned to Kit.

'Indeed,' said Kit. His senses were screaming at him now. And the message they were communicating was that they were being followed. There was nothing else for it. He walked straight over to the policeman standing guard.

It would be fair to say that *Gardien* Jacques Dubois had just about had enough of the tourists. Although the day was overcast, it was getting warmer. He'd been standing at the entrance to the barricades over an hour without a break. He wanted to smoke. He wanted a coffee. He wanted a seat and a chance to take his damn coat off. More than anything else, he never wanted to see an English aristocratic tourist again. To a man, and it was usually men, they thought they had a divine right to march across crime scenes to order people around or play cards.

Just at that moment Kit appeared before the roasting constable. Despite his discomfort, there was a certain satisfaction to be reaped from sending the rich on their way with a few well-chosen words. One look at Kit Aston and Dubois knew exactly what he was dealing with. This was an exceptional example of the cursed breed. Dubois' mouth twitched into a sneer. He was past the point of listening to their bad French. Instead, he was on the point of dismissing the Englishman out of hand and humiliating him in front of his friends and his particularly fetching lady friend when he felt a hand on his arm.

Kit was surprised to see the man who had suddenly appeared beside the policeman.

'Lord Aston, what a pleasant surprise.'

'Your young man has been following us for a day or two now so it can't be that much of a surprise.'

The man had the good grace to laugh, and he acknowledged the truth of this. Kit turned to his party and said, 'I imagine you already know that this is my wife, Mary, my aunt, Lady Frost and her friend Betty Simpson. And this gentleman is…'

'Rufus Watts of Scotland Yard,' finished the man with a smile.

'Your young man is to be congratulated,' said Kit, glancing towards the man who had been following them. Then Kit turned to the others and said, 'May I introduce someone I met a couple of years ago in Paris, Inspector Briant of the Sûreté.'

'Captain Briant, now.'

'My congratulations, Captain Briant. Well now that we're all acquainted, perhaps we can step inside, and you can apprise us of what has happened.

11

Briant nodded to Dubois who, with a great show of reluctance, stood aside to allow Kit and the others past the barricade. The group walked towards the casino. Briant began to explain what had happened. He didn't spend any time building up the drama.

'Monsieur Blanc, the general manager of the casino, has been murdered.

Kit stopped dead causing a minor pile up behind him and a few sharp words from his aunt that Briant's excellent command of English had no trouble in comprehending.

'Sorry, Aunt Agatha,' said Kit sheepishly. 'Blanc dead? Good Lord. Do you have any suspects?'

'No, Lord Aston. He was murdered last night but the body was only just discovered this morning. He went to his office sometime close to midnight and locked the door. The cleaner found him this morning when she opened his office to clean it. He was lying alongside his desk. We believe he has been poisoned.'

They had reached the doors of the casino when Briant stopped. He looked at Kit as if wrestling with a decision. In this case, if Kit was judging him correctly, it seemed there were no good answers. Briant did not look happy. Finally, he decided.

'Lord Aston, I will make a strange request of you and your family and friends.'

'Go on.'

'It will suit me well if your aunt continues to do the work that was requested of her by Blanc.'

Agatha, who spoke French fluently, stepped forward when she heard her name mentioned.

'Lady Frost, I know that you have been employed to investigate instances of unusually high success against the casino.'

Kit glanced at the young detective beside Briant and nodded once more. It appeared the young man had done a thoroughly good job.

'Do you know who asked her?'

'Yes,' replied Briant, glancing at Agatha rather like a man given a sure-fire tip for a horse race, disbelief followed by curiosity.

'May I ask why you are making this request, Captain Briant?' asked Agatha.

Briant smiled and nodded towards the casino.

'The case is officially in the jurisdiction of the local police. Specifically, the Inspector from the Nice police, and an examining magistrate, Inspector Saimbron and Monsieur Charpentier. I am not sure if they appreciate my presence.'

Kit raised an eyebrow at this and replied with a smile, 'Now you know how this feels, Captain.' Briant smiled and acknowledged the jibe. 'But it does throw up an interesting question,' added Kit. 'What exactly are you and your men doing here, Captain?'

'Let us go inside,' said Briant, neatly avoiding the question but giving Kit and the others something that would interest them more. A chance to see the murder scene.

They passed through into the entrance hall of the casino. From there they headed towards Blanc's office. Briant glanced at Mary. Kit had been dreading this. He knew that it was already asking too much that he be allowed to into the crime scene. It was pushing things too far for Briant to expect him to invite Mary, too. Mary saw the exchange of looks between the two men. She had suspected that this would be a step too far for the man from the Sûreté.

'Mary can be my and Mr Watts' translator,' said Kit looking at Briant in the eye.

A smile creased Briant's lips. He nodded to Kit and then, for sake of form said, 'I must warn you that we have a dead body in here, Lady Mary.'

'I was a nurse in the Voluntary Aid Detachment,' said Mary, holding Briant's gaze.

A shadow passed over the face of the policeman as if a thousand memories, all sad, descended upon him. Kit had wondered before, in Paris, if Briant had served. He now knew, without question, he had.

At this point, Agatha, and Betty, disappeared. Neither were particularly happy about this but recognised that there was no choice. More staff were coming through the entrance accompanied by the police. Briant knocked on the door and entered immediately without waiting for a reply.

The office was as Kit had found it a few days previously although with the marked difference of two men dusting for fingerprints, two ambulance men crouching down over a corpse and two older men staring open-mouthed at the arrival of Mary. At that moment, they resembled the dead body lying on the ground.

'Briant, what is the meaning of this?' exclaimed the older of the two men. Kit noted that he wore a pince nez which pretty much condemned him in Kit's eyes. This was unquestionably a martinet.

Briant held his hand up to the older man, which appeared to enrage him further. Kit suspected that this had been Briant's intention. The other man was a little older than Briant, probably early forties, and unquestionably a detective. He was dressed a little shabbily and didn't care who knew it. He smoked a cigarette with casual disdain and an amused look on his face. Kit liked him immediately.

Briant introduced the first man as the Examining Magistrate Charpentier. The second, as Kit surmised, was Inspector Saimbron. There was a shrewdness in his eyes, Kit noted. He stayed silent, smoked a cigarette, and sized Kit up in a swift glance. Then he turned to Briant and ignored Mary and Rufus Watts.

'May I introduce Monsieur Aston,' said Briant eyeing Kit closely. Kit acknowledged him and then the two men. 'The other gentleman is Monsieur Watts from Scotland Yard, and this is Mademoiselle Cavendish.'

It would be fair to say that both Kit and Mary's eyes fairly popped out of their head at this. Kit shot the young man a glance once more. This had been very impressive work in a short space of time.

'Mademoiselle Cavendish is acting as a translator. They were asked by Monsieur Blanc to investigate unusual gambling patterns in the casino. I gather they have some expertise in this area.'

Charpentier, however, was having none of this. His chest was puffing out and there was a distinct redness around his gills that suggested an explosion was imminent. At this point the little police artist stepped forward. Dressed in his light cotton suit, his straw fedora at a jaunty angle and long hair falling over his collar, probably the last thing that the situation needed was for Watts to say, 'Bonjour,' in an accent that was a hammy version of theatrical English. Sure enough, this tipped the examining magistrate over the edge.

'Captain Briant, this is an outrage, sir. It is bad enough that you have inveigled yourself onto this case but now you bring in outsiders. English no less.'

Mary turned to Kit and began to translate.

'This man is a fat head of the highest order.'

'Yes, I spotted that,' replied Kit in a low voice.

'Captain Briant,' exclaimed Charpentier, 'I demand an explanation.' He stamped his foot as he said this. There was a moment of silence as everyone registered that he really had stamped his foot. Kit glanced towards Saimbron. The detective dragged on his cigarette with stained fingers and rolled his eyes.

Watts, meanwhile, turned to Mary with eyebrows raised and a twinkle in his eye for a translation. Mary's face remained straight as she said, 'I think he wants to skin the two of you alive…with a spoon.'

'Dessert or soup?' asked Watts.

Briant could hear all that was being said and was fighting his own battle between anger at the unwelcome British guests and a very strong desire to burst out laughing. His admiration for the young woman was growing exponentially.

'Monsieur Charpentier,' said Briant pointedly ignoring the use of his title, 'if you will give me a moment to explain. The English are here at the express invitation of Prince Albert. If you have a problem with this, then you will need to take it up directly with His Serene Highness.'

There was an edge to his voice. Just enough to suggest impatience. This was noted by the examining magistrate. While it certainly made him no more pleased, there was a noticeable deflation in his preening prickliness.

'I shall,' snarled Charpentier impotently. Everyone took this to mean that he wouldn't and that his wings had been clipped. Briant emphasised this by turning away from Charpentier and addressing Saimbron directly.

'The reason they are here today is that they can provide some assistance to us in the investigation. Monsieur Watts is a police artist. He was asked to create likenesses of the men who have been winning large sums from the casino. I think that perhaps we could call upon his talents in speaking with the casino staff, don't you think?'

Saimbron nodded and spoke for the first time.

'Scotland Yard police artist?' asked Saimbron addressing Watts directly. His shrewd eyes seemed to read the man before him in an instant. There was just the hint of a crinkle at the corner of his eyes although his mouth remained set.

Mary turned away from Saimbron and said sotto voce to Watts, 'Careful. He's no fool.'

'Yes,' said Watts to Saimbron, nodding enthusiastically. The he turned to Mary and looked her directly in the eye, 'Yes, indeed. Good-looking though.'

Blanc was removed from the office just at that moment by the two ambulancemen. There was a moment of silence as they performed this sad task. The tension in the room dissipated. It was as if all realised the task that faced them required a pulling together rather than petty politics. Certainly, this was the case with Saimbron and Briant if Kit read their faces correctly. Charpentier was still in a lather but was, by now, ignored.

Saimbron, who had been perched on Blanc's desk, slipped off it and strolled over to Watts.

'Come with me,' said Saimbron in broken English. Watts glanced at Kit and then turned to follow Saimbron. Meanwhile, Mary seemed on the point of following Watts and Saimbron when the inspector raised the palm of his hand. This stopped Mary in her tracks. Once outside the office, Saimbron stopped Watts and looked him up and down. And said in French, 'Are you really a police artist? And don't pretend you speak no French.'

Watts grinned sheepishly and then knelt. He unlatched his small suitcase. Inside where the various materials of the trade. He opened it out for Saimbron to see.

'Happy, dear boy?'

Saimbron nodded and then motioned with his finger for Watts to follow him. Without looking back, he asked 'Do you need anything?'

'Not at the moment, thank you, but I shall need a photographer when I'm finished.'

Saimbron stopped and said, 'To make copies of the suspects for our men?'

'No, silly boy. I want some pictures of me outside the casino as a souvenir.'

The inspector spun around and marched forward towards a group of casino workers that included Agatha and Betty. He was shaking his head, but Watts couldn't see if this was in amusement or anger. He was profoundly unworried either way.

Inside Blanc's office, Briant explained in more detail what had transpired the night before.

'The cleaner found Monsieur Blanc dead around eight in the morning. You did not meet the doctor, but he believes Blanc had been dead at least eight to ten hours. Inspector Saimbron will speak to the staff with Monsieur Watts and establish who was the last person to see him and when.'

Mary duly translated this for the benefit of Charpentier rather than Kit, of course.

'Cause of death?' asked Kit remembering, at the last moment, to ask in English.

Briant waved a hand to stop Mary continuing with the charade on translating for him.

'Poison, we believe. A glass has been taken away for examination. In essence, we think that Blanc carried the poisoned drink into his office after some time in the casino.' At this point Briant began to act out the scene. 'He took a drink and set the glass down here. Then before he could sit down, the poison began to act, and he fell where you saw him.'

Kit nodded as Mary translated and replied, 'I can see that there are some books and papers on the ground. He must have guessed what had happened. Perhaps he was looking for a pen or paper to tell us what had happened, or the murderer was here, too, and looking for something.'

Briant nodded and replied, 'Yes, this is what Saimbron said, and I agree with you both. The question is what might he have been looking for?'

The examining magistrate was following all of this with a brooding air of resentment. It was now clear to him that the Englishman knew his job. So too did Briant. It seemed that Saimbron was taking the side of Briant. This left him out on a limb. He oversaw the investigation but without a say in how it would be conducted. He knew that either Briant or the Englishman could call upon a higher authority if they needed and further undermine him. For the moment he could only sit there and steam silently.

'Do you think there is any connection with the people who have been winning so much in the casino?' asked Kit.

Briant shrugged but he shot a glance at Kit to suggest that he stop anymore inquiries in this direction. Kit nodded and they stood for a few moments at a loss as to what to do next. Briant suggested that they leave the two men to their job of locating fingerprints and that they join Saimbron.

This was one dismissal too many for the unfortunate Charpentier. He glowered at Briant and muttered that he would have an audience with Prince Albert that very day. Briant smiled and touched his hat. Kit would have done likewise but the scowl that greeted Briant was enough to put him off such a provocative act.

'Will you join me for a coffee?' asked Briant once they'd left the office of the former general manager of the casino.

They sat down in the bar of the casino and Briant called over a member of staff and requested coffee for the three of them. Briant's subordinate looked forlorn at not being included.

'This is Lieutenant Boucher, by the way.'

The young man shook hands with Kit and Mary. Then Briant asked him to join their other colleague, Saimbron.

After Boucher had left, Kit smiled at Briant, 'Your young man was thorough.'

Briant glanced in the direction of Boucher, 'He has potential. Now, if we could talk about the reason why you are here and what you must do.'

Kit had been expecting this and realised that this was the point at which he would be told that he and the others could not become involved in the investigation. It seemed like a trope of detective fiction and yet here he was again.

'You wish us to stay out of the investigation?'

Briant did not smile but humour radiated from his eyes.

'I may need you but, yes, Lord Aston, Lady Mary, if you please, confine yourself to the task that His Serene Highness has assigned to your aunt. The gambling is not my affair. In fact, as you have seen, the murder investigation may not be my affair either but, while I am here, I shall make it so. But if I could ask one thing more of you, Lord Aston.'

'Yes, Captain.'

'Please keep me informed of your inquiries related to the gambling. If you should chance upon a connection, then you will, of course, let me know.'

'Of course,' smiled Kit.

'You will speak with me first. I will liaise with Saimbron. He is a good man I think but I don't really know him. I want to be sure my instincts are correct.'

'He seems pragmatic.'

'This is my view, too,' agreed Briant. 'One other thing. When you are enjoying all that this beautiful country has to offer and not investigating, you might be interested to know that Monsieur Blanc kept a file on many of the casino's patrons. I imagine one or two of the patrons would have been shocked by what it said about them.'

'It sounds as if the number of possible suspects has just increased,' observed Kit.

The coffees arrived which prompted the two men to move away from discussion of the case. Briant congratulated the couple belatedly on their marriage. Under close questioning from Mary, Briant was forced to reveal more details of the case in which Kit and Briant had first met in Paris. The newspapers at the time had labelled it, *The French Diplomat Affair*.

About an hour later Boucher arrived clutching some pieces of paper. He was accompanied by Saimbron. Kit guessed that these were some of the first efforts by Rufus Watts. This was good news as it meant that he had established his credibility with the police. More worrying was the look on the young man's face. Kit felt his senses tingling. Then Boucher set down in front of Briant, Kit and Mary one of the drawings. Briant looked at it, but it meant nothing to him. Mary, however, put her hand to her mouth and looked at Kit.

'Do you know this person?' asked Briant.

'Yes,' replied Kit coolly. 'It's my Uncle Alastair.' He looked up at Boucher for an explanation.

Boucher waited until Briant gave him a nod.

'He was one of the last people seen drinking with Monsieur Blanc last night.'

Kit sat back in his seat and exhaled. Just at that moment Harry Miller arrived and, seeing Kit and Mary, headed directly over towards them.

'Harry, I'm glad you're here,' said Kit. He turned to Briant, 'Perhaps Harry could take Monsieur Boucher to my aunt's house to bring Uncle Alastair over so that we can clear this up.'

12

Alastair Aston wasn't usually at his best in the morning. Let it not be said that he was a cantankerous chap or, indeed, mean of spirit. But morning was a beastly time of the day for any man with a convivial nature forced by circumstance, and let us say now, choice, to submit to the sociable essence of his being. Staying true to his character had required him to fall into bed but a few hours earlier.

Light was now streaming through the white shutters with enough intensity to end a dreamless sleep. His eyes opened slowly in a manner that suggested they'd been welded together during the night by a mischievous imp; he groaned and immediately regretted not closing the shutter to block out all light.

A face appeared up close. Ella-Mae stared at him and satisfied herself that he was alive and, if not well, then likely to live another day. Her appearance had the usual effect of taking Alastair completely by surprise and thereby potentially expediting an early demise in the man who was now into his early sixties.

'For the love of…why do you keep doing that?' exclaimed Alastair, covering his head with a pillow. When he removed the pillow, Ella-Mae had left the room as noiselessly as she'd entered it. On the bedside table was a cup. Propping himself up on his elbow, he girded himself for what had to be done. The foul-looking drink was just as foul-smelling. He grimaced and looked away. However, if the drink was not persuasive, his headache was. He looked back at the greenish liquid and felt something rise in his stomach. In such an enfeebled state, he knew he had no choice. Snatching the drink in one hand he downed it in two mighty gulps and fell back onto the bed to wait for its restorative embrace.

Twenty minutes later he was shaken awake. Alastair let forth a volley of words that, by their passion, indicated grievance more than eloquence. However, the sight that greeted him was uncommon.

Ella-Mae was glaring at him in a manner that was worrying. Her anger was all too evident but there was fear in her eyes too. This cowed Alastair somewhat. As his eyes began to focus more clearly, it became apparent that they were not alone in his room. Harry Miller was standing at the foot of the bed with another young man that he did not recognise. Even if he did not know who the young man was, he certainly knew his profession. This was a policeman.

'Good morning,' said Alastair, from behind the bed cover. 'How can I help you?'

'You're under arrest, you old fool,' hissed Ella-Mae angrily.

'Under arrest? Whatever for?' demanded Alastair, his senses clearing up rapidly thanks to the foul concoction that Ella-Mae had given him earlier and a rising sense of panic. His mind, still fuzzy from the previous evening's endeavours, began to scroll through possible reasons for the presence of the police. They had been rather rowdy walking along the port. Giuseppe almost certainly rang the doorbell of several apartments and had someone tried to steal a policeman's headwear? Perhaps that was the other night.

'Murder, according to Harry,' snarled Ella-Mae.

'Murder. You seem in perfectly good nick to me,' pointed out Alastair.

'Not me, you fool.'

Alastair wasn't sure if it was appropriate for his servant to address him in such an informal manner, especially in company. However, the gravity of the situation was all too clear and, to be fair, he'd called her a lot worse over the last few decades. He glanced at Harry Miller partly to understand better the situation, partly to see at least one sympathetic face.

'It's true, sir,' explained Miller. 'There's been a murder at the casino. I understand that you were seen speaking with the victim last night. This is Lieutenant Boucher from the Sûreté. His lordship thought you should come in and meet with the police to explain what happened.'

The previous evening was rather like a painting by the original Impressionist, JMW Turner. It was composed of fragments: vague, intangible scraps which, when taken together, formed an impression of a whole idea. Yet the idea was imperfectly rendered; it was an emotional rather than a physical outline. In short, he'd had a rather jolly time. He'd drunk a lot, laughed a lot, chatted to many people and, somehow, ended up in his own bed.

'I see,' said Alastair, which was an exaggeration both metaphorically and in reality. 'You want me to come now?'

'I believe that is what his lordship wants.'

'Well in that case…' said Alastair in a weary voice.

Half an hour later, Alastair was in the Mercedes-Benz and on his way to Monte Carlo. A coffee and a croissant had ignited his senses and filled a gap. He felt better; more importantly he felt ready. He was not a murderer and he had Kit as well as Agatha to ensure that justice would be served. This was reassuring. In fact, the ludicrousness of the situation was becoming more and more apparent. Had it not arisen from such tragic circumstances, a man such as Alastair Aston, secure in the knowledge of his innocence and the presence of two outstanding detectives, might have enjoyed the spotlight as prime suspect.

He sat back in the car, gripping his cane between his legs. He glanced at the young man beside him and smiled. The young man, unsure of how to respond, frowned in reply. Alastair's smile widened. He turned his attention to the view of the Mediterranean. It wasn't being seen to best effect due to the overcast sky, but it was, as ever, a magnificent sight. One or two yachts were sailing in the calm grey sea. He wished he could be out with them.

It wasn't until they pulled up outside the casino that a few butterflies began to appear in Alastair's stomach. His assumption of innocence along with Kit and Agatha's omnipotence was just beginning to see the first signs of doubt as he was ushered through the barricades and the crowd that had now assembled in Place du Casino.

There's nothing like being led by a policeman through a crowd to set you thinking. In Alastair's case his thinking was focused entirely on a large wooden frame with a sharp blade that descended at a rapid rate of knots to separate a chap from his bonce. Beads of sweat assembled on his forehead like troops about to go 'over the top'.

The sight of Kit and Mary was, at least, heartening. He tried to smile but was aware that his nervousness was becoming all too apparent. Nervousness in Alastair's mind equated to a guilty conscience.

'Uncle Alastair,' greeted Kit. 'May I introduce you to Captain Briant and Inspector Saimbron.'

Hands were duly shaken which did give Alastair some reassurance. The four men and Mary headed off to an empty office that was used by Blanc's secretary. They sat down, all facing Alastair, which unnerved him somewhat.

'Monsieur Aston,' began Briant in French. There was no pretence around language. The assumption was that all in the room spoke French. In this regard, the French are almost as delightfully open-minded about language as their cousins across the English Channel. Like England, France has spent many centuries invading and colonising countries around the world. Consequently, the Gallic race have a high regard both for the precision of their language and its efficacy as a lingua-franca.

'Can you tell us how you came to meet Monsieur Blanc last night and your memory of the time you spent with him?'

'Monsieur Blanc is the man who died?'

'He was murdered,' said Briant with an undue emphasis on the word 'murder'. Alastair's eyes widened and he grinned nervously.

'Very unfortunate. I hope that you are not for one second suspecting me of having committed this ghastly crime.'

Neither Briant nor Saimbron responded. Instead, they fixed their eyes on Alastair with no little impatience. Kit, meanwhile, wasn't sure whether to be amused by the charade or irritated. There was clearly no way his uncle was a murderer. Even the merest hint of this from the detectives would be going too far.

'Very well,' replied Alastair. 'I must confess, my memories of last night are somewhat vague. You will have to give me some moments to collect them. I did not arrive at the casino until after ten. I'd been out to dinner and enjoyed a few drinks with some friends.'

Boucher leaned forward with his notebook and asked, 'Who were these friends?'

Alastair glanced nervously at Kit and then returned his attention to the detectives. The grimace that passed for a smile returned to his face. If he was trying to convince the detectives of his guilt, thought Kit, he was making a jolly good fist of it.

'I've met some people since coming here a couple of weeks ago with my sister. Rather like me, they have a certain bias towards revelry. The gentlemen have styled themselves, rather silly if you ask me, as "The Bluebeard Club".'

Mention of this name was like an electric charge passing through Briant and Boucher. Both sat upright and frowned. This was noted by Kit who shot Mary a quick glance. Whatever jest may have been intended by the men in question, this was obviously the last thing Alastair would have been advised to say.

In a voice that almost chilled Kit to the bone, Briant asked Alastair, 'tell me more about this Bluebeard Club.'

Alastair shut his eyes and tried to order his thoughts about the previous evening.

13

The previous evening:

Giuseppe Russo rubbed his stomach and smiled benignly at the men and women before him. Russo was sitting in an Italian ristorante with three other men and three women. On the table lay enough empty plates and glasses to set the table at the Wedding of Cana. He caught the eye of Yves Fournier and his smile widened, a wicked gleam in his eye. Fournier knew what was coming. He groaned and rolled his eyes.

'Here we go,' he said.

Russo shrugged and patted his stomach deliberately.

'Come on, Yves, I want to hear you say it. Italian cuisine is the best and you know it.'

'I know nothing of the sort, Giuseppe and, if I may say, you know it. Yes, Italian cuisine ostensibly has much to recommend it. It's very straightforward for a start: tasty, simple to prepare and,' he added, gesturing expansively around the table, 'you certainly believe in quantity.'

'But…' interjected Russo.

'But come on now, Giuseppe. Where is the subtlety? Where is the sophistication? The mystery?'

Russo laughed and added, 'Of course, it is but peasant food whereas French food is for the refined palate. Just like ours.'

'Exactly, Giuseppe. I know you are mocking me. Well, you can have your fun. I know I am right, and in your heart, you know this too.'

Russo laughed, waved his hand, and said '*Cavallo*.'

'Why do we not call upon our guest. A neutral observer in the never-ending war of words and forks.'

Alastair Aston grinned nervously. He'd long suspected that he would be called upon for jury service at some point in the evening. The friendly rivalry between Russo and Fournier covered food, art, music, and literature. The debate the previous evening on the merits of Proust versus Svevo had gone long into the evening. Entertaining, frivolous, and academic, as Alastair had pointed out, coming, as he did, from the land of Shakespeare, Dickens, and Austen. This brought the rest of the table against him much to his and their amusement.

Of course, in the matter of cuisine, Alastair knew that he had no leg to stand on. British cuisine was rightly regarded with something close to disdain. He couldn't even suggest American cooking for it was no better but at least its quantities matched or even surpassed that of the Italians. Personally, he found French cooking every bit as fussy as their language. But despite spending most evenings of the previous week with these men in a highly convivial manner, he did not yet feel secure enough to join in the gentle chaffing. Diplomacy would be the order of the day with a hint of self-deprecation.

'I could not separate either country. You both excel in this area and one day you may reach the dizzy heights of my own country and its roast beef.'

Howls of protest greeted this calumny along with great laughter. Philippe Redon, the other man at the table threw a napkin at Alastair. This caught him by surprise but within seconds napkins were flying in all direction. Two of the ladies joined in, Josephine Redon was built like an Alsace farmworker and could inject some genuine heat into her missiles. Alessia Russo, the wildly flamboyant wife of Giuseppe, brought great passion to the fun fight but, sadly, little sense of direction in her aim. Only Elsa Fournier refrained from joining the battle. She smiled serenely at the horseplay but was happy to remain neutral. She was from Switzerland.

Alastair patted his pocket to search for a panatela cigar. He could not find one; then he was handed one and smiled.

'Not sure what I've done with my case,' laughed Alastair.

'What say we go to the casino?' shouted Russo once the play fighting had ceased. 'I feel my luck is in.'

He looked around the table to see if there was support for continuing the festivities a little longer. Alastair was certainly all for this. He had not been to the casino in this company, and it seemed like a capital idea. The others thought so too.

'The walk will do us good,' said Mme Redon. This settled the question and before long the group was marching along Boulevard des Moulins. Fournier took Alastair by the arm as much for support as for friendship. He was a large man in his sixties with suspiciously black hair and a black handlebar moustache. Like the other men he was retired after a successful career in commerce.

All the couples had been married before; all were either widows or widowers. Being with them made Alastair wonder why he had never re-married after losing Christina. Had it really been four years? But he could never remarry. After losing Penny to Lancelot, he thought that he could never love anyone else and then he'd met Christina in San Francisco. She'd proved him wrong then; perhaps he was wrong now. He doubted it, though. When she had passed away a part of him had died too. Something of his spirit and energy had gone. Within twelve months he'd all but retired from work. And then Algy, dear Algy had gone to prison.

Now he had Dain, the woman his son would marry one day, to take care of. There was also the shelter for young women he'd created as a memorial to his late wife. Besides which, the prospect of introducing anyone to Ella-Mae terrified him. Yes, a widower he was and a widower he would stay.

The walk to the casino was relatively short which was just as well as Alastair had felt like he was carrying Fournier. However, he was too polite to point this out.

They arrived at Place du Casino. Redon and Fournier paused forcing Alastair to do likewise. Redon pointed his thin cane at the casino which was lit in an orange glow against the black night. It was an inspiring sight yet, in essence, the primary purpose was no different from the riverboats on which Alastair had spent close to a year of his life – separating the gullible from their money.

The chill of the night forced them to move along to the casino entrance. They strolled through the *Salle Renaissance* into the *Salle Europe.* It was crowded tonight. Mme Fournier's face sank as she looked around. Alastair had some sympathy with her. He also liked her better than the other women. She was still a beauty and must have been quite something in her younger days. Now she was in her forties, slender, obviously cultured, and quite a lot less flamboyant than Mme Russo and the volatile Mme Redon.

'Do you gamble?' asked Redon taking Alistair's other arm. Now it must be said that Alastair deferred to no chap when it came to games such as stud poker. He found *vingt et un* and Baccarat a little unmanly, somehow. He smiled graciously and admitted to enjoying the odd flutter now and again. A discreet curtain was drawn over his late-night games in San Francisco speakeasy establishments and the year spent on a Mississippi riverboat.

Once inside they headed directly to the *vingt et un* table. The game was being played for relatively low stakes.

Alastair looked around to see if Agatha or Betty were present but there was no sign. His sister had been at the casino earlier and had probably retired for the evening as Kit and Mary were in Cannes.

Mme Redon joined them at the table while Russo took the other ladies away to find a table for them to sit down and chat. Alastair rather envied him. He would have preferred to sit with the attractive Mme Fournier and enjoy a cigar. However, the enthusiasm of Redon and Fournier was too infectious, and he decided to join in the spirit of the occasion.

Initially, Alastair played with a careless insouciance treating those twin imposters, twenty-one and busts with the same casual disregard. However, the sight of Fournier slowly building a decent size mountain of chips began to stir the competitive instincts latent within any Aston worthy of the name. Just as he was clawing back some of his negligible losses, Russo came over and suggested that a spell on the roulette wheel would be just the ticket. Smiling reluctantly, Alastair abandoned his seat and joined the others, including all three ladies, at the roulette table. There were fewer people around now, so they were able to take over one of the tables.

Alastair had a system that he had employed over the years to good effect on the riverboats in the United States. In fact, on his first arrival in the New World, he had spent his first summer gainfully employed in one such establishment as a croupier. It hadn't quite put him off playing the game as a casino customer but since then he'd been more aware of the advantage the house enjoys. This was over five percent in many cases. Consequently, his preference had always been for games of chance where he did not have to compete against the house. His system was a classic of its type.

Grabbing a napkin, he wrote down the numbers one to five. Crossing out the top and bottom numbers, he added them together which made six. Then he placed six one hundred Franc chips down on red. If you won, you took the next two high and low numbers. The idea would be that he repeated the exercise until all the numbers were crossed out and then, depending on how things were going, one could start the process over again. Of course, it was advisable to retire when in profit. The casino would always beat you in the long run.

Mmes Redon and Russo did not appear to have any system. True to form, they played with all the restraint of a child in a toy shop. In this, they were matched by their husbands who knew no fear nor, apparently, anything about probability. The Fourniers played more conservatively and enjoyed greater success as a result. Of course, success is relative. None of the group were likely to wipe away their savings in ill-advised speculation on the gaming tables.

After twenty minutes they took a break and retired to a table to end the evening on a *digestivo* or three. By this stage, the men were flushed with happiness and a good deal else besides. The casino was quieter now as the patrons slowly disappeared into the night.

A man appeared from nowhere and hovered over the table like a spectre. Alastair was on the point of ordering a drink from him when he noticed that his appearance had put a dampener on the gaiety of the party.

'Auguste, how good to see you,' said Russo. Even in a foreign language, Alastair could detect more than a hint of forced jollity. Perhaps only Mme Redon was immune to the chill that had descended on the group. She stood up and offered both her cheeks to the new arrival. Mme Fournier glanced up and with little obvious sign of pleasure was kissed by the man called Auguste. He ignored Mme Russo entirely, but this may have been as much to do with where she was sitting.

Fournier turned to Alastair and said, 'Auguste, have you met our new friend Alastair? He is an Englishman. Alastair Aston, this is Auguste Blanc.'

It was a close-run thing as to whose eyes widened more: Alastair's or Blanc's. Although they had not yet met, the name of each was clearly familiar to the other. Blanc bowed in a very French manner, certainly enough to turn the corners of Alastair's mouth downwards.

'Perhaps I could show Mr Aston around the casino?' suggested Blanc.

This was met with more approval by Alastair's friends than by Alastair himself. It felt as if they were fobbing Blanc off on him, yet he could see by the look on his host's face that he was keen to have a few words in private.

'I would be delighted,' said Alastair with a grin wider than a drunk Cheshire Cat's. He rose from his seat and felt Blanc take his arm to lead him in the direction of the *Salle Renaissance*. When he was far enough out of earshot he said to Alastair, 'Mr Aston, am I correct in thinking that you are related to Lady Frost? She mentioned to me that she was holidaying with her brother who she called Alastair.'

'Yes, Agatha is my sister. She did mention you, Monsieur Blanc.'

They headed towards the bar where Blanc offered Alastair a cocktail on the house. Alastair was too much of a gentleman to turn down such a generous offer.

-

'And did you go into his office by chance, Monsieur Aston,' asked Briant, when Alastair had finished relating the events of the evening.

'No, we stayed at the bar and then I found an excuse to return to my friends. I don't wish to speak ill of the dead, but I did not find him easy company. I felt like he was pumping me for information.'

'Really? How so?'

'He was interested in how I came to meet my friends. He referred to them as the Bluebeard Club although I'm not sure he was really on good terms with them.'

'As you said,' replied Briant. 'What made you think this?'

Alastair grinned nervously and chuckled. This was a habit of his whether he was in a good mood, drunk or worried. He patted his breast pocket. A cigar was always useful to buy time when faced with probing questions, especially in a second language.

Seeing this, Briant took a case from his pocket and opened it. Inside were the long panatela cigars favoured by Alastair.

'Oh, thank you,' said Alastair, taking one. Briant lit the cigar with a match. 'Very good,' he acknowledged, holding the cigar up to the detective.

Briant closed the cigar case and showed it to Alastair. It was silver with an engraving on the front: 'AA'

'Good lord,' said Alastair, his eyes widening. 'Where did you find it?' He patted his breast pocket again and looked around him. It would be fair to say Kit and Mary were shocked at this moment. How did Briant come to have his uncle's cigar case? With a rising sense of panic, Kit realised there could only be one explanation.

'We found this,' said Briant, 'in the office of Monsieur Blanc. We also found two cocktail glasses in the office. Monsieur Aston, we will need your fingerprints. In fact, I think you will need to come with us.'

'Where?' said Alastair, his heart sinking like a litre of vodka in a Russian lighthouse keeper's hand. Briant looked back at him stony-faced. 'I see. I don't suppose I can have my cigar case back.'

Briant snapped the case shut and pulled it away.

'No.'

14

'And you just sat by and let them arrest him?' exclaimed Agatha angrily.

'What would you have me do, Aunt Agatha, stage a getaway? Alastair is not going to see sixty again and I'm not exactly Charlie Paddock.'

Agatha looked at Kit up and down and replied drily, 'Charlie Chaplin more like.'

Even Mary couldn't resist chuckling at this, but she put a hand on Kit's elbow anyway to show some moral support for her husband. The fallout from Alastair's arrest was just beginning to make itself felt. No one believed that Alastair was guilty of anything other than being a dupe.

'The fool,' snarled Agatha with particular vehemence. 'The trusting fool. "Useless" would have read this Bluebeard Club in a flash.' She snapped her fingers to make the point.

Kit nodded. It was true. It was entirely plausible that Alastair understood all too well that this Bluebeard Club were company he would have been better off not keeping, but clearly something had drawn him to them. It was in his uncle's character to like fast company. His tendency was more towards moth and flame than hedgehog. His patronage of half a dozen speakeasy bars in the Bay area was a source of pride to him and no little revenue for the establishments concerned. Unlike Agatha's late husband who was an exceptionally shrewd judge of human nature, Alastair could not resist going against his better judgement and running with the wolves.

Now they, or to be more precise, Alastair, was in a pickle. Agatha was quiet now and, just for a moment, it seemed to Kit she looked every one of her seventy plus years. Then she spied Kit looking at her. She read the sympathy in his eyes. This was enough for her back to straighten, for fire to ignite in her eyes and the old spirit to come flooding back.

'No use looking at me like that. We have a job to do now, Christopher. Between us, we must clear Alastair's name and find the real culprit.'

They were in the Hotel de Paris at this moment having a late lunch. Alastair had been taken to Nice by Saimbron but with an assurance from the inspector that Kit's uncle would be well looked after. At this point there had been no suggestion that he was under arrest, notwithstanding Agatha's comments. However, the murderer had planted his uncle's cigar case in the office and Kit had no doubt that one of the glasses would be proven to have Alastair's fingerprints. At this point they would have something of a case. How long would it be before the murderer was able to plant more bogus evidence pointing towards a motive, which was the one thing lacking now?

'You know this chap, Briant, Kit. What's he like?' asked Betty. There was concern etched all over her face, yet within her tone and even in the question itself was the optimism that was always bubbling away inside her great heart.

Kit paused to consider his answer. The truth was he rated Briant highly but…

'He's a good man. Nor is he a fool. I think he'll understand all too well what's happened, but he can only work within the limits of the law.'

'Meaning?' asked Agatha, leaning forward, and fixing her intelligent eyes on Kit.

'Meaning that we are not quite so beholden to the norms and rules of society. We can cheat if need be.'

Agatha and Mary nodded their approval at this. Betty nodded too but had no earthly idea what Kit was driving at. But it certainly sounded exciting. 'I think Briant knows Uncle Alastair is innocent. In fact, I'm certain of it. We have to consider why Briant is here in the first place. His patch is Paris. I'd love to know why he and his man are in the south of France.'

'Can't we just ask Briant? suggested Mary.

Kit gazed at Mary with love, tenderness and, he hoped, no little desire. The final point was noted by Mary and answered in a hint of a smile.

'I have no doubt, my dear, you could make Briant confess all. The only problem is I'm not sure I'd be happy with the methods you might employ.'

'He is rather good-looking,' said Mary, 'in a dark, suave manner.'

Kit ignored this point and continued, 'The problem is Briant is unlikely to share anything with us. Yet, equally, he will happily see me and all of you investigating this off our own back, if we, paradoxically, don't tell him and then, do.'

'I think I understand,' said Betty, who plainly didn't.

'So, he will turn a blind eye?' asked Mary.

'Yes, for the moment. Did you see the way he reacted to the mention of the Bluebeard Club?'

'Yes,' nodded Mary. 'Do you think he's here because of them?'

'Hard to say, but if I were a betting man…' replied Kit. He turned to Agatha and continued, 'You say everyone is talking about this Bluebeard, Henri Landru? It could be that the police are unusually sensitive about this subject or…'

Agatha finished the sentence.

'There's one or two more out there.'

-

Notwithstanding the loss of his beloved Penny to his brother Lancelot, the loss of his wife Christina to illness and then losing his son, in a manner of speaking, to the law, Alastair Aston always considered himself one of life's 'fortunates'. In his case, fortune had been both good and bad; fortunes had been made, then lost, and then made again but throughout out it all, Alastair remained as cynically upbeat as the next man.

So, when it became apparent upon their arrival at the police station in Nice that there were no free police cells, Alastair suggested that the Hotel Negresco might be the next best choice in the holding cell options. He would pay, of course. This highly unusual choice of detention location was met with shock initially, followed by some hilarity and then the highly pragmatic Provencal detective recognised that it was not the worst idea he'd heard in his twenty plus years on the force.

The Negresco, if you haven't been fortunate enough to spend time in Nice, is a hotel from the Belle Epoch that sits grandly on Promenade des Anglais overlooking the beach like a happy memory of a time before war, flu, and communism. His suggestion was, much to his surprised relief, accepted.

For Saimbron, who had been taken aback by the absurd proposition, it was a chance to enjoy a little luxury that a life spent dealing with the very worst of humankind had denied him. The thought of sitting in a police cell that was likely to be rank and uncomfortably hot, questioning a man that ducked whenever any wasp appeared, admittedly they were large wasps, struck the inspector as an unnecessarily squalid way to spend the afternoon.

By four, the two men were enjoying a very English afternoon tea in the airy café at the Negresco. Around them were rich, well-dressed American and English tourists. It was Saimbron's observation that each year, more and more American and English people were finding their way down to the Cote d'Azur. For Saimbron this was a mixed blessing. He was French enough to understand that it would be a boon for the tourist industry after the dark years of war. However, if it was a boon for the tourist industry, then the same could be said for the criminal world. Tourists were easy marks. And if Saimbron's instincts were as acute as he thought they were, there was no bigger mark than the charming, albeit nervous, Englishman chuckling away in front of him.

In such a fashion, Saimbron was able to learn more of Alastair's association with the Bluebeard Club.

-

'I think it was down at the beach where I first met them. As it was a nice day, not too hot, I thought I might take some sea air.'

In fact, Alastair had spent an enjoyable afternoon in a bar that bordered the beach. It was there that he spotted the modestly attired but obviously attractive Mme Fournier, walking alone on the beach just where the Mediterranean met the sand. She stood gazing out at the cerulean blue sea. Then, much to Alastair's satisfaction, walked in that sensual manner of hers towards the bar that Alastair had located for the afternoon.

She sat three tables away from him and ordered a coffee. Her fair hair and fresh complexion suggested someone in her early thirties. It wasn't until later that he was shocked to realise she had just turned forty-five. Her blue eyes were wide set and sadly intelligent. Just when Alastair had thought to ask the waiter if he would invite her to join him, a large man, of the French variety, arrived and appeared to lay claim. Alastair had smelled his after shave before he'd seen him.

The man seemed much older than the woman despite his suspiciously black hair. His attentiveness towards her, while old-fashioned even to Alastair's eyes, seemed sincere. Overbearing almost. She met this with forbearance; she was neither happy nor sad at his presence. A little later another couple joined them.

'This was the Russos. Mme Russo seemed in an energetic mood.'

By energetic, Alastair meant that she was tearing a strip off the unfortunate Monsieur Russo for paying too much to a shop keeper for a Panama hat. His refusal to allow her to strike a more equitable bargain, at least as far as she was concerned, was an act of cowardice. Russo pointed out that they were hardly short of money.

'To which she said that he was short of money. Not her. Of course, Fournier laughed uproariously at this although I fancy Russo, himself, although he was smiling, was less amused by it. However, after this explosion, the air seemed to clear, and they chatted away. At least the two Italians and Fournier did. Mme Fournier said little.'

This was her way. Alastair couldn't decide if it was shyness or the fact that Fournier was larger than life. It was he, of course, who invited Alastair over to join them.

'How did this come about?' asked Saimbron.

It was a presage of a role that Alastair was to play often when with this group.

'I could hear them arguing among themselves. It was friendly enough. The topic of the debate was who were the most revolutionary artists. Fournier was arguing, as usual, for the French team: Braque, Rousseau, Duchamp. The two Russos were equally passionate in their advocacy of Futurism. They were waving their hands around like bookies on a racecourse. Anyway, doesn't Fournier come over and inquire if I was French. Now I had noticed him looking at me from time to time.'

Fournier had noticed Alastair was eavesdropping on almost every word that the two couples were saying. The shaking of the shoulders as he chuckled at one outrageous comment after another only encouraged Fournier to come over. Out of the corner of his eye, Alastair saw the large frame of Fournier amble over towards him. He felt a sudden wave of embarrassment as he realised that he'd been caught out looking at the woman who appeared to be Fournier's wife.

'Excuse me, sir, but are you French?'

Alastair glanced up faking a surprise he certainly wasn't feeling.

'Me? No, no, I'm English,' replied Alastair in fluent French.

Fournier turned to his companions and repeated what they had probably heard anyway.

'But you are alone?' asked Fournier, waving the palm of his hand around the empty table. You should be a detective, thought Alastair. He smiled at his own joke but to Fournier it seemed he had embarrassed the poor Englishman. 'Forgive me, but I wanted to suggest that you join us. We are in the middle of a debate that requires an impartial observer to arbitrate. And providence has provided us with the most disinterested of nations to do this.'

Disinterested, thought Alastair. We were not so disinterested over the last few years when we were bailing you out against Germany.

'Of course,' grinned Alastair. 'Shall I?' he asked, rising from his seat.

'We would love you to join us. Wouldn't we?' asked Fournier turning once more to his own table.

The two Italians immediately chorused that they would, although disappointingly, the woman who had attracted Alastair's original attention merely stared meekly at the ground. It was as if she deferred to her overbearing husband's wishes in everything.

-

'And that was how it started,' explained Alastair to Saimbron, who was now smoking one of Alastair's panatela cigars. He waved the cigar at Alastair and nodded his approval. Alastair smiled reluctantly. This was the second cigar the detective had taken. Mind you, Saimbron had suggested that Alastair, at least, retrieve them from the cigar case before Briant kept the case as potential evidence.

'After that they invited me out to dinner, and I saw them a great deal.'

'How did you come to call them the Bluebeard Club?'

'That was Mme Redon who coined the name. I met her and her husband that night. She said to me that I could become an honorary member of their club, indicating the three men. Naturally I asked what club this was, and she told me.'

'Did you, or the ladies, not find this strange? I mean it is a name with much significance here in France now. You have, no doubt, heard of the Henri Landru case.'

'Naturally, but the three ladies, well certainly Mme Russo and Mme Redon anyway, did not appear unduly worried by the sobriquet.'

'And Mme Fournier?'

'She is a little different from the other ladies,' said Alastair.

'How?'

She's divine, thought Alastair. Beautiful, intelligent, and calm. The others are mad; well, they all are in one way or another. But that's what makes them so captivating, he supposed.

'She's less demonstrative,' answered Alastair. 'A little shy. I think she's happy to let Monsieur Fournier take centre stage.'

Saimbron nodded at this. His cigar was nearly finished and for one awful moment Alastair thought he would eat further into his dwindling supply. Then, to his relief, the detective said, 'No more. My wife will know I've been smoking. She's always at me to give up.'

'They have a way, don't they?'

This certainly struck a chord with the Frenchman and for a few minutes he treated Alastair to a delightfully indiscreet and utterly disloyal dissection of his wife's manifold ways of undermining him. Publicly. Alastair laughed sympathetically as men do when in the presence of aggrieved husbands. Neither considered the possibility that Mme Saimbron might also be sharing with a friend similar tales of woe caused by her insensitive and selfish mate. On such firm foundations are built every successful marriage.

It was early evening now. Alastair gazed out at the ice blue sea and the periwinkle sky. In any other situation the two men would have happily shared a cognac and swapped stories of an interesting life led. Alastair liked the inspector and suspected the feeling was mutual. They were now sitting on the terrace of the room Alastair had booked.

'I can stay here this evening?' asked Alastair with more than a hint of hope in his voice. 'I'm sure one of your men can be persuaded to stand guard. I certainly am long past making daring escapes.'

'I see no reason why not,' replied Saimbron.

Just then there was a knock at the door. Saimbron leapt to his feet and went to answer it. It was one of his police sergeants. They chatted in a low voice, and then Saimbron turned to Alastair. His downcast features told their own story.

'I'm sorry, Monsieur Aston, but we must return to the police station.'

15

Kit and Mary strolled around La Condamine market in Places d'Armes. Agatha and Betty had returned to the casino which was now reopened to a very curious public and probably doing a roaring trade. It was in the small marketplace that they ran into Ella-Mae and Natalie, Agatha's French maid. The two ladies were sitting in a café enjoying a coffee. Around their feet were several bags of food shopping from the market. Mary's eyes widened.

'Gosh, I'd forgotten about Ella-Mae. We have to tell her.'

Kit nodded. This was not going to be easy. For around thirty years or more, Ella-Mae and Alastair had been fighting like two alley cats over a scrap of fish in a garbage can. It was unlikely either could envisage life without the other. Despite the utter conviction that Kit felt of his uncle's innocence and a similar level of certainty that Briant and Saimbron shared this, there was no question that the mounting evidence would persuade Monsieur Charpentier, the examining magistrate, to make life unbearable for both policemen. He might even bring someone new onto the case if he felt they were dragging their feet. At this point, they would be in trouble.

The face of Ella-Mae betrayed some inkling that the situation was not going well. One look at Kit told her that it was calamitous. Despite her fear, she took the news well. While she was a little too young to remember the Civil War, she had been born into a family of freed slaves. Her life had not always been so privileged. Her eyes momentarily welled up and then she regained control. A clue to this was her rather un-servant-like reaction to news that Alastair would probably spend a night in a police cell. It bore an uncannily resemblance to the lack of sympathy that Agatha might have exhibited.

'Damn fool.'

Kit heartily agreed and had to smile when she said it. He took her hand and reassured her that he would do everything in his power to find out the truth. Ella-Mae nodded, and her face resumed its stony countenance. Natalie also took her hand and smiled encouragingly. She, of all people, knew that Kit and his extraordinary family were more than capable of uncovering what had really happened.

'Who is this Bluebeard Club?' asked Ella-Mae after a few minutes.

'Good question. We need to find out more about them.'

'Did they frame him?'

Kit was certain they had, but proving it was another matter and said so. Ella-Mae lapsed once more into a sullen silence. Neither Kit nor Mary tried to bring her round. They knew it would be no use. She was fearful, angry, and sad in equal measure. They all were to a degree.

'I think we'll need to deploy Harry on this.'

Mary perked up at this. A smile appearing on her lips for the first time in hours.

'You mean break in?'

'I was thinking that he could tail them initially and then we would see if we needed to take things as far as that.'

'I could help,' said Natalie. 'If there are three couples, I could follow someone too.'

Kit nodded and agreed that this was a good idea.

'Count me in,' said Ella-Mae. 'No one ever notices me.'

This was as true a statement as Kit had heard all day. Ella-Mae could have given lessons in stealth to a Gurkha.

'I'll need to speak with Alastair and find out where they live. I gather they all have a place in town which is a stroke of luck. Hopefully, they confine themselves to moving around on foot. One hardly needs a car in Monaco.'

'Just a yacht,' added Mary. 'And a balloon. I feel I'm always climbing in this town.'

Kit grinned and tapped his leg, 'Yes, I'd rather noticed.'

-

'What do you mean I have to spend the night in a police cell?' exclaimed Alastair. 'Are you mad?'

'No,' replied Kit. 'I'm afraid there's nothing else for it.

It was just after seven in the evening at the Commissariat de Police in Nice. Alastair had left the Negresco somewhat reluctantly to return to the less salubrious surroundings of the police station. Saimbron was on the point of departing himself when Kit arrived with Briant. Alastair knew there was little point in arguing but felt that a show of defiance was, at least, in order.

'Can you enlighten me as to what purpose this could possibly serve. I'm hardly likely to run away, am I?'

On this point Kit wasn't entirely convinced any more than he was by Alastair's show of rebelliousness. His uncle had often talked about his times in jail, invariably following evenings of immoderate sociability. Of course, these had been in his younger days.

'Captain Briant and Inspector Saimbron clearly don't think you're a criminal. But they must progress the investigation because there's too much evidence pointing your direction. I've convinced them that this Bluebeard Club needs to be investigated. In fact, I don't think Briant needed much convincing on this score. So, it seems your framing may provide an opportunity that would otherwise have been denied him.'

'You mean I am to suffer here,' at this point Alastair broke off his wounded appeal and pointedly looked around the small, grey cell. It was a convincing performance. His face displayed the hurt, his posture slightly slumped but not so much as to exaggerate. 'How could you, Kit? To reduce me, your old uncle, to such deprivation to lure these ghastly people into thinking they've put me in the frame.'

'Glad you agree,' smiled Kit brightly.

'But I'd booked a room in the Negresco,' came the plaintive reply from Alastair. Now there was genuine regret in his tone. By anyone's estimation, an evening's incarceration in the walnut wood confines of the Negresco Bar surrounded by beautiful people listening to jazz music would have been just the ticket when facing a murder charge. Now such hopes had been dashed on the rocks of duplicity. He was to be bait.

'I'm sure you'll survive, Uncle,' said Kit with an uncharacteristic lack of sympathy.

A quick glance towards Briant and Saimbron confirmed to Alastair that the game was, for the time being, up. He slumped onto the bed and threw his feet up and put his hands behind his head.

'Very well. I'll need something to read. More cigars, too, would be welcome. Now, can you tell me, what time is breakfast served?'

-

Probably for the first night in six weeks, Kit and Mary enjoyed more sleep than Kit's notoriously late-rising uncle. The night for Alastair was not quite as horrible as he intended to make out to his nephew it had been. Calm reflection on his pitiable situation helped him recognise that it could be a bargaining chip for the future. All the same, years of soft living in San Francisco had left him unprepared for the joys of a sleeping on a hard bed and flat pillow, all with the possible prospect that it would be for naught. Quite what would come from it, Lord only knew.

However, despite the prospect of the sword of Damocles, Madame Guillotine herself, Alastair remained chipper about his prospects. His soul rarely took a turn towards the tormented unless an indecent amount of alcohol consumption the previous evening was involved. The alarming aspects of his situation had not yet sunk in. And why would they? There were Kit and Agatha to look out for him and even Mary was showing more than a little promise. More importantly, he was innocent. Common sense would prevail, and the true criminals brought to justice. He had no doubt who they were. For a few seconds his thoughts became darker as he thought of the Bluebeard Club.

Who, though? Was it all of them or just one man using them as a Trojan horse?

His first thought was Fournier. Now that he'd had more time to consider him, he realised he did not like him. His overbearing manner, particularly with his wife, was unpleasant. Yes, he could be charming company when he wanted to be; funny, intelligent, and generous. Lurking underneath this facade was a darker spirit. This was good, thought Alastair. Years of reading detective novels had not been in vain.

He called the guard and asked for a pen and something to write on. Pen and paper were duly obtained, and Alastair paused for a moment and considered the blank sheet in front of him. At the top of the page he wrote, 'The Bluebeard Club'. Then he began to scribble some notes on his former friends. With any luck, he reasoned, they would help Kit and his sister. While he did not doubt the capability of the French detectives, he knew salvation was in the hands of his peculiar family.

It took him an hour to write but he was satisfied with the result. He read it over once and added a note or two. Just as he was finishing, he heard the door being unlocked.

The Bluebeard Club

Yves and Elsa Fournier

Fournier is a blowhard. Likeable on first acquaintance and often very good-humoured hes (sic) a bit of a bully when you know him better. The way he treats his quiet and very good-natured wife is quite beastly. He made his money from munitions, or some such thing. Elsa is his second wife. His first died over a year or two ago from tuberculosis. Personally I wouldn't be surprised if he topped the first one. Hes (sic) a powerful man and I wouldnt (sic) want to be on the wrong side of him.

Mme Fournier is a widow. I believe her husband was at Verdun. She is from one of the French-speaking cantons in Switzerland. She is very quiet and seems in fear of her husband.

Philippe Redon and Josephine Redon

Redon is a martinet. You can tell he is ex-army. His ridiculous mustache (sic) and pompous manner. He would like to be insouciant and sophisticated. Hes (sic) neither. A knave of the first rank. He has a bit of Napoleon about him. No wonder we nearly lost the war with twits like him leading those poor brave men. I am quite skeptical if he would have either the brains or the courage to kill anyone. Hes more interested in how his mustache (sic) looks.

She and Mme Russo are like Cinderella's ugly sisters even uglier cousins. Quite how she and the other managed to entrap these two men is beyond me. I wouldnt (sic) trust

M Redon as far as I could throw a cask of wine. She and Fournier would have gone well together.

Giuseppe and Alessia Russo

Oddly I quite like Russo. Certainly more than the other two men. Of course hes (sic) ridiculous in his own way but unlike the others I think he knows this. He is well travelled and once lived in New York. He was married to an American lady but she died just before the start of the War. He came over to Europe before the situation became a horrible stalemate. I am skeptical (sic) that he could have killed anyone. Hes (sic) smart enough but hes (sic) more interested in eating good food and drinking from what I can see. Hes (sic) retired now but was in insurance I believe. That could mean anything of course.

I believe he met the present Mme Russo just a few months after his own wife died. It just shows that when the goddess of fortune is in a particularly prickly mood it can take away with one hand and give you Lucretia Borgias (sic) little sister in the other. I gather shes (sic) quite wealthy herself. Shes (sic) the daughter of a count. (Dracula probably)

16

Kit was the first to arrive the next morning to see Alastair. This had been the source of an argument between him and Agatha. In the end it was felt that Agatha, whose mood, it must be said, was unlikely to provide much consolation to her incarcerated sibling, should visit in the afternoon. This provided the second argument of a febrile morning in Agatha's Cap-d'Ail villa. She had announced her intention to quit the assignment given to her by the prince to devote her energies to freeing her brother. She was mid-argument with Kit on this topic when she'd seen a look on her nephew's face that she knew, and loved, so well. She'd frowned, studied him for a second and asked, 'What are you thinking?'

Kit shrugged and shook his head. It was a thought that he could scarcely bring himself to utter. But the seed had been planted.

'You're not suggesting that this Bluebeard Club might be connected to the gambling operation, are you?'

One of the things that both Kit and Agatha adored about Mary was that she was as quick on the uptake as the next English amateur fictional detective. Her eyes suddenly widened, 'Do you think that Monsieur Blanc was in league with them?'

This was flying ahead very quickly but Kit could not deny that this was exactly where his mind had been traveling.

'It was just a thought,' admitted Kit.

Agatha and Mary both sat back in their seats at the same moment and a reflective glint entered their eyes. Betty poured some more tea. It was an article of faith with Betty that detective work was best fuelled, nay, inspired by the consumption of tea. This was particularly appropriate at those critical moments in a case when cool appraisal of known facts had to be mixed with imaginative leaps of thinking. Betty was convinced that American policemen would have no need for guns if they placed a similar trust in the remarkable properties of tea. Her theory was still in its early stages of development, but she was convinced there was something in it.

'Very well,' said Agatha at last. 'I shall visit Alastair this afternoon. If what you say is true, then it could mean that the Bluebeard Club will be ready to strike again, and soon.'

'You don't mean murder?' said Betty.

'Of course not. I meant they might feel safe to attack the casino,' said Agatha with just a hint of impatience.

Betty was slightly affronted at Agatha and replied, 'That's what I mean, you don't mean murder.'

Agatha rolled her eyes while Mary, despite their predicament, had to stifle her laughter.

-

Kit was greeted by Alastair like a long-lost son upon his arrival in the small jail cell. His delight intensified further when Kit removed from his pocket around twenty panatela cigars. This would keep his uncle going for a couple of days. In return, Alastair handed Kit his morning's work.

Kit read through the notes made by Alastair in silence, stopping only to check on a misspelt word or three.

'For the love of God, Kit, are you a teacher?'

'You spelt "traveling" with two "l's", this is the American spelling. Scepticism has "c" not a "k".'

Alastair made a face at Kit whose eyes were studying the notes intensely. There were more important things to be getting on with than pedantry over Americanisms.

'Perhaps when you've finished pointing out the spelling mistakes, Anne Sullivan, we can move onto the grammar.'

'Don't start me on the grammar,' replied Kit, not looking up. For the next couple of minutes Kit studied the two sheets of paper intensely. When he'd finished, he glanced towards his uncle and smiled.

'I'm glad it meets with your approval, grammar aside.'

'I could care less about the grammar, really, Uncle Alastair.'

'Now you sound American, Kit,' said his uncle laughing

'Thanks, it must be all the books Aunt Agatha gives me to read. Anyway, your summary is very clear. Who is your money on?'

Alastair looked downcast at this question. He shrugged and replied, 'The three of them are all capable. Fournier is a blowhard, Redon is ex-army and probably sent thousands to their death, so he is inured to killing and Russo is volatile enough.'

'And the wives?'

'I would be worried that Mme Fournier will be the next victim. He's a very cruel man that one. The other two, yes, I could see them slipping something into a man's drink while batting their eyelashes at him.'

Kit folded the paper and put it into his breast pocket. They chatted for a few minutes about what would happen next. Alastair gazed bleakly at Kit when informed that he faced the prospect of another day or two in the cell. Then a more reflective mood fell upon him as he reached into his pocket and extracted two of the cigars Kit had brought him. He offered Kit one of the cigars, but it was met with a shake of the head.

'Do you mind if I do?'

'No, please go ahead. It's your cell.'

Alastair looked around him and a wicked grin creased his face, 'Rather fetching, isn't it? Dark grey is such an underrated colour.'

'Uplifting.'

'Very. I was thinking a nice Matisse would help break things up a little. What do you think?'

'Undoubtedly. Would you not prefer a Bouguereau?'

'All that naked flesh? It would be a cruel reminder…' reflected Alastair as he lit his cigar.

The restorative effect of a cigar for a man of a certain age should not be underestimated. Aside from its medicinal properties which, to be fair, are probably nil, it gives a chap a certain air of enlightenment; a meditative soberness that hints at an intelligence which one is far too humble to acknowledge yet can't quite hide either.

It was in such a mood of contemplative inquiry that Alastair asked Kit, 'Tell me, Kit, did you and Lancelot talk much about marriage?'

Kit was taken aback by the question on several levels.

'Hardly. You know how father and I are, and he's probably about the last person to dispense guidance on the topic of matrimony.'

A shadow swept over Alastair which made Kit instantly regretful about his outburst.

'Yes, I see what you mean. My purpose in asking the question was not to highlight Lancelot's failings as a husband or father.'

'Or brother,' pointed out Kit, bitterly.

Alastair looked at Kit with a sadness in his eyes.

'Well, perhaps I wasn't much of a brother either.'

'Nonsense, anyone would have reacted badly to what he did.'

Alastair shook his head and changed course. This was not what he'd wanted to discuss.

'The purpose of my inquiry related to you and Mary.'

A look of alarm passed through Kit's eyes, and they widened like a ham actor's in a silent movie.

'I was taught about the birds and the bees a long time ago, Uncle Alastair.'

Alastair laughed and replied, 'Quite. I mean something else. You know, the two of you became engaged rather quickly. I know there was the meeting during the war, but you'll admit it was like something from a comic novel.'

Kit wasn't quite sure that he was a character in a comic novel. Detective story perhaps. He decided to stop interrupting Uncle Alastair and allow the circulatory inquiry to reach its final destination.

'What I'm trying to say to you, Kit, is that marriage is tricky. It's not easy. Right now, nothing could seem simpler or more fun. But it won't always be this way. Women are more complicated than we are. They don't always know what they are feeling, they won't tell you what they are thinking, and they'll feel hurt when you don't understand what they want.'

'Jiminy,' said Kit for wont of anything else to say.

'I know,' agreed Alastair. He took a few puffs on his cigar to allow time for him to continue this theme.

'What should I do if this mood descends on Mary?' Kit was all ears now. He remembered the arguments between his own father and mother. Back then, before it was obvious to him that his father was cheating, he could see the anguish that both his parents were feeling. Even he, as much as he adored his mother, couldn't understand why she was so distant with his father on occasion. Later, he understood more.

'There's nothing you can do my boy. She will feel this way and not know why. But you must promise me one thing.'

'Yes,' replied Kit.

'Don't be angry. I remember there were times when Christina could be so exasperating. We would argue. Then she would cry. And, of course, I would feel such remorse. I still feel it now. I knew so little at the start. I was like you. It was exciting, fun and Christina was, well, I won't go on, but we were young. Anyway, Mary is an absolute ripper, Kit. I can't tell you how proud I am of you that you have someone like her to love you. You're a very lucky man.'

'I know.'

'But the Mary you know is only a small part of who she is. This is what I mean by the rush to marriage. Don't misunderstand me. In your shoes I'd have done the same. This is when you will really come to know her. What you learn you may not always like, and what you like may not always be what you'll see. And what you see will likely not be what she is feeling. Do you understand?'

'No.'

'Good, because if you'd said "yes" then I'd know that you hadn't. For better and for worse, Kit. For better and for worse.'

A knock on the cell door told Kit that he had to leave. They parted with a shake of the hand and a brief nod. This was all that was required between two men of an English persuasion.

-

A few miles away a conversation was taking place between Mary and Agatha of such striking similarity that one could have been forgiven for thinking that the older principals had planned it before the arrival of the honeymooners. And before one of them had been accused of murder most foul.

'My dear,' said Agatha at breakfast in the villa. 'I've been meaning to talk to you when we had some time to ourselves.'

Mary looked up in curiosity at Agatha. Usually, which is to say, always, Agatha had a resolution to her gaze, a stony conviction that was as superior in its reasoning as it was unshakeable in its faith. However, on this morning, there was more than a hint of hesitation and, extraordinarily in one so thick-skinned, even embarrassment.

'Yes?' asked Mary.

'I don't know if you had any conversation with your Aunt Emily about marriage.' The look of horror on Mary's face suggested that this had not been the case and it was also the last thing she would have wanted.

'That would be no,' suggested Agatha, reading Mary's reaction perfectly. 'I hope you won't find it presumptuous of me to say something on the subject.'

'No, Aunt Agatha. I'm all ears.' Mary folded her arms on the table and fixed her eyes on Agatha.

'Very good,' replied Agatha although her evident discomfort suggested it was anything but. 'The early days of marriage are undeniably a magical time, Mary. We don't need to dwell on this.'

Mary could not have agreed more on both scores.

'What I wanted to address relates more to the reality of spending one's life with a man. Do you follow?'

Mary nodded but remained worried where this was leading.

'Christopher, as I have often acknowledged, is unusually impressive for his sex. A man like this, and I speak not just as his aunt, is sadly, all too rare a specimen. However, for all the good things that Christopher is capable of, he is still subject to the limitations of his gender.'

Agatha nodded hopefully towards Mary. Mary nodded back, transfixed by this extraordinary soliloquy.

'Men are, for wont of a better expression, uncomplicated. They are driven by things that I neither understand nor want to, frankly. If one is to believe the theory of evolution, then once upon a time Christopher's male ancestors were alone, hunting mammoth and whatnot while we were back at the caves making soup and rattling bones at babies.'

'I'm jolly well glad I wasn't around then,' chipped in Mary.

'I couldn't agree more, my dear. Horrid existence. Anyway, to address the key point, men are fundamentally solitary animals. We have civilised them as best we can but I'm not sure you can ever fully tame them. From time to time…'

If this was going where Mary thought it was going then a line would unquestionably have to be drawn and Aunt Agatha needed to understand this. What was good for Lancelot Aston would certainly not be good for Kit.

'Aunt Agatha if you're suggesting that I should sit back and allow Kit to stray…'

'Good Lord no,' exclaimed Agatha. 'If he's stupid enough to do that then you have my full permission to shoot him.'

This was, perhaps, taking matters a little further than even Mary might be prepared to go, but it was certainly reassuring to know where her loyalties would be lie.

'No, what I was driving at is that you must let him be alone sometimes or with his friends. Do not begrudge him this time. I remember the Byzantine machinations of "Useless" when he wanted to escape for a few snifters with his friends when all he had to do was…'

'Beg?' suggested Mary grinning.

Agatha appraised Mary. There was a softness in her eye. Then after a few seconds a half-smile appeared on her lips.

'You'll do.'

17

A couple of hours after the heart-to-heart chat with Agatha, Mary found herself sitting in the Mercedes-Benz outside a block of apartments on 'The Rock'. The apartment block had a spectacular view of the Mediterranean, principally because it was located beside a cliff that overhung the sea. A few hundred yards further along the Avenue was the cathedral of Monaco, then the *Palais du Justice* and finally the palace itself.

The white paint of the art deco building was peeling in some places. Outside, a lonely dog slept in the warm morning sunshine. It was a building that, despite its extraordinary situation, was in a poor state of repair. Lying near the apartments was a dead rat. It was almost as if it had been thrown out of the window of one of the apartments.

None of which mattered to Mary. She was one hundred and five pounds of quivering resentment. A few minutes earlier Kit and Captain Briant had met up outside the building and then gone in together. Mary sat in the car; steam poured from her ears. It was the hottest day since they'd arrived on the Riviera, although Egypt had been hotter. However, this was not the source of the wildfire burning in her eyes. As much as she tried to deny it, she was angry that, once more, she was confined to the car while the men did the policework. Never did the unreasonable expectations of society clash more with her own aspirations than in these moments when she could not be allowed to participate as an equal partner in an endeavour.

The role of surveillance was better than nothing, but experience had taught her it could be frightfully dull. She yearned for an opportunity to go under cover as she had the previous year at the Roslings' house*. Memories of this had softened over time. Back then she'd felt intensely the guilt of deception and even betrayal. Now she would have been prepared to accept this in return for a more active role in helping a man she had come to adore to regain his freedom.

Harry Miller glanced at Mary in the mirror. He could tell what she was thinking for he felt this himself. Stealthily breaking into a house at night in search of information rather than jewels was preferable to sitting in a car staring at a house. He turned his attention to the sea which peeked in between the branches of the trees in a narrow strip of park that led to the overhanging rock face.

'I wonder what they're saying,' said Miller after a few minutes of silence.

'Oh, don't, Harry,' said Mary, moodily. 'Much rather be in there.'

'I agree,' replied Miller glumly and turned his attention to the dog napping near the entrance to the block, its tail flicking every so often.

The plan was for Kit and the policemen to question the Fournier couple first. Around twenty minutes later, Lieutenant Boucher would visit the Russo household while Saimbron would arrive at the Redons. Staggering the arrivals had been Briant's suggestion as it would be interesting to see the reaction of the other households as Fournier phoned each of them to warn of the arrival of the police. The visits themselves would, ostensibly, be about gathering evidence on Alastair whose guilt was assumed. The ulterior motive was to find how the Bluebeard Club would react firstly to the news about Alastair but then with one another.

-

As they met on the street outside the apartment, Kit handed Briant the notes made by Alastair. Briant cast his eyes over them then handed it back to Kit.

'My English is passable but perhaps you could translate?'

Kit suspected that Briant's English was more than passable but read through it anyway. Then they entered the apartment building. The dog in the entrance opened one eye to check them over. As guard dogs went, he was already enjoying semi-retirement. Kit stroked him behind the ear than followed Briant up one flight of stairs.

Outside the door of the apartment lay the morning newspaper. Briant reached down to pick it up. He showed Kit the headline.

MURDER IN THE CASINO

'It would make a good title for the sort of book my aunt or uncle might read,' said Kit.

'Not my taste,' replied Briant. 'Lacks subtlety.'

Kit smiled and replied, 'Yes, I suppose it does.'

The detective knocked on the door. Moments later a young maid opened it. Briant held up his police card and said, 'May we see Monsieur and Mme Fournier please?'

Kit and Briant were ushered into a large apartment. It was at least as large as Kit's in Belgrave Square and there was a terrace outside. The two Fourniers were sitting enjoying breakfast there. The maid scurried over to tell them of the new arrivals. A look of alarm spread over Fournier's face like a pall. This meant nothing of course. It was rare that the arrival of the police heralded good news.

The apartment was tastefully furnished in the art deco manner. The walls were a dark green colour but the light flooding in through the terrace meant the interior was far from gloomy. French Impressionist paintings decorated the wall. Kit did not recognise any of them. In the corner of the room was a mouse trap. Even here, thought Kit. Then he turned his attention to the terrace.

Kit watched Fournier rise from the table and glance in. A frown hung over his face. He seemed to order his wife to stay seated and then came in through the lounge doors that led to the terrace. A nervous smile traced across his lips rather like a rodent encountering a peckish python and a potential escape route at the same moment. Fournier was tall, burly and was already sweating like roadworker at midday.

'Gentlemen, how can I help you?' asked Fournier, gesturing towards the sofa. 'Can I offer you a coffee?'

'No thank you,' replied Briant. 'My name is Briant. Captain Briant from the Sûreté. May I introduce Lord Kit Aston. He…' Briant paused for a moment. It hadn't occurred to him about how he would make this introduction, much to Kit's amusement.

'I work with the police in Britain, Monsieur Fournier,' interjected Kit in French. 'I believe you've met my Uncle Alastair.'

The three men sat down, and Fournier appeared to relax visibly.

'You are Alastair's nephew. This is a great pleasure. We have only recently met your uncle, but he is already a great favourite with my wife and me.'

'Where is your wife, Monsieur Fournier?' asked Briant.

'She's outside taking breakfast,' replied Fournier, making no suggestion to bring her in.

'May we see her as this concerns her, too.'

Fournier could not hide his annoyance at this request, but he nevertheless instructed the maid to bring his wife.

These were his exact words. This caused an exchange of glances between Kit and Briant.

Mme Fournier arrived a minute later. Kit and Briant rose from their chairs although Fournier remained seated. One year of wedded bliss had now released him from any obligations of good manners towards his partner in life. Kit could see immediately why his uncle had been so taken by Mme Fournier. Her beauty was child-like. Fair hair bubbled underneath a blue ribbon with one strand falling over her wide-set blue eyes. There was fear in those eyes and Kit was not entirely convinced this was due solely to their presence.

She sat down beside her husband after being introduced and immediately reached for his hand.

'Is something wrong?'

Briant said nothing. Instead, he showed the front page of the morning newspaper. It was a coup de theatre on Briant's part. Kit was unsure what reaction the detective had been looking for, but to his eyes, the shock that registered on Fournier's face was, unless he was an excellent actor, genuine. Mme Fournier gasped and buried her head in her husband's shoulder.

'Monsieur Blanc was poisoned sometime in the early hours of yesterday morning. You were not aware of this?'

'But no,' said Fournier, still dazed by the news. 'Who could have done such a terrible thing?'

Briant glanced at Kit and then replied, 'We arrested Alastair Aston yesterday.'

Kit noted that he did not say "charged". The reaction was, once more, immediate, and authentic.

'Alastair? But this is madness,' exclaimed Fournier. 'He is a gentleman. Why would he do such a thing?'

This was the obvious hole in the theory, of course. Unless Alastair had hitherto well-disguised tendencies towards psychotic violence, then making the charge of murder stick would be a challenge for someone of the meagre talents of Monsieur Charpentier. Briant wisely ignored the question and redirected it towards them.

'Why do you think he might kill Monsieur Blanc?'

Now the reaction to this was more interesting. Both Fourniers paused for a moment to consider their answer. This was natural as the question required them to do more than simply to take in shocking news. However, the highly tuned senses of Kit and Briant recognised something else. As they agreed afterwards, unless they were mistaken, each could think of a very good reason why someone might want to do away with the director of the casino. A few seconds passed and then Fournier laughed at the absurdity of the situation.

'But Monsieur Aston had only just met Monsieur Blanc.'

Briant was on the point of suggesting that for all they knew, Alastair could have met him before when he felt Kit touch his arm lightly.

'How did he meet Monsieur Blanc?'

A shadow passed over Fournier's face as he realised that this might very well have been a trap. He felt the grip of his wife's hand tighten. Briant, meanwhile, smiled and nodded.

'We, that is I and my friends, introduced him to Monsieur Blanc. We were not sure if he'd met him before.'

'Your friends?' asked Briant, even though he already knew the answer. Fournier provided the names while Kit kept his attention on Mme Fournier. Throughout the interview she stared at the ground, too fearful to speak. Or perhaps she was not allowed. A glance down at the way they were holding hands suggested that Fournier was tightening and loosening his grip to direct his wife's silence.

'And how did you and your friends know Monsieur Blanc?' It was asked disingenuously, by Briant, like an afterthought; just to clarify some details.

Fournier stammered at first, searching for an inspiration. This told Kit two things: the news of the director's death was a surprise, otherwise he would have been better prepared. Yet, and this gave Kit cause for optimism, Fournier had something to hide.

'Well, you know,' blustered Fournier. 'Monsieur Blanc was a marvellous host. I'm sure he made it his business to know everyone who visited the casino.'

'Indeed,' said Briant, seeming to agree with this. Then he asked, 'Did you visit the casino often then?'

'From time to time,' admitted Fournier.

Briant looked around him and then smiled.

'You are renting this apartment, or do you own it?'

'We are renting until the end of summer. Just for six months,' said Fournier with a smile that suggested he was beginning to recover some of his composure.

'So, you only came here in early March.'

'Yes.'

'How often had you seen Monsieur Blanc over this period?'

'Perhaps two or three times. We do not visit the casino often.'

Kit noted that Mme Fournier seemed to squeeze Fournier's hand at this point.

'Yet Monsieur Blanc knew you well?'

'I wouldn't say well,' replied Fournier hurriedly. 'But tell me, where is Monsieur Aston now?'

'In a police cell in Nice,' replied Kit. 'He's naturally very upset.'

'Of course,' nodded Fournier. 'Perhaps we can visit him?'

'I'm not sure that will be possible,' answered Briant rising from his seat. This signalled the end of the interview. Kit rose too, and Fournier showed them to the door. He thanked Briant for his kindness in sharing the news personally. Kit had to acknowledge his impudence in treating Briant as a messenger boy rather than owning the fact that he might be a suspect. The smile on the detective's face and the twinkle in his eye suggested he thought so too.

Outside the door, Kit put a hand on Briant's arm. They stood outside the door and listened. A lifetime spent in English country houses catching out servants listening at doors had desensitised Kit to the questionable morality of eavesdropping. It was as much a weapon in his armoury as putting Harry Miller's old skills to good use through nocturnal visits in a suspect's house. Kit did not doubt that he would be required to deploy this rare talent once more.

The two men glanced around surreptitiously. No one was around. Each put an ear to the door. They found their reward.

'What have you done?' shouted Fournier to his wife. 'Did you do this?'

Mme Fournier could be heard breaking down in tears.

'No!' she screamed. 'No, I haven't. It wasn't me.'

'Tell me?' roared her husband. 'Don't lie.'

'I'm not lying. How can you say this?'

Fournier's voice changed tone. Gone was the anger. In its place it became a soothing whisper, only just about audible to Kit and Briant.

'I'm sorry, my dear. I don't know what came over me. Forgive me, my sweet.'

Then there was silence. When it persisted for over a minute, Briant indicated to Kit that they should leave. The face of Briant was set to stone, however. And Kit had a better idea of what had brought the man from the Sûreté down to the Riviera.

*The Phantom (Kit Aston Book Three)

18

Lieutenant Thierry Boucher glanced at his watch and then up at the sun splitting the Riviera sky. It was a little after eleven. He rolled his finger around the rim of his shirt collar where it meets the neck. It was hot. He was hot. Still, much better to be here than in a Parisian backstreet with his stomach churning.

At twenty-eight he was two years into a police career that had been delayed by a small matter involving a neighbouring country. His rise through the ranks had been rapid. A combination of arrogance, intelligence and no small ambition had propelled him to the attention of one Inspector Briant. The inspector, as he was then, recognised a lot of himself in the young man. He used his growing influence to move Boucher to his team. For the next six months he gave the young man hell. Every mistake was jumped on, every achievement ignored. His object was to see what the young man was made of. As it turned out, the young man who was impressing him almost daily had a spirit that had been forged in the fire of Marne and then Courtrai. After a year, Boucher was promoted and then promoted again a few months later. Nothing was said but he guessed the captain liked him.

The apartment block was on the outskirts of the Principality on Boulevard de Ouest which bordered Moneghetti, the less affluent part of Monaco. After a brief conversation with the doorman, he walked through the hallway to the ground floor apartment. A knock on the door was followed by the sound of a dog barking. A large dog if Boucher was not mistaken. Moments later he was greeted by a dressing gown-clad Philippe Redon. The dressing gown was a surprisingly flamboyant purple silk number. For a moment Boucher thought that he'd put his wife's on by mistake.

'Go away,' shouted Redon which was a trifle unwelcoming by any standard until Boucher realised Redon was speaking to their pet. The pet, in this case was a Dobermann. It was as evil a beast as Boucher had ever seen and he'd seen his fair share.

Boucher introduced himself, showed his police identity card and asked to enter. The former colonel bristled at the impertinence of the young man but as he was no longer a soldier there was little he could say. His unfortunate exit from the army was a never-ending source of frustration to him. It meant he was no longer able to send pups like this unwelcome visitor off with a few choice words to peel potatoes in a barrack room kitchen.

'I suppose you'd better come in,' said Redon moodily.

He reached down and took the Dobermann who, it transpired, was called Mimi, and led the killer into a bedroom and closed the door. This unjustified exclusion brought the worst out in Mimi who began to bark furiously and claw the door. Boucher was to spend the next ten minutes with one eye on a door that seemed likely to give way under the ferocity of the attack by the big black guard dog.

The apartment was a good size although the interior did surprise the young detective. The Redon's seemed to be unaware that they were French and in the era of Art Deco. Instead, it was tastefully furnished in the manner of an English country house just before the butler murders his employer. Brown seemed to be a particular favourite of the couple. Wooden tables, wooden chairs, brown leather

Chesterfield sofa and a wall of books on wooden shelves with reddish brown covers. Wherever you looked it was brown. At this point, Redon's purple gown represented a welcome flash of colour in the monotone interior.

Mme Redon appeared just then with a face like a Marseilles sailor intent on starting a street fight. She was wearing trousers and braces which framed her ample bosom in a way that had Boucher's eyes popping out of their sockets.

'Who is this, darling?' asked Mme Redon, smiling dangerously as she registered the impact she'd had on the young policeman.

'A policeman, my sweetness,' replied Redon with moustaches twitching nervously.

Mme Redon made a show of coolly appraising Boucher. The young man was certainly an improvement on the preening popinjay she'd married. For a moment she imagined him taking out his handcuffs and twirling them slowly around his finger in a manner that suggested she could be his prisoner if he so desired. She certainly did.

It was time for Boucher to step up to the boule circle as his dear old father would say.

'May we sit down?' said Boucher hoping that there was no hint of pleading in his voice. His desire to evacuate the flat and the hungry eye of Mme Redon as well as Satan's favourite pet was overwhelming. She reminded him of a praying mantis he'd read about at school. The females had a nasty habit of disposing of their mate once he'd performed his duty. Any minute now he expected her to lick her lips. Thankfully the two Redons sat beside one another on the sofa.

'Monsieur Redon, Madame, I'm sorry to tell you that your friend Monsieur Auguste Blanc was found murdered yesterday morning.'

Boucher announced this in a matter-of-fact voice, but his eyes were fixed on the couple to capture their reaction.

'What?' cried Redon, needlessly. He was on the point of asking if this was some sort of joke because it was in poor taste when his wife interrupted. As usual.

'What happened?'

'We are trying to understand this. I believe you met with Monsieur Blanc the night before in the casino.'

The Redons turned to one another. Both looked shocked by the news. So was Mimi if her howling was any guide. Boucher tried to ignore the pleading of the desolate Dobermann and push on with his interview.

After the initial few seconds of shock had receded Philippe Redon immediately worked out where this was heading. He erupted out of the chair and exploded at Boucher, 'What are you suggesting, you young oaf?'

Boucher was aware that Redon was ex-army. He'd seen enough of this class to do him several lifetimes. He stared back at the former colonel unapologetically and without fear. The intensity of Boucher's glare and the silence that accompanied it might have cowed many a man, but Redon had not reached the rank of colonel without being made of sterner stuff. However, in the presence of his wife, that stuff was pure terror. Once more she interrupted him.

'Can you tell us what happened?'

'He was poisoned sometime after he was seen talking with you. Can you tell me what you recall of that night?'

Redon, bristling with resentment at the young policeman and his wife, fell into a sullen silence. Mme Redon took over. Her calm voice had a notably soothing effect on the quarrelsome colonel.

'Well, not a great deal unfortunately. Monsieur Blanc only stopped for a few moments to greet us. As he hadn't met one of our party, Monsieur Aston, an English gentleman, he offered to show him around the casino.'

'That was the last time you saw either man?'

'No, Monsieur Aston returned around fifteen minutes later.'

'It was closer to thirty minutes, my dear.'

'What time was this?'

'Just before midnight,' replied the colonel. His manner had changed completely as if he now understood that it was in his self-interest to cooperate.

'How was Monsieur Aston when he returned?'

This confused both Redons. In a comically choreographed moment, they shrugged simultaneously. Redon said, 'I didn't notice any change. He is always good-humoured. He does not take life or himself very seriously.'

'I see,' said Boucher. 'You are sure that Monsieur Aston and Monsieur Blanc did not know one another.'

Once more they shrugged. This time Mme Redon replied, 'It did not seem so to me.'

At this point the phone rang in the apartment. The former colonel turned and walked over to the side table and picked up the phone.

'Hello?'

He was silent for a few moments as he listened to a voice at the other end. His manner changed though. Boucher could see him turn visibly paler. He nodded and said goodbye.

'Who was that dear?'

'Of no importance. Just some business I must conduct.'

The rest of the interview saw Redon revert once more to a monosyllabic manner that appeared to infect his wife. She was obviously taking her cue from her husband's manner and the drawbridge was well and truly pulled up.

-

Around the same time that Boucher had knocked on the door of the Redon household, Saimbron was engaged on a similar mission with the Russos. They lived in an apartment overlooking the port. Saimbron nodded to the doorman and showed his card. The doorman looked distinctly unhappy at admitting the policeman but realised he probably had no choice.

The Russos lived on the first floor. Saimbron straightened his tie as he looked in the mirror outside the apartment. Then he knocked on the door. He was met by an elderly maid who looked like she needed people to look after her. She sounded Italian. Saimbron wondered if she'd been with the lady of the house for a long time.

The first person to meet Saimbron was Mme Russo. She was dressed in a silk dressing gown and exuded polite hostility. Saimbron was used to the nervous suspicion that descended on someone when confronted with an officer of the law. It turned everyone into a naughty school child because almost certainly, they *had* done something wrong.

Moments later, her husband appeared with a welcoming smile. Hand outstretched, he approached the policeman. Saimbron smiled back. After all, it cost nothing to do so, and he wanted them to relax.

'My apologies for this intrusion,' said Saimbron. He introduced himself and asked if they could all sit down. The apartment was impressive. The view from the terrace was the port of Monaco and the deep blue of the Mediterranean.

'You have a beautiful apartment.'

'It belongs to my wife,' smiled Russo proudly at the scowling woman beside him. Saimbron knew the background but pretended to be confused. 'My wife's late husband owned a factory that made yachts.'

'I see,' said Saimbron. On Briant's suggestion, he already had men looking into the death of Mme Russo's late husband. 'Doubtless you are wondering why I have come here.'

'On the contrary, Monsieur Inspector, I suspect it is in connection with the death of Monsieur Blanc yesterday.'

'How did you hear of this?' asked Saimbron.

'I was passing the casino yesterday evening and I met with an acquaintance. He told me of the tragic circumstances.'

'Unusual circumstances, you mean.'

'Indeed,' agreed Russo. 'Have you any idea who murdered him.'

'We are holding one man presently.' Saimbron kept his eyes fixed on the couple sitting opposite him. They betrayed no obvious sign that they knew where he was heading with this. If anything, Mme Russo was showing signs of fear now, rather than outright enmity. 'You know him I believe. Monsieur Aston.

'What?' expostulated Russo. Even Mme Russo seemed shocked by this revelation.

'Ridiculous,' said Mme Russo dismissively. 'He wouldn't harm a fly.'

'Why do you say that?'

'Have you spoken with him?' asked Mme Russo. 'He has not a single violent bone in his body. You are making a mistake, I think.'

'Why do you say that?' This was one of Saimbron's favourite questions. He'd probably asked it several thousand times, often in the same interview.

'My wife is right, inspector. This is not a violent man. He treats life as a joke, like all Englishmen. Why would he want to kill Monsieur Blanc?'

'Why do you think he wanted to kill him?'

'That's the point,' said Russo. 'He wouldn't. He'd only just met him.'

'When was this?'

Mme Russo's eyes narrowed at this point and the hostility returned. Her face was a mask of hatred in fact and

Saimbron suspected that her husband would be on the receiving end of a tongue lashing when he left. To be fair, Russo was no fool and he immediately realised that in his loyal defence of his new friend he'd allowed the shrewd-looking detective an opening to pry a little into their affairs. There was nothing for it but to forge ahead and make the best of a bad job. He didn't have to look at his wife either to realise that he was in trouble. It was something in the aggressive way his wife was breathing. Like most men, Russo could always tell when the doghouse beckoned.

'We were in the casino the night before last, and Monsieur Aston was with us as he has been for the last week or so. Monsieur Blanc came over. He is a very sociable man and knows everyone. Everyone knows him. Except, as it turned out, Monsieur Aston. Blanc, as you will find out, is always at pains to be the most generous host and invited Alastair to join him on a tour of the casino.'

'What time did they return?'

'Around midnight. No, before, because that is when we all left.'

'Did you see Monsieur Blanc after he had been with the Englishman.'

'No,' said Mme Russo.

'Did he say what they had done or where they had gone?'

Mme Russo had a hard gleam in her eye, and she replied with a certain finality, 'No.'

Just then the phone rang. The maid answered it and then turned to the two Russos.

'It is Monsieur Fournier.'

If Mme Russo had been showing signs of anger before, the raging fire that erupted in her eyes at that moment told Saimbron that it wasn't just her husband who was in for a verbal rinsing. She leapt out of the sofa like she was sitting on a hot plate. She confined the conversation to single words with one syllable and then hung up without a goodbye.

Saimbron saw that she was distinctly paler. Her husband, too, was more agitated now. He guessed that the police had not only visited all the people Aston had been with, but they had done so at the same time. They were all, now, very much under a microscope.

Russo knew this was a problem. A very big problem indeed.

19

Late afternoon in Agatha's Cap d'Ail villa saw the return of Mary and Harry from their surveillance operation on the Fourniers and Redons respectively. Betty had played her part too by volunteering to follow the Russos. This had required her to spend most of the morning and a good portion of the early afternoon sitting outside at a bar near the yachts in the harbour.

Agatha looked suspiciously at her friend upon her return and asked, 'Have you been drinking?'

'A little refreshment, my dear. Nothing more.'

The credibility of this statement was somewhat undermined by Betty placing a firm hand on the side table to maintain her stance. It was greeted with a derisive snort from her friend which Betty happily ignored as usual. Spying Kit waiting at the dining room table, she made her way over carefully to join him and the others in sharing what they'd witnessed during the day. Betty arrived safely at the table having steadied herself on a couple of occasions and sat down with great dignity.

Mary joined her and shot her husband a knowing smile. Soon everyone was in in place. Agatha confirmed that Alastair was in good spirits having seen him earlier. Kit asked Mary to open the batting and relate what she'd observed in her time with the Fourniers.

'The Fourniers stayed in their house until just before lunch,' reported Mary. 'Then I followed them to a restaurant near that little beach at Lavrotto. I must say that man is perfectly beastly.'

'I gather,' replied Kit, remembering what Alastair had said. At the time he'd though that it was more a symptom of his uncle's growing affection for Mme Fournier. Meeting her husband had convinced him that something else was afoot in this relationship. 'What did you see?'

-

Monsieur Fournier and Elsa Fournier emerged from their apartment around midday. Fournier was wearing a beige-coloured suit and a Panama hat. He might have been described as a fine, if rather severe, figure of a man. Tall, perhaps a little heavy but not overweight. The contrast with his wife was striking. Mme Fournier wore only a light blue cotton dress which emphasised her slender build and pale skin. She carried an umbrella to shield herself from the sun. Fournier walked ahead of his wife as if he was too embarrassed to be seen with her. Mary already felt her hackles rising.

The couple walked for a few minutes down the street before turning off, arriving at a small square, *Place da la Visitation*. There were several hansom cabs in the square. The couple climbed onto one of them. Mary overheard them ask to be taken to the beach. A minute after they departed, Mary took one of the other open hansom cabs.

'I'm a little late for an appointment,' said Mary. 'Could you go quickly?'

A small restaurant was the Fournier destination. It was situated just across from the beach. There were several outdoor tables with parasols. The waiter greeted them both warmly as they entered which suggested to Mary that they were regular customers. At this point Fournier walked straight over to a table without a parasol. Although Mary could not hear what was being said, it was clear that his wife was dismayed with the choice. Her shoulders slumped and she pointed to a seat underneath a parasol that would give her shade. Fournier waved away her objection.

Mary gave the Fourniers a few minutes to settle at their table before arriving in the restaurant and taking a table towards the back, in the shade. From this position she was able to view Mme Fournier. There was no question that she had a fragile beauty that many men would be attracted to. This made her husband's treatment of her all the more baffling.

The couple ordered and then waited in silence. Both seemed content to gaze out onto the beach. The better weather had brought out several mothers, or nannies, with small children. Was it Mary's imagination that Mme Fournier gazed wistfully towards them? Mary wondered if she had any children. She was perhaps not too old to have a child now. Mary judged her to be no more than forty. Fournier seemed quite a bit older. There was at least ten years between them, perhaps more.

A few minutes passed and it was clear that Fournier was growing impatient for the waiter's return and their order. He said as much to Mme Fournier who replied that they had not been there so long.

'Nonsense, my dear. Why there is only us and that young lady over there in the restaurant. It's weak-minded to think anything other than they are taking too long.' His voice was gentle, but the tone was icily dangerous. 'Why we must have been waiting fifteen minutes or more.'

He tapped his waistcoat pocket in search of something. He frowned momentarily, then stood up and began to search his pockets.

'What is wrong, my dear?' asked Mme Fournier.

'I can't find my watch. Is this another one of your little mischiefs, my dear?' The question appeared innocent, but Fournier's tone was dark.

Mme Fournier grew even paler. She shrank into the seat so much that Mary had to resist the impulse to fly over and give the arrogant bully a piece of her mind. And that piece was vitriol.

'I didn't do anything, I swear. Look at me,' cried Mme Fournier. One look at her would have convinced the most sceptical of sceptics. This woman was innocent and living in fear.

'Open your bag.'

Mme Fournier glanced down at her bag. Terror spread over her face like an infection. Just at this moment the food arrived at the table, forcing Fournier to sit down. He paused for a moment to allow the waiter to leave them alone and then he turned sharply to his wife and hissed, 'Open your bag, please.'

She hesitated for a moment then reluctantly lifted it off the empty seat. Fournier tore the bag from her hands and opened it up. Then, with a look of triumphant contempt, extracted a pocket watch from inside the bag.

'How do you explain this?

Mme Fournier stared at the watch in speechless horror. All power of communication vanished, and her eyes shifted from her bag to the watch and then up to her husband who, although seated, seemed to tower over her. Finally, she found her voice. It was barely a whisper and Mary could just about hear her.

'But why would I do something so wicked?'

The look on Fournier's reddened features and angry eyes asked 'why indeed' but he said nothing. He turned away from his wife and tried to eat some of the food but angrily gave up. Meanwhile, Mme Fournier could not bring herself to eat and wept quietly.

'It's too much, Elsa. You need help, my love. Stealing my watch. Always moving the painting from the wall. Why do you do this?'

'I don't. I don't know,' she replied before covering her face with her hands.

Mary's food arrived a minute later. The thought crossed her mind to carry the plate to the Fournier's table and empty it over the ghastly persecutor's head. In fact, it raged within her like a forest fire. Whatever she could do to make this man pay she would do with a happy heart.

-

'He sounds like a charmer,' said Kit when Mary had finished relating the story. 'It certainly supports Uncle Alastair's view of him as a tyrant.'

Agatha, along with the rest of the table, had been listening in silence, her face was a mask but there was anger in her eyes. Finally, she spoke. There was a restrained passion in her voice.

'I'd have handed him his hat a long time ago. I have come across men like this before. They are bullies. They prey on women who are of gentle character, and they can often be violent. I am very concerned for this woman's welfare. I don't know if Alastair had mentioned it, but when I asked him who had coined the term 'Bluebeard Club' he said that he'd heard it from Mme Redon first, but she claims that it originated from this vile man. He wears it like a badge of honour.'

Mary looked horrified at this, 'You don't think that he's planning to murder her?'

'Far from it, my dear,' replied Agatha enigmatically. 'Far from it.'

This was too much for Betty. A combination of her anger at the story told by Mary, the libations she had enjoyed while waiting for the Russos to appear, and her usual impatience at being several hundred yards behind Agatha on the uptake made her thump the table.

'Is he planning to kill or not?'

'I think what Aunt Agatha,' answered Kit, 'is suggesting is that this beast is mentally torturing his wife to such a degree that he is making her question her own sanity. In doing so, he is either preparing the way to have her committed to an asylum or…'

'Suicide,' chipped in Mary as the horrible realisation of what was happening hit her.

'Why would anyone do this?' asked Betty.

Kit and Agatha stared at one another and then Agatha said, 'Money. I imagine he would inherit everything if she died whether at her own hands or in an asylum. I doubt someone so fragile would survive long in one of those places.'

Attention fell on Harry Miller next. His day tracking the Redons had been even more uneventful than Betty's.

'Mme Redon did not leave the apartment at any point when I was there,' began Miller. 'Monsieur Redon only appeared after lunch. He went into the town centre for an aperitif around four, four-thirty.'

'Did he meet anyone?' asked Kit.

'Yes, as a matter of fact. He was joined by a small man who looked a little shabby, at least compared to Redon.'

'You'll have to give a description to Rufus.'

'Where is Mr. Watts anyway?' asked Agatha.

'He went to Nice after lunch. He'd finished his work at the casino. I asked him to pop in and say hello to Uncle Alastair,' replied Kit. "I think the police wanted to see him too.'

'I'm sure Alastair will enjoy that,' said Agatha. Kit wasn't sure if she was being serious or not so ignored her.

'I say,' said Betty, who often started sentences in this way and duly did so. 'The Russos made a late appearance too, just after three. They met a small man wearing a rather shabby suit. You don't think it was the same man?'

Kit raised an eyebrow at this which told Mary that he was one hundred percent certain that it was.

'Perhaps,' said Kit, thereby confirming both Mary's and everyone else's assumption that it was one and the same person. 'I think, in the spirit of cooperation, Harry, that you should go to the police station in Nice and share what you have seen.'

Miller looked a little downcast at the prospect of voluntarily entering a police station. His pre-war career as a burglar meant that old habits die hard. Kit smiled in sympathy at his manservant's reaction. He shrugged in a we-have-no-choice manner that he normally reserved for those times when Agatha or Mary were being particularly unreasonable.

'How long did Redon and this man meet for.'

'Only a few minutes. I couldn't hear what was being said, they spoke in low voices, but I don't think that they particularly liked one another. There were no handshakes or salutations.'

'Did you notice anything similar, Betty?' asked Kit.

'I did,' said Betty, eyes widening. 'The Russos looked like they were chewing wasps when they were with him. There was definitely an atmosphere.'

'Could you hear what was being said?' asked Agatha sharply.

'No, the bar was full of Italians,' commented Betty. Everyone nodded and this was considered sufficient explanation. 'The man didn't stay long and there was certainly no fondness in their farewell. What do you think this all means?'

Kit sat back in his chair at the head of the table. It was too early to say who the man might be. Until they could identify him it was academic. The key to this was Harry Miller.

'I think you should make your way over to Nice as soon as possible. I'll ring Inspector Saimbron and tell him you're on your way. If you are able, try and obtain a carbon copy of whatever Rufus creates. The police will want to keep the original to make photostats.'

Agatha rose from her seat, full of business.

'If you are going, you may want to replenish his supply of reading material and those filthy cigars.'

Agatha took two books from a sideboard and a box full of cigars. Kit and Mary took one look at the cover of the book on top and had to choke back their laughter. '*The Wayward Nurse*,' by Ivor Longstaff. The blurb read, 'Her prescription read love and the doctor was just the man to fill it…'

'I didn't know you had his new one, Agatha. I've been wanting to lay my hands on this Longstaff for a while now.' exclaimed Betty. 'Bags it when Alastair has finished.'

'Ivor Longstaff?' asked Kit, one eyebrow raised suspiciously. Betty nodded enthusiastically. Kit decided to keep their meeting focused on the next things that needed to be done rather than dwell on the nom de plume of a hack writer.

'After you've provided your description, you can bring Rufus back to meet everyone here this evening.'

'Ahh,' said Agatha.

All eyes turned to Agatha.

'Yes?' said Kit and Mary in unison.

Agatha looked at her nephew and then Mary. It was difficult to read what she was thinking at that moment. She had that ability to turn herself into a sphinx when she wanted to.

'You and Mary should come to the casino with me this evening. There's someone you need to meet.'

Kit and Mary both grinned immediately. It wasn't too hard to guess who it was.

'Oh?' Who are they meeting?' asked Betty.

20

Much later that evening, a taxi drew up outside the casino. Out stepped Kit, Mary, and Agatha. Despite the heat earlier, the night was distinctly chillier. Summer was not here yet. They skipped up the steps into the casino. Agatha led Kit and Mary towards the office that they'd been to the day before last. A slender, well-dressed lady greeted Agatha with a smile and ushered them into the office.

All signs of police activity had been taken away. The office looked ready to welcome its next inhabitant. Poor Blanc thought Kit. Life goes on. Mary was impressed by the office and went to the wall which displayed a painting by Jean-Honoré Fragonard. Mary thought it ghastly. A voice from behind took her by surprise.

'I see you're admiring the Fragonard. Do you like it?'

Mary and Kit both spun round and a small man with penetrating eyes entered.

'Your Serene Highness,' said Kit, bowing.

'Lord Aston, I believe?' said Prince Albert I of Monaco.

Kit smiled and replied, 'Strictly speaking I am Lord Christopher; my father is Lord Aston. Most people call me Kit, though.'

'Like Kit Carson, the American scout?'

'Yes,' exclaimed Kit, enthusiastically.

'I am a great admirer of Kit Carson. I should love to have met him. A very inspirational man.'

'Yes, a trapper, explorer, Indian agent, and Civil War soldier. He lived several lives, each one as exciting as the other. It's probably the only thing my dad and I see eye to eye on,' said Kit, a hint of sadness in his voice. Albert picked up on the note of melancholy and put a hand on Kit's arm. The he turned his full attention to Mary.

'And this beautiful young woman must be Lady Mary. Your adopted aunt has told me so much about you.'

Mary glanced at Agatha who could not hide the look of pride on her face. To be fair though, she did try.

'I hope I'm not as bad as all that, Your Serene Highness,' grinned Mary.

'You know your aunt well,' laughed Albert. 'Do you like the Fragonard?'

'It's lovely,' lied Mary.

'I was never very keen on it myself,' replied the prince looking at the riot of colourful foliage surrounding a wistful young woman in a garden.

At this point Mary began to giggle and admitted, 'I'm sorry, I wasn't telling the truth. I just didn't want to be rude.'

Even Agatha's eyebrows shot up at this, but the prince began to laugh uproariously.

'I see what you mean, Agatha,' said the prince, clearly delighted with his new acquaintance. 'Now perhaps we can sit down and talk about this tragic situation.'

Albert sat behind Blanc's desk and studied the three people in front of him. Kit and Mary intuitively understood that they should wait for the prince to begin.

'Auguste worked for me for over ten years. I am heartbroken at the thought that his working here has, in some way, caused his death.'

Kit could not have agreed more on this point but did not feel it appropriate to explain why just at that moment. The prince fixed his eyes on Agatha. There was no hiding the affection he felt.

'Agatha, I know that you helped me in the past, but I cannot ask you to look into this matter. It is something for the police. I met with a man the other day, Monsieur Charpentier. He is the examining magistrate.'

'Frightful man I gather,' said Agatha.

The prince laughed and neither confirmed nor denied this. 'He was most particular on the subject of outside interference. I think he was referring as much to Captain Briant as Lord…sorry, you, Kit. I appreciate that you will be very worried for your uncle. I have no doubt of his innocence in this matter and I'm sure justice will be served. However, it is important that we leave this matter to the authorities. Our situation with regard to France, as you will appreciate, is a delicate one. While I may share your views on some of the officials I must work with, I cannot risk being seen to be, how shall I put this, unhelpful or obstructive.'

'We understand,' said Agatha speaking on behalf of them all.

'For this reason, I think that we need not trouble you further on the matter that I asked for your help on.'

Kit and Agatha had been expecting this and it was now time to declare openly their position.

'I would beg you to reconsider, Your Serene Highness,' said Kit. 'I think that the matter that you brought Aunt Agatha in to investigate may not be finished.'

Albert looked surprised at this.

'Why do you say this? Surely with police everywhere, this man or men will not return now.'

'On the contrary, sir, this is exactly when I would come. The casino manager is out of the way, confusion and fear will reign. I would say this is the perfect time to strike.'

This gave Albert pause for thought. He looked back and forth between his visitors. A shadow fell over his face as a thought struck him.

'Do you believe, and I hope you will be frank with me, that Auguste was connected with the man or people who have been winning so much from us?'

Agatha touched Kit's arm and replied, 'We should not discount the possibility but nor are we accusing him of anything. Both Christopher and I have always wondered why no investigation took place before my arrival.'

'Ah,' said Albert in the manner of a man who was about to correct a misapprehension, 'that is not the case. I believe Auguste did have his man look into the matter.'

'His man?' asked Kit.

'Yes, a rather devious former detective named Dupin, like the Poe character. Rene Dupin.'

'Former detective?' asked Kit.

'Yes, he was with the police force in Nice but left under a cloud, I gather. I never inquired much about him, but he was a rather seedy character. However, Auguste swore by him. He used him to trace gamblers who left without paying their debts. I understand he had a knack for finding them and ensuring they fulfilled their obligations.'

Blackmail had never been so regally endorsed, thought Mary, trying not to smile.

'I wonder if we could speak to him,' said Kit. In fact, he was angry and so, if he was not mistaken, by her breathing, was Aunt Agatha. This was something that Blanc should have briefed them on. He glanced at Agatha; his eyebrows raised. There was a fire in her eyes, now.

'I'm surprised Auguste did not mention him,' said Albert, thoughtfully. There was silence in the room as the group shared the same thought and it was a thought that did not reflect well on the late manager of the casino. Albert rose from the desk, went to the door, and opened it. He spoke a few words to someone who, Kit guessed, had been listening to their conversation.

Moments later a woman appeared. She was the same lady they'd met outside the office. Her hair was tied back in a neat bun; she could have been anywhere between forty and sixty. She curtsied to Albert.

'Mme Cotille, would you be so kind as to locate a telephone number and address for Rene Dupin? Thank you.'

Mme Cotille nodded and disappeared from the room. Kit glanced at Agatha and seemed to be unhappy about something. Albert observed this and waited for him to speak.

'I think it would be wise to share this with the police,' said Kit in the manner of a man who has just had his nails pulled out.

Mme Cotille returned two minutes later and handed a note to the prince containing the details of Rene Dupin. Albert looked at the note then smiled and nodded to Mme Cotille. She left the office just as the prince handed over the note to Kit.

Kit pointed to the phone on Auguste Blanc's desk.

'May I?'

Albert held his palm out towards the phone in a be-my-guest manner.

Kit put the receiver to his ear and dialled the number on the paper. There was no answer. He put the receiver back and dialled another number. This time he spoke to an operator. He asked to be put through to Inspector Saimbron.

'Inspector it's Lord Aston….We may have a lead for you to pursue. Do you know a Monsieur Rene Dupin?'

21

Rufus Watts's day had begun, as it usually did, around nine-thirty in the morning. It was rare that he would grace the corridors of Scotland Yard before ten. Such was the lacerating prowess of his tongue, senior officers fought shy of persuading him to follow more regular hours. He probably worked longer than most. His lifestyle choice was more night owl than early bird. Very often he would stay late at the home of the Criminal Investigation Department before ending the night in some low rent bar; the less salubrious the better when the mood took him.

The previous day had been akin to a day at the factory. Not that Rufus had ever been to such a place, but he imagined that no factory worker could have been quite so manually employed as he had been by the French Police over the previous twenty-four hours. By his estimation he produced around twelve likenesses from his exhaustive interviews with casino staff.

His first appointment of the day was not until two in the afternoon when he would meet Alastair Aston. He was aware that his drawing had probably contributed to Alastair Aston's unfortunate current situation, but he felt not a jot of guilt about it. Moral responsibility lay with those who committed crimes, not those who uncovered their vile deeds. As to the innocence of Kit Aston's uncle he was in no doubt, but he'd been in the police long enough to know that appearance was no guide to innocence any more than lies indicated guilt.

After a leisurely breakfast, Rufus used his morning for a spot of sightseeing. A walk down the hill from the Place du Casino offered the opportunity to view the beautiful, masted yachts moored all along the port. Rufus was a man of taste, and that taste ran from refined to vulgar without so much as a pause in the middle for thought. He sat in a café for an hour gazing out at the sea, the rich people walking by and the elegant motor cars which made him want to howl at the moon for the fates that had denied him the wealth that he would surely have used and joyfully abused to the full.

He took the train into Nice and settled himself at a fish restaurant just behind the port at Nice. The *bouillabaisse* was exceptional, washed down by half a bottle of white wine. So, it was with a light heart if not a spring in his step that Rufus announced himself at the police station in Nice. Oddly, the French policeman seemed more accepting of the long-haired artist than many in his own country, used as they no doubt were to being in the presence of the artistic temperament.

Saimbron greeted him warmly. The pictures by the artist had helped identify everyone that had been seen speaking to the murdered casino manager. He didn't begrudge a conversation with the man they had in the cell.

'Please come this way, Monsieur Watts. Our guest has had quite a busy day with visitors. First Lord Aston and later his sister.'

'Tell me, Monsieur Inspector,' asked Rufus, 'Have any of his friends visited him yet from the Bluebeard Club.'

The inspector smiled and looked shrewdly at the Rufus.

'No. They seem reluctant to visit a police station. Strange, don't you think?'

'Very,' agreed, Rufus, removing his fedora.

Saimbron led Rufus down a dingy corridor that was thankfully poorly lit. It was a place of misery. Rufus felt a chill in being in such dank surroundings where humanity had been excised and replaced by despair.

From inside his cell, Alastair heard the footsteps echoing down the corridor. He had his feet up on the bed and was reading a book provided by Kit from Agatha's extensive collection of high literature, *Maid of Death* by Max Bloode, one of Agatha's favourite writers. He had just arrived at a critical point in the drama when the maid in question has enticed the farmer's son to the barn where she would, quite literally, have her evil way with him when the cell door opened. Alastair rolled his eyes and slammed the book down on the bed. Even here, incarcerated in a foreign country for a murder he had not committed, he couldn't get a moment's peace to feed his intellect.

The cell door opened, and a small man was ushered in. He was wearing a light, cotton suit that fitted him perfectly. His tie matched the handkerchief that had been stuffed into his breast pocket expertly enough to resemble a waterfall. Alastair rose from his bed and smiled.

'Am I addressing the man that put me in here?'

'At your service, sir,' said Rufus mimicking a bow and a wave of the hand that would have been considered excessive even in the court of the Sun King, Louis XIV.

'Please take a seat. Can I offer you something? There may still be some stale bread left.'

The door closed behind them leaving the two men alone. Alastair gestured towards the wooden chair and Rufus sat down after first brushing the top with his handkerchief.

'I trust they are treating you well.'

'Oh tolerably,' said Alastair.

The eyes of the artist strayed over to the book lying on Alastair's bed. The lurid cover showed in the foreground an attractive young woman wearing a night shift with barely sufficient material to accomplish its duty.

'Interesting,' said Rufus.

This could have been a comment or a question. Alastair opted for the latter interpretation. He glanced down at the book and smiled.

'A deeply moving meditation on the human condition.'

The eyes of the artist hovered over the young man in the background. He appeared to have mislaid his shirt. His torso, and arms were positively throbbing with vitality.

'So, I see,' said Rufus. 'They both seem to be in tip top condition.'

Alastair ignored the dry scepticism in the tone. He smiled shamelessly and said asked, 'To what to I owe the pleasure?'

'I've finished off a few more of the artist impressions of the patrons. Would you like to see them? Perhaps you might recognise someone who was speaking with the dear departed Monsieur Blanc.'

Alastair perked up at this.

'Do you have mine by any chance? I'm rather curious.'

A smile spread over Rufus Watts's face. He opened his case and shuffled though a wad of paper. Finally, he pulled out Alastair's impression with the flourish of a magician introducing a rabbit from his hat. Alastair took the paper from the artist and studied it for a few moments.

'I must say, you're rather good.'

Rufus bowed humbly. While Alastair continued to examine his features, the artist took a sheaf of papers and set them down on the prison bed. Alastair returned, not without a pang, his portrait picked up each of the three other impressions in turn. Two of them had spoken with Blanc while he was with him at the bar. The other was unfamiliar.

'Is this of any help?'

'Yes, I believe so. Don't forget, the police need to be able to trace the movements of these men. Therefore, if you were with Monsieur Blanc at the bar around eleven-thirty, then they know that these men were there too. It's a very useful way of cross-checking everyone's story.'

'Yes, I see that it is,' said Alastair.

'Is there anything you need? I can pass on a message to your relatives?'

'Well, a few more books wouldn't go amiss and I'm running a little low on my panatela supply. He took out a cigar and showed it the artist.'

'I shall let them know.'

-

In fact, Agatha had anticipated such demands and upon Harry Miller's arrival a couple of hours later, he made his way to Alastair's cell carrying a fresh box of cigars and a couple of new books to help him pass the time. He was led into the cell by a large policeman who had missed his calling as a store Santa Claus.

The policeman inspected the small box for anything that might assist the Englishman in escaping from custody. Then he looked at the two books. His eyebrows shot up as he examined the covers. He handed the two books to Alastair with an amused grin. Alastair ignored the look with great dignity. Alastair held the two books with the cheery reverence of a schoolboy with a new train set. The door of the cell closed as the gaoler let himself out.

'*The Wayward Nurse, Axe of Revenge*. Oh, very good. I shall enjoy these books,' said Alastair enthusiastically, leafing through the top one. 'They really do provide a wonderful way of exercising one's mind.'

The cover of *Axe of Revenge* displayed a man carrying a bloody axe. The axe-wielding man had long matted hair, mad eyes, and a smile that had moved beyond malevolent to beatific.

'Capital. Of course, Axe is a play on words for Acts,' explained Alastair.

'Yes, I think I understood this, sir,' said Miller drily. Alastair shot Miller a glance and then smiled to himself.

Suddenly a horrible thought occurred to Alastair. He recoiled in horror. The bloody axe all too closely resembled a guillotine. The smile faded from his face.

'Perhaps I'll start with *The Wayward Nurse*.'

Miller stayed for ten minutes with Alastair and updated him on their surveillance as well as the mysterious individual who had met up with all the couples. Alastair could shed no further light on who this was. Miller banged on the door of the cell to be let out. Then he was led from the basement upstairs to the office used by Saimbron. Waiting for him there was the inspector and Briant. A half-smile crossed the face of Briant when Miller arrived.

'Monsieur Miller,' greeted Briant before adding in English. 'A pleasure to meet you again. I hope you are keeping well.'

And out of trouble added both the captain and Miller in their thoughts.

'Yes, sir, very well,' replied Miller in French. He'd made a point of learning some of the language during the war. It had kept his brain active during the long weeks between engagements with the enemy. It had also kept his mind off the impending engagements.

'It was good of you to provide support in the surveillance of this Bluebeard Club. Perhaps you would remind Lord Aston his assistance in this matter is no longer required. He will understand, I'm sure.'

'I'll tell him, Captain.'

'Good, now perhaps, with the help of the extraordinary Monsieur Watts, you can shed some light on who this man is that visited Monsieur Aston's friends. Saimbron, who had remained silent throughout until this moment rose from his seat and went to the door. He spoke to someone in rapid

French and then returned to his seat. Moments later Rufus Watts appeared.

First Miller described the man that he'd seen. As he did so, Watts showed him various facial types, hair types, eyes, noses, mouths all drawn by him. Little by little the composite was built up using the cards with the various parts. Then Watts took the composite and began to sketch it on a fresh piece of paper. He worked slowly and methodically to create a lightly sketched initial likeness. Then, with Miller guiding him, he made alterations and added subtle shadows to enhance the features and make the face more three-dimensional. The process took less than an hour.

Finally, Watts took a separate piece of paper and created a full body picture using an impression of the larger portrait combined with guidance on the build of the man and the clothes he'd worn. This was a relatively rapid process and took less than twenty minutes. The two pictures complete, Watts and Miller left the office they'd been given and walked down the hall to Saimbron's office.

Briant was no longer there but the inspector was. He looked up from his desk when the two men entered. Watts placed the two pictures on the desk. There was more than a glow of satisfaction in him when he saw the reaction they provoked. The inspector's eyes widened, and he shot the artist a glance.

This was what Watts lived for. Not for him the reviews of an over-educated, under qualified art critic or the squalid acclaim of a mercantile class that purchased art with their ears rather than their eyes. No; praise and criticism of art were the same to him. They meant nothing. The role of art was to provoke a reaction. If he read the face of Saimbron correctly, and of course he did, then the reaction of the detective towards his impression of the man who'd met various members of the Bluebeard Club was recognition.

There was no greater testimony to Rufus Watts' art than this.

Just at this moment the phone rang. Saimbron's eyes never left the picture. He grabbed the phone, irritated at the interruption. A voice could be heard by the others.

'Lord Aston,' said Saimbron turning towards the two men. For the second time in the space of a minute, the inspector's eyes widened.

'Yes, I know Rene Dupin,' he said after a few moments. 'I'm looking at a picture of him now created by your Monsieur Watts and Monsieur Miller. This is the man that met with the others earlier in Monte Carlo.'

-

A fly buzzed around the small apartment in a token effort to be a fly. It was just too damn hot that evening. In the end the fly gave up and came to rest on the forehead of the man sprawled on the sofa. The sofa in question had seen better days, but not many. The room was small and dark. The furniture was mostly second hand except for a few choice items that were probably third hand. The apartment was one of ten in a crumbling block in Nice Nord. Even burglars were wary of walking in this area at night.

The fly soon had company on the forehead of the man. No territorial scuffle ensued. Each was content to patrol their area and ignore the other. They also ignored the banging on the door and the shouts coming from outside. The shouts grew louder as did the banging. When the door crashed open, four flies decided it was time to move onto pastures new.

Inspector Saimbron stepped through the door followed by two officers. They were all armed and their guns were pointing into the living room of the apartment. The three men stared down at the dead body of Rene Dupin. The clue that he had been murdered lay in the bullet hole in his forehead. Saimbron motioned with his gun for the two other men to search the flat. This was a job that could be measured in seconds rather than minutes. It was a two-room flat. All the windows were closed. One of the men came back from the bedroom. He shook his head.

Saimbron glanced at the other policeman and then back to Dupin. He was holding a framed picture in his hand. It showed two young men. Both soldiers. Jean-Francois and Pierre. His throat tightened and his eyes lost their focus.

'We need a doctor. And find someone from forensics,' he whispered at last.

The man nodded and left the apartment. There was no time for sentiment. The past was the past. Saimbron looked around the room for some sign of who had visited. There was nothing. No glasses. No semi-full ashtray. Nothing. The murderer had come in and either caught Dupin sitting in his sofa or, more likely, been invited in and shot him while he sat down. Saimbron exhaled and felt like sitting down himself. He'd hoped to return home half an hour ago. That was not going to happen now. He reached into his pocket and pulled out a packet of cigarettes. He lit one and offered another to the other policeman. This was accepted.

'Start with the apartments next door and go door to door. Someone must have heard something.'

'Yes, sir.'

He looked down at Rene Dupin. The man had been his colleague. A friend. Rene had chosen a different path, one that lay somewhere between right and wrong. He'd lost the trust of the police force he'd served for fifteen years. He'd lost the trust of his friends, his wife. He'd probably stopped trusting himself. Now he was no more. Saimbron doubted many would mourn his passing. Even though Dupin had been shot, Saimbron knew deep down that he'd had been killed by the same hand that had murdered Auguste Blanc. Insofar as he'd ever thought that this could be the Englishman, he was even less convinced now.

-

Around eleven that evening Saimbron returned to the police station. The place was empty as he arrived. A sergeant at the desk barely acknowledged his arrival. Great security he thought. He wondered how many prisoners might have escaped while this idiot slept at his post. Tiredness overwhelmed him. He couldn't raise the energy to raise hell.

He trooped into the station reluctantly. All he wanted to do was go home. However, a sense of honour brought him back to his office. He felt it was only fair to inform Alastair Aston that he would be released within the next twenty-four hours. The original intention of jailing him seemed to have served a purpose, albeit a tragic one. Rene Dupin was dead because the murderer, or murderers, had felt safe enough to kill him because they did not think the police were after them. In doing so, it was evident they did not need to have Aston as a scapegoat. Clearly, Rene Dupin had represented too big a threat to be allowed to live. Bigger than the need to have a finger pointed at the Englishman.

It was a weary trek down to the cells. Oddly, there was no guard. Saimbron frowned. This was not right. Another example of the lax security. He would have to have a word with the chief. Then another thought struck him. He stopped and listened for a sound. He could hear noise coming from the Englishman's cell. A low murmur. From his side holster he took out a revolver and moved noiselessly to the cell door. He threw the door open and jumped inside with his gun in front of him.

Alastair and the guard looked up in alarm. They were both sitting on the bed. From where Saimbron was standing it looked as if Aston had been reading from a thin book with a rather vivid cover featuring a nurse. Saimbron put the gun away and glared at the guard. Aware that his life was no longer in mortal danger, Alastair began to chuckle. He turned to the guard and said, 'We can read the rest of it tomorrow, Edgar.'

'You'll be out tomorrow,' replied Saimbron.

'Excellent. I knew justice would be served,' said Alastair but Saimbron was already heading out of the cell.

22

Harry Miller parked the Mercedes-Benz just outside the police station in Nice. He jumped out from the front and opened the door for Kit and Agatha. It was a beautiful morning. The sky was an unbroken blue and there was no trace of wind to leaven the heat that bounced off the ground and pummelled the skin.

They were met at the entrance by Briant. He smiled a greeting and took them to Saimbron's office first. The inspector was with Monsieur Charpentier. This was potentially an ill omen and nothing on the face of the little examining magistrate suggested good news.

He bowed stiffly to Kit and Agatha and invited them to sit down. Kit noticed the trace of a smile on the inspector's lips. Their eyes met. The inspector, far from being put out by the actions of Charpentier, seemed amused. The examining magistrate was sitting in Saimbron's seat behind a desk. His two hands were on a cane which was propped on the floor. He attempted a smile but then thought better of it.

'Lord Aston, you will be pleased to learn that Monsieur Aston is to be released from custody this morning.' Charpentier glanced at the two detectives, and added condescendingly, 'We can find no evidence to support his continued confinement, nor indeed, any obvious motive. You are free to take him away.'

'Thank you, Monsieur Charpentier.'

'I would like to add, however, this is now and always has been a police matter. I have written to Prince Albert in Monaco and requested that he release Lady Frost from her commission in the casino. We will take it as a kindness if you cease to have any involvement in anything to do with the murders and, in addition, the irregular gambling observed in the casino. Furthermore, we would request that Monsieur Aston makes no effort to meet or communicate with those men who describe themselves as the Bluebeard Club. Is this clear?'

'Very,' replied Agatha. Something in the compliant tone of his aunt's voice told Kit that the examining magistrate's views had been noted and would be duly ignored. Kit remained silent and waited to hear what other restrictions would be imposed. Thankfully, Charpentier appeared to have run out of things to stop them doing. A strange silence descended on the office. Kit looked at each of the three Frenchmen waiting to hear what was to happen next.

Briant was the first to realise that Charpentier had finished. He jumped to his feet.

'Perhaps we should release the prisoner.'

Charpentier nodded curtly. This was the end of the meeting. Kit and Agatha rose from their seats. Briant and Saimbron led them downstairs to the holding area. Once more, and to Saimbron's evident irritation, there was no sign of a guard. As they approached the cell holding Alastair, they heard him reading aloud, in French. His French was arguably better than either Kit's or Agatha's. The group stopped and listened to what was being said.

'How could you have known that the table was round and not square? Only if you had been in the room. Only if you had been the killer of Montague Mogg, Nurse van Dyck. Or should I say, Candy Noinkers or Daphne Rodhunter or whatever name you go by.'

Inspector Bellmop stood over the killer nurse, a cruel smile twitching the corners of his mouth. She bent her head and began to sob softly.

'Yes, it was me, Inspector Bellmop. I killed him like I killed all the others.'

What others? This was news to Bellmop.

'There was that the baker's boy, Arnold Whiffle, and Hamilton Minge, the Earl's son. Now, let me see. Who else? Oh yes, the Tollyring couple. I enjoyed killing them.' She began to giggle. It seemed so funny now. She added more names to the list, so many that Bellmop was struggling to capture everything she was saying. When she'd finished the list, it encompassed twenty-two victims. Mostly male.

'You're going away for a very long time, young lady. But before you do, there's just one thing you need, kid.'

Bellmop bent down. He caressed her cheek then his hand grabbed her hair suddenly. He pulled her face up to his and kissed her hard. Then he let her go, leaving her panting for more.

'Take her away, Chopper.'

Bellmop's faithful sergeant, 'Chopper' Todgeman took Nurse van Dyck's hands and put handcuffs on her wrists. She stared at Bellmop, yearning in her eyes. He walked out of the library and didn't look back.

The End

'*The Wayward Nurse*,' whispered Agatha to the others listening outside the door. 'Not one of Longstaff's best, I think. I am not so keen when you know who the murderer is from the start.'

'Indeed,' replied Kit looking sideways as his aunt, trying to refrain from laughing.

Inside they heard Alastair speak again.

'I have to say, Edgar, she folded rather quickly. I might have tried to deny it a little longer. But Bellmop always gets his man. Or woman.'

'*Bellmop est magnifique*,' said Edgar the police guard. The two men turned around as the door opened and they were joined by a frowning Saimbron, and an amused Briant. Kit and Agatha remained outside.

Briant accompanied them back to the waiting car. He shook hands with Alastair.

'I'm sorry for the inconvenience of this all. Could I ask that you refrain from visiting the casino for a day or two longer. As you may imagine we have your friends, or former friends I should say, under surveillance.'

'Quite right too,' said Alastair.

'May I make one request from you, Lord Aston?" asked Briant.

'Of course,' said Kit.

'May I avail myself of a lift into Monte Carlo. I need to meet Sergeant Boucher.'

Twenty minutes later they were travelling along the Grande Corniche. Kit marvelled at the feat of engineering that had created the coastal road. It was remarkable to think that it was built in the time of Napoleon I. Each new corner revealed a spectacular view of the Mediterranean, sunlight glittering like jewels upon the sea.

Alastair, unaware of the request by Charpentier for Kit and Agatha to disengage from investigative work, began to talk about the state of play of the case. This was borne of a natural curiosity given his involuntary role in it but was also prompted by two days of reading nothing but detective fiction.

'How goes the case, then? I gather there was another murder.'

Briant smiled and replied politely, 'Yes. Bad news for the victim but good news for you.'

Alastair grinned back but was unsure if this was appropriate.

'Ah, yes. Quite. Have you hauled in the Bluebeard Club yet? Given them the third degree?'

'Not yet. We need more evidence.'

'Was my pen portrait of them of any use?'

Briant shrugged and looked towards Kit and Agatha. She shifted in her seat; this was as sure a sign as any that a withering assessment was but seconds away. Sure enough…

'It was very useful, but I didn't think much of your grammar.'

'Grammar?' scowled Alastair.

'Nor the American spellings,' added Agatha.

'Well, I apologise,' said Alastair huffily, 'with an "s". In my defence, with a "c", I was under just a smidgeon of pressure. Pedant.'

'No need to be like that,' said Agatha.

The drive was around twenty minutes and they pulled up outside the café near the Hotel de Paris. Boucher was sitting there, a look of impatience etched across his face. As soon as he saw the Mercedes-Benz he leapt up from the table. Briant was out of the car before it had stopped moving.

'Sorry I am late,' apologised Briant. 'Shall we leave for the Fourniers now?'

'No need,' replied Boucher. 'The three men arrived at the hotel five minutes ago.'

Briant frowned, 'Couldn't you have followed them to listen in to their conversation?'

'How would you propose I disguise myself because Redon would recognise me?'

Briant swore out loud just as Kit, Alastair, and Agatha appeared. This caused him to redden slightly.

'What's wrong?' asked Kit.

Boucher explained the problem to him. All three members of the Bluebeard Club were meeting down in the sauna of the Hotel de Paris. Kit shrugged and replied, 'It's a pity you no longer want us on the case, I might have had a suggestion for you.'

Briant's eyes narrowed but there was an amused discernment there too.

-

If the other two members of the Bluebeard Club found Fournier's aggressive bonhomie overwhelming, then they kept their counsel. While relations remained outwardly cordial, the strain was beginning to show for all three. No longer were there mock debates on important matters of the day. An air of resignation hung over the three men like a morning mist that would not vanish. They were thoroughly tired of one another. What had started out as a pleasant distraction from their matrimonial bliss had then become a wider circle including that from which they wished to escape. Their relationships had slowly corroded under the intense assault of shared secrets.

'Pour some more water over the rocks, old fellow,' said Russo to Redon. The three men were clad in towels and sweating profusely under the dry heat of the sauna. Redon, instantly regretting his decision to sit near the stove, did as he was bid. A hot jet of steam rose and nearly scalded the colonel. A few choice words followed that would have found favour in a barrack room but caused one or two of the other gentlemen in the sauna to raise a disapproving eyebrow.

'What do you make of the departure of our friend in Nice?' asked Russo guardedly.

'Yes, that was a surprise,' agreed Fournier looking at Russo meaningfully.

'Of course, it was a surprise,' snapped Redon, still burning from his mismanagement of the stove. 'But what does it mean?'

'You're asking me?' said Fournier. His face was irritatingly unhelpful. Redon's eyes began to bulge in an unattractive way that suggested an explosion was imminent. However, the presence the other men acted to cool his pressure gauge if not exactly his body.

'Gentlemen,' said Russo in a voice that was almost a purr. 'I have given the matter of what we should do a great deal of thought today.'

'Go on,' said the other two men in unison.

Russo looked at the other two men in the sauna. They were minding their own business which meant they were most likely hanging on every word spoken.

'I propose we go through with what we were going to do. Tomorrow night. What have we to lose?'

The two men looked at him as if he was crazy. Russo had anticipated such a reaction however and held his hands up to mollify them. Redon noticed something on Russo's arm.

'What on earth is that?' asked Redon, a shade rudely.

'A tattoo,' said Russo with a shrug. 'A youthful folly. He held his inner forearm out so that they could see it.'

'It looks like a fish,' said Fournier.

'A deadly fish. None deadlier. It's a killer whale. An orca. Anyway, we digress. I think we should go on as planned tomorrow night. We've done nothing wrong,' said Russo, before adding, 'Have we?'

The other men were not so sure.

'Don't you wonder about the last few days?' asked Fournier.

Russo smiled and shrugged. They took that as 'no'.

'Bit of a coincidence, don't you think?' barked Redon in a whisper.

'Perhaps, but why should we worry?'

The other two men looked at him as if he was mad.

'Nothing has come from it,' pointed out Russo. 'Surely it would have by now.'

'Perhaps,' acknowledged Fournier. 'I still think it's a risk and not just because of what's happened.'

'Why then?' asked Russo, genuinely surprised.

'It's Elsa. She's…' Fournier looked around and stopped himself. 'You know.'

A shadow passed over Russo's face. He leaned into Fournier, 'And who is to blame for that? You treat her abominably.'

'Rather goes with the club, doesn't it,' replied Fournier mirthlessly.

'We need her,' agreed Redon.

'Pah,' said Fournier angrily. 'I've seen water with more backbone than her. I don't know what I was thinking when I married her. Ignore beauty, gentleman. It matters not in marriage; a lesson for us all.'

'A lesson for next time, maybe,' grinned Russo. This made Fournier smile, but Redon remained stone-faced.

They were silent for a few minutes. Russo's request for more hot water on the rocks was rebuffed by Redon who invited him to do it himself. The effort was obviously too much; Russo remained seated on the wooden bench.

'So, gentlemen, what is it to be?' asked Russo.

A few moments passed. Fournier glanced at Redon. Then, after a pause, Redon nodded curtly. Fournier did likewise.

'Excellent. We'll prepare tonight and tomorrow. Instead of a maximum of one table, we shall try and cover two tables over the course of the afternoon and evening. Who knows? We may be lucky. Dare we hope for three tables?'

This caused the other men to raise their eyebrows. They looked sceptical but something else was there now. A fire in their hearts and a light in their eyes: the glint of greed.

'Will Elsa be ready? We'll need her.' asked Redon.

The look on Fournier's face was chilling, 'She will be.'

23

'And that was the end of the conversation. They all left immediately. Naturally I couldn't follow them. I left it for a few minutes and then went out of the sauna. Fournier was in the swimming pool. Russo had left and Redon went to the bar.'

Rufus Watts looked around with some satisfaction at the rapt audience. He was in Agatha's villa at Cap d'Ail. Sitting at the table were Kit, Mary, Agatha, Alastair, Briant, Saimbron, and Boucher. In the palm of my hand, he thought. You never lose it lose it, Rufus, old boy, you never lose it.

'What were your impressions of them?' asked Mary.

This was an interesting question and very female. Rufus rubbed his hands together. What could be more heavenly than sitting amongst his peers in a beautiful villa in the south of France being asked to perform a character assassination? Heaven. Pure, unadulterated, heaven.

'Well as you ask,' smiled Rufus. 'Monsieur Fournier is a sunless presence. A bully and a pig. Nothing less. He despises his wife. In fact, I would go as far as to say he despises women generally. They are chattels for his beastly needs. The other two men fear him a little, I think. All three are volatile but there is violence within this man.'

'Sounds like a charmer,' said Agatha looking archly at Alastair. What he saw in this company she still couldn't fathom. Of course, such implicit reproach was water off a duck's back to Alastair who had enjoyed this for over sixty years. He smiled at his sister raised his panatela in salute and sat back in his chair to enjoy his cigar.

'Russo seems the shrewdest of the three rather like a cat with two bulldogs. He's smarter and weaker than the other two. I suspect he feels contempt for them both. I'm certain of it, even. Sometimes he would look at them like they were both idiots. He wouldn't be far wrong from what I saw.'

'And Redon?' asked Boucher. He had been eyeing the extraordinary little artist with great curiosity. Rufus turned to the young policeman and studied him in amusement. He knew what was being asked, why it was being asked and he cared not a jot. Instead, he waved his hand in a manner that was as dismissive as it was balletic.

'Oh, dear Monsieur Redon. Oh dear, oh dear, oh dear. Well, he is an interesting fellow. A former army officer, too. I can see that he has trained himself to walk like one, yet he just can't help himself. He skipped at least once when he walked out of the changing rooms. I have never seen a man take so long over changing and trust me I have seen a good many. When I appeared in the room, he was rubbing skin cream into his face and body like a prima ballerina. Needs it too. His forehead has more lines than Hamlet. He looked at me once or twice too. You say he'd married? Ha!'

Rufus laughed at this idea and shook his head. Kit thanked him for the report and then turned his attention to the three policemen. It was clear that despite the words of Charpentier, they had tacitly agreed to ignore the examining magistrate. It also helped that Kit had invited them to the villa for dinner. All three were enjoying the first of five courses that would be served this evening.

'It strikes me, and no doubt all of you, that the three couples are the sharpers that rooked the casino so badly.'

At this point Kit held up two pieces of paper. Both were artists impressions created by Rufus based on the descriptions provided by the casino staff of the two people who had won so handsomely several months previously. The hair was different, it was darker, but there was no mistaking the faces of Russo and Elsa Fournier. The former had a moustache but was now clean-shaven.

'Congratulations, by the way, Rufus. These are extraordinarily accurate.'

Rufus bowed humbly to Kit and tried not to beam too much. It was all in a day's work for him. So was praise.

'Two questions arise from this. One was always the view of Aunt Agatha. The other came from Mary. Ladies?'

Kit glanced at his wife. Mary smiled back at him. Meanwhile, Agatha, took over the meeting. It was time to get a move on and she was a woman who had made it her mission in life to get weaving.

'I have no proof of course, but I believe Auguste Blanc was working in league with these people. I suspect he would have happily spent the next few years rinsing the casino from time to time to build up his pension. However, things went wrong somewhere along the line, and it seems to me that one or all the actors in this drama decided to cut Monsieur Blanc out of the deal. The missing piece for me was why these people, who are outwardly successful and rich in their own right, should want to help Blanc.'

'Blackmail,' said Mary from the other end of the table. All eyes turned to Mary. All that is except Boucher who had barely been able to keep his eyes away from Mary since he'd arrived at the villa. Mary continued once the impact of her interjection had faded.

'Monsieur Blanc, probably with the assistance of Rene Dupin, had something on these men and women. He used this to involve them in a scheme to, I can't say rob because it's perfectly legal, win money. Large amounts of money. How much he shared with his co-conspirators we can't know, of course. As far as I can see, this can be the only explanation as to why these people would agree to such a scheme.'

'Of course,' said Kit, taking over again, 'we are now left with the conundrum of proving this. We can all speculate on what hold he had over these men. However, Captain Briant, Inspector Saimbron, I suspect that you may have more on this than you have thus far shared.'

'If we do have such information, why should we share it?' asked Briant, before eating a piece of exquisitely cooked veal. He raised his fork appreciatively to Agatha in acknowledgement that she had a good table. Agatha nodded back. 'I mean, I can see merit in everything you say. What are you proposing?'

Kit's eyes met with Briant, and he felt like applauding. This policeman was exceptional in every way. Where others could only see the ground in front of them like bloodhounds sniffing for clues, Briant saw the whole landscape. He saw not only the panorama; he was able to gaze into the future and see how this vista would change as circumstances changed. All in all, he was a man to be reckoned with. Kit knew that he had to offer something in return before Briant would share so much as a syllable of intelligence with him.

Thankfully, he had prepared for such an eventuality. He smiled and noted that Briant, too, smiled and seemed to relax visibly as if he knew he was going to enjoy immensely what he was about to hear.

'I have an unusual proposal, Captain Briant, Inspector Saimbron.'

Briant's smile widened. Both Boucher and Saimbron were a little confused but, equally, they could not help but observe Briant's reaction. They suspected he knew what was coming. And they would have been right in this assumption.

'There are two things I think we can offer that, you have to admit, would not be either possible or, indeed permissible, for you.'

Briant began to chuckle at this observation and even Kit could not help but join him. Proposing breaking the law to policemen is not for the average amateur detective, whether British or, indeed, from the nobility. He put his palm out to give permission for Kit to continue.

'Notwithstanding our friend Charpentier's injunction on Aunt Agatha and Betty's involvement with the casino, I think we should risk one more night. With your blessing, of course.'

As if on cue, Betty arrived late to the dinner table. On her back was a bag of golf clubs. Everyone looked up and Betty's face suggested that it had not been a successful day.

'The greens were horrible. Anyway, what have I missed?'

Agatha rolled her eyes and jerked her head upward to indicate to Kit to carry on.

'Aunt Agatha and Betty will patrol the casino and keep an eye on the actions of this Bluebeard Club. Now, if our suspicions are correct, they are involved in some sort of card counting exercise. Aunt Agatha, would you care to explain?'

Agatha licked her lips and leaned forward as if relaying top secret information in a bar full of spies. Her eyes gleamed like a bulldog before bacon.

'*Vingt et un,* is an unusual game insofar as it gives the player the best chance to beat the house. Theoretically the house still has the advantage by a few percent but even this does not discourage gamblers. Now, if my theory is correct, the odds can be tipped towards the player if they are able to count the cards. Now, you may wonder how this is possible. Well, it is. This is not a simple matter of counting cards. It's just a name. The process is actually quite complex. What you must remember is that, unlike games such as poker where the same deck of cards is used, in *vingt et un*, the cards come out of a shoe, and they are not replaced. The shoe gradually empties. This is important. For someone who has been following the cards from the start, if they are able to remember what cards have gone then they can begin to estimate probabilities with greater accuracy towards the end of the life of a shoe. Now, how they do this, I am not sure. Nor am I certain of how they grade the level of advantage one shoe has over another. Clearly, they have a system. I imagine this system somehow codifies the advantage they may have. This is where it becomes interesting.'

To be fair to Agatha, it was already very interesting. The table was hanging on every word uttered by this remarkable woman.

'When I spoke to the dealers and asked them about card counting, they dismissed the notion out of hand. They said they would have spotted if someone was playing from the start of the shoe until the end. Not just that, the player would have to have remarkable powers of concentration to remember the cards that had been dealt and then deploy calculations of probability on top. So, I asked, what if more than one player was in on this system. They said there was no way for the two players to communicate without them knowing. This, of course, is arrant nonsense. A simple code could be developed to relay the relative attractiveness of the deck. I didn't say that to them.'

'That was kind of you,' chipped in Alastair who was puffing contentedly on his cigar. Agatha ignored him.

'How can you tell if a deck is attractive?' asked Mary.

Agatha licked her lips once more. This was always a prelude to relaying a piece of information that only she was privy to.

'High cards favour the player because it helps them make twenty-one. Lower cards increase the risk for players. Conversely, high cards present more risk to the dealer who is looking to reach sixteen at least. So, we return to thinking of each table representing an opportunity. If you place someone on a table playing for small amounts of money and counting the decks down until the last deck, you can use probability theory to deduce which table offers the greatest potential gains. Assuming the ladies or, indeed, one or two of the gents play at a table for a while then they call over the one who has the mathematical capability to apply the coup de grace.'

'Russo,' said Kit. Briant nodded at this. 'Russo worked for an insurance company. Now, as we are talking about probability, what are the odds that he was an actuary?'

'Pretty high I would say,' said Betty, who had been transfixed by how far they had come.

'You mean low, dear,' said Agatha. 'If the odds are low, it means a higher probability of the event happening.'

Betty nodded as she always did. It was better this way. Why hold them up explaining something she had no earthly interest in?

'Based on Monsieur Watts's intelligence, and once more, thank you for your spying mission, we believe all three couples will be in attendance tomorrow night.'

Rufus Watts was pleased by the acknowledgement of his contribution. It had been something of a rush to get to the sauna without arousing suspicion from the Bluebeard Club members. He was less sure if he liked being described as a spy. There was something a little tawdry about it, but he decided not to point this out.

'And while they are away, I suspect that you will use this time advantageously, Lord Aston.'

'Yes,' replied Kit.

'I had a feeling Monsieur Miller's skill would be brought to bear at some point,' said Briant.

Kit shrugged and replied, 'I couldn't possibly say. Now, inspector. Perhaps you could share with us what you have been working on.'

'Anything in particular?'

'Yes. What brought you to the Cote d'Azur and what can you add to what we've told you about this Bluebeard Club.'

'A clear brief,' smiled Briant. 'Very well. Colonel Redon served his country during the war. However, he left the army under clouded circumstances. I think that, based on Monsieur Watts's observations, we can speculate on why. His first wife died two years ago. We are still trying to establish how. Mme Redon is a widow like Mme Fournier. From the war. I gather that Redon and her husband were friends. There is no suspicion surrounding the deaths of either spouse. Monsieur Russo, as we know, worked in insurance. He spent ten years in the United States of America before returning to Europe when the war had finished. His first wife died from natural causes. It seems that he met his present wife while she was organising an insurance policy for her husband. I gather the husband was many years older than she. He died, once more of natural causes, and Madame Russo inherited a sizeable estate and received a significant pay out from Russo's insurance company. However, I understand her estate was not the nest egg she had been hoping for. Unknown to her, the first husband was heavily in debt. Perhaps you are seeing a theme here.'

Everyone around the table nodded.

'As you may have surmised, given the attention Henri Landru has received recently, the authorities in Paris are keen on identifying other so-called Bluebeards. A task force was set up to investigate men who had been married twice or three times. This was just to re-examine the circumstances by which they were widowed. More suspicious cases were sent to us.'

Briant indicated himself and Boucher.

'One such case was Monsieur Fournier. This is his third marriage. His first two wives died while still relatively young and, in both cases, he'd made a substantial amount of money from the insurance claim. In each case the insurance was handled by...'

'Monsieur Russo.'

'Correct. Of course, when Monsieur Aston heard them describe themselves as the Bluebeard Club, well this was a potential break in the case. Alas Monsieur Aston's noble sacrifice in jail perhaps yielded less than we had hoped.'

Mary was incensed by what she'd heard.

'But isn't there enough in what you have said to investigate more directly?'

'No, Lady Mary. There is not. The two wives of Monsieur Fournier died in a manner that did not arouse suspicion.'

'Were there post-mortems?' persisted Mary.

'I understand there were not,' said Briant. His face looked grave. It was clear he was far from happy relaying such information. It reflected poorly on how the French authorities conducted inquests following deaths that were deemed unusual. 'I make no excuse for how this was handled. You understand?'

'Well, what happens now?' cried Mary. 'Do we simply wait for Fournier to kill his wife? He treats her abominably.'

'I think it is unlikely that he will take such a risk at this moment.'

'Do you know if he has taken out a similar insurance policy with his wife as he did with the others? pressed Mary.

'He has,' admitted Briant. A shocked silence descended on the room. The stakes in this game had been raised considerably.

'If what you say is true, then whoever killed Blanc and probably Dupin, was looking for documents that would incriminate the club. It's possible they have found what they needed and now feel free to pursue what Blanc originally wanted them to do only this time they will keep the money they win. If this is the case then whatever you have planned, Lord Aston,' at this point Briant's smile returned, 'may prove invaluable in bringing a murder case and a conspiracy to murder on these people.'

-

A few miles away in an apartment on Avenue St, Martin, Fournier regarded his wife with a pitiless stare. She gazed back at him bleakly. Her shoulders hunched. She was moments away from crying. He wondered what was on her mind. Her poor, damaged mind. He shook his head and walked over to the sideboard. Above the sideboard was a light patch on the wall where a picture had once hung. Bending down he reached behind the sideboard and, sure enough, he found the picture in question. It was a photograph of his previous wife. Slowly, deliberately he put the framed photograph back up on the wall.

'Why do you keep doing this, my dear?' There was no hiding the patient cruelty in his tone. Its low rumble oppressed the senses and chilled the atmosphere in the room. She shook her head then looked away. Her shoulders began to shake.

'No, my dear, please, believe me. I didn't touch it.'

'So, it was the maid, was it?'

'She hates me.'

'Well, I shall ask her when she comes tomorrow morning.' Fournier's tone had switched to a snarled sarcasm that was, if anything, even more humiliating for his wife.

'You do believe me, don't you?' cried his wife.

Fournier said nothing in reply. He sat down and rubbed the palm of his hands on his face. What was he to make of this? His wife was manifestly lying. To blame the young maid only added to the slow erosion of her dignity. Just like her mother. Elsa had confessed to him at the start of their relationship that her mother had died in an asylum.

'You should retire, my dear,' said Fournier.

'Are you coming too?'

'Soon,' replied her husband.

She crept away like a pickpocket. As soon as she was gone, he leapt to his feet and began to pace the room. There was so much to think about. He reached for his pipe and lit it. For a while he gave himself up to the pleasure of the tobacco. It freed his mind of the events that lay ahead, the things that had to be done.

Finally, he drifted towards the bedroom. His wife was asleep or, at least, pretending to be so. He sat on the bed softly by her side. He put his hands up to her neck. They hovered there for a moment. It would be so easy. So easy.

Damn Russo.

24

The mood in *Casa Russo* was, as ever, characterised by a fake optimism about the day that lay ahead. They had each reached the marriage equivalent of a Greek island in their relationship. It was too hot to move elsewhere and, at least, you still had the good food and wine. It would be unfair to say they heartily detested the sight of one another; however, readers of this chronicler will know that truth is always and always will be the servant to entertainment. Neither, yet, had the courage to kill the other. It was probably too soon after their previous 'bereavements'. But time waits for no man or woman.

Russo grinned dementedly across the table at his wife in greater hope than expectation. Mme Russo did not return the favour, although on this morning her husband had managed a rare foray into her good books. Like most married women, she made it a rule to dispense the occasional favour, but the norm was keeping her mate in a state of permanent suspense by carefully spreading eggshells for him to tiptoe around.

'Are you looking forward to tonight, my dear?' asked Russo before sipping his coffee.

Mme Russo restrained herself from snapping back that the scheme had been her idea and he'd merely convinced the others to join it. He was but a vehicle. An important vehicle, none the less. Perhaps it would be better to be nice to the chump for once.

'Yes, very much, dear,' trilled Mme Russo. 'The important question is, are you? We need you at your best tonight. That enormous brain of yours, my dear. I'm so proud of you.'

Mme Russo glanced down and saw that she'd laid the strawberry jam a little bit too thickly onto the croissant. She scraped it all off and started again.

'No drinking tonight, remember? Or during the day, for that matter,' added Mme Russo. Her tone was distinctly sharper. Like a father rebuking a child *before* they've done anything wrong.

'Of course, my dear,' said Russo hoping that his disappointment was not too evident.

'And the others are ready?' This was a more pertinent point. The unspoken fear that the best plan was always a hostage to its weakest practitioner.

'Fournier assured me that Elsa would be ready for tonight.'

Mme Russo shook her head. As much as she detested the very sight of the browbeating oaf, she sometimes had an unsisterly sympathy for his palpable frustration at being with such a timid non-entity as Elsa Fournier. Her job was as simple as she was. Count the number of cards below eight that came out of the shoe. What could be simpler? A child could do it. But then again, this was a child in a woman's body. Unquestionably, there was a porcelain prettiness to the face that might, for a while, snare a man before the brittle truth became clear.

'Perhaps I will call on them later,' said Mme Russo.

'I'm sure they'll appreciate that, my dear,' said Russo just about managing to keep his face straight.

-

A conversation on a not too dissimilar topic was taking place in the Redon household. Mme Redon looked at her husband feeding their Dobermann with a piece of prosciutto and shook her head. There was no question where his affections lay. They were sitting on the terrace of their apartment and although barely nine in the morning, the heat was already causing a line of perspiration to break out on her husband's forehead. She wondered for a moment how the wax in his moustache did not melt. An image of burning wax falling on Mimi passed through her mind. Not that she'd anything against the poor animal. She reserved her derision for the owner of the moustache although she appreciated that she had gone into the arrangement with her eyes open.

He needed legitimacy. She needed a backer.

It was hardly his fault that the money, his former wife's money, had been lost. The men in her life had been, without exception, made from poor quality material. Her father and brother were prime examples. Her father was a failed stockbroker who took his own life after, yet another series of investments went up in flames. Her brother had even less aptitude for the business and had lost a sizable portion of her husband's money on a speculation in Algeria. Apparently, there was no oil in Algeria. It had taken a few hundred thousand Francs to establish this. A few hundred thousand Francs of *their* money.

'Do you think I should go and see Elsa?' asked Mme Redon. She was going to see her anyway, but the silence was becoming oppressive. It would be an opportunity to spend some time with Fournier. Now there was a man. He knew how to make a woman feel special. A little shudder ran through her body.

Redon glanced up from Mimi and smiled.

'Yes, I think that's a good idea. Fournier knows what needs to be done,' said Redon before turning adoringly to Mimi. The Dobermann rested its head on his knee; every so often it would look up and lick his face. Redon giggled happily. 'Look what he's doing, dearest.'

Mme Redon hadn't the energy to point out that it was difficult, sitting where she was, to ignore such a risible sight but thought better of it. Was it worth it? Was he worth it? She'd pondered this question many times. The answer was, invariably, yes. He understood her needs and accepted that they had to be fulfilled elsewhere. He, too, wanted something else. The *quid pro quo* worked quite well but she missed living with a man who shared her interests and desire to explore pleasure without any preconceptions, without restraint. Or better still, with restraint. Two husbands, two weaklings were the sum of her marital achievements. Both men were frauds in their own way. But then again, wasn't she?

As the former colonel, the man who had spent a war many, many miles from the front giggled at Mimi's affection, she decided a visit to *Chez Fournier* was a necessity. Perhaps she would give Alessia Russo a call. Her husband was pivotal but, then again, so was Elsa Fournier. She and Alessia could stiffen Elsa's spine for what lay ahead. If they could find it, that is.

-

The fears of the two households were not misplaced. The morning had not witnessed the Damascene conversion that Fournier had hoped for. In truth he had not expected it. Instead, Elsa Fournier took to her bed and lay there still as a gravestone claiming a headache. In the face of such weakness, Fournier was not the sort of man to let it pass without comment. He sat on the bed, his voice as soft and hot as lava.

'Yes, Elsa, rest. I will need you strong and alert for later.'

'I can't,' sobbed Mme Fournier.

'You will.' His whisper was like the howl of a wounded animal who is even more dangerous now. It was barely ten in the morning, yet Fournier was already reaching for a bottle of whisky. He reserved the Scotch for when he was in a bad mood, for it was certain to make it worse. And he wanted nothing more than for Elsa Fournier to understand he was in a foul temper.

By the time he left the house at midday, he was in a festering state of barely contained violence. At the cab rank there were no cabs. This caused the first minor explosion of the morning as he screamed a volley of invective at a sign. A cat walked past, stopped to look at him in curiosity before disappearing into some bushes as a stone came flying in its direction.

Fournier walked down the hill to Le Condamine. He was to meet the other couples there for lunch. Walking across the small square, he spied them together at a table. There was no wine, only water. Mme Russo spotted him, and the others turned around.

The mercury began to rise rapidly as he saw the knowing looks on their faces. The lack of surprise. His face glowed red as the two foes that had trailed him since childhood appeared once again to mock him: anger and humiliation.

The humiliation was his and his alone. Russo and Redon were married to strong women. Women who did not need to be ordered around like children; women who knew what was needed; self-reliant and wilful women. A wave of hatred rose as he thought of his own wife lying in bed feigning illness. Her beauty, as he'd found out, was only skin deep. There was nothing else underneath. Not even the wealth he'd hoped for. She would pay for those lies. She would pay for the beauty that had beguiled him, fooled him, lulled him into matrimony.

She would pay. Just like the others had.

-

The mood in the Aston household was a mixture of excitement and sadness. The excitement was felt by all. None would admit it, but they all lived for such adventure. Yet the sadness was there too, for Alastair would soon be going back to the United States. He'd been away for two months. It was time to return. He would take the train up to Paris and then onto Cherbourg where he would join the RMS Aquitania for New York. Sitting at the breakfast table, they could hear Alastair getting in the way of Ella-Mae as she packed. The argument ricocheted back and forth like the gunfight at the OK Corral. Alastair was on the receiving end of the worst of it, rather like the Clantons forty years earlier.

Kit smiled at Mary as they listened to the exchanges. Betty, meanwhile, seemed unusually apprehensive about the evening ahead. Agatha's face was a mask but there was unquestionably a conflict going on. One felt her melancholy as much as one could sense the excited glow in her eyes.

Sensing the discord within Kit's aunt, Mary walked over and sat beside her. She took her hand and grinned. Agatha was delighted and showed it by rolling her eyes and demanding to know what Mary wanted.

'It feels strange just sitting here. I wish we could go out and do something,' said Mary.

Kit felt disloyal for rather enjoying a break from having to think too hard about anything, or perhaps it was fatigue. The last few weeks had been as blissful as they had been physically exerting. He couldn't stop smiling. Only an unaccountable sense of shame stopped him from jumping in the swimming pool. It was rather hot. His prosthetic leg felt uncomfortable and even Sam was capable of no more than sleeping in his basket. He did this a lot nowadays. He wasn't at his best in this weather, concluded Kit.

'You should tell us about some of the cases that you've worked on. You always keep them so secret,' said Mary suddenly, fixing Kit a killer stare that made him wish he was alone with her. 'It makes me wonder what you were up to.' Not nearly as much as I'm up to now thought Kit trying to suppress a smile.

'Oh yes, Kit. Why don't you? It'll take our mind off what's coming up later,' said Betty with her usual puppy-dog enthusiasm. 'Aldric is always mentioning one case or another.'

'He is?' said Kit, with a frown which only made Mary's smile widen. 'Such as?'

'He says there was one before the war that involved explosions,' answered Betty.

'Really?' Kit was now thoroughly confused and not a little bit worried by where the conversation was headed. Spunky enjoyed tremendous sport by telling outrageous porkies to his Aunt Betty. He shook his head and reached for his cup of tea. At that moment Alastair appeared looking as flustered as ever following a bruising encounter with his maid.

Betty wasn't taking "no" for an answer and pressed on regardless, 'Yes. He asked me to ask you about the case of the Maharani's Dildo.'

Kit almost choked on his tea and began coughing. He waved away Mary whose face took on a look of concern.

'By the way, what is a dildo?' asked Betty looking at Kit. In fact, Mary and Agatha were also looking at him intently. Behind them, Alastair stopped dead in his tracks. His eyes widened and he spun around.

Kit who had recovered his voice if not his senses suggested, 'Perhaps Uncle Alastair can enlighten you.'

Alastair had begun creeping away at this point but was forced to stop. He turned around and a nervous smile appeared on his face like an allergic reaction. He looked daggers at Kit but stepped forward nervously.

'I believe it is a massage implement used in the Far East.'

'Sounds interesting,' said Betty. 'Perhaps I can find one for my back. All those years playing golf; there's a price to be paid.'

'I wouldn't do that, Betty dear,' said Alastair. 'It's a very ancient device. Probably only found in museums and the like.'

'But how did it cause explosions?' asked Mary, the light of scientific inquiry shining from her eyes. She turned from Alastair to Kit. At this point Kit was unsure if she was onto Spunky's jest or not. As good an actress as she was, and he was aware she had played many roles on stage at school, he doubted that even she could carry off this *ingénue* role quite so truthfully. Anyway, it was time to nip this in the bud.

'There was no such case. I must have a word with dear old Aldric. I fear he enjoys making me sound like a cross between Sherlock Holmes and Allan Quartermain,' said Kit, much to the disappointment of the ladies and Alastair's evident relief.

'What shall we do now?' asked Mary, drumming her fingers on the table.

Kit reached over to a sideboard near the dining table. He grabbed something and then placed it on the table. It was a pack of cards. He raised his eyebrows towards Alastair.

As has been alluded to earlier in this chronicle, Alastair had spent some time on a Mississippi steamboat. It was there that he learned the dark arts of gambling with cards. Alastair rolled his eyes and joined the group at the table.

'What had you in mind, dear boy?' asked Alastair taking the cards from Kit and performing a feat of juggling with the deck that would have found favour in a children's party and sent hardened gamblers heading for the exit.

'Practice,' said Kit.

-

Just before Agatha, Betty and Natalie were due to go to the casino, Kit saw his aunt outside on the terrace. There was a faraway look in her eyes. She sat down at the table. Just at that moment she seemed wearied by the events that had taken place and burdened by the pressure that would be hers to bear later. She saw Kit and waved him over. Kit appeared at the French doors.

'Mary too,' said Agatha.

Mary appeared and she walked alongside Kit past the swimming pool and sat down at the table. Mary glanced at Kit and squeezed his hand. She could see that something was on Agatha's mind.

'Ready for this evening?' asked Kit.

Agatha seemed not to be listening then she waved the question away.

'After this is all over, I will travel to Morocco to see the grave. It's been too long.'

Kit and Mary nodded but said nothing. Both sensed this was not what Agatha wanted to tell them. Then she switched subject.

'Have you given much thought to where you will live? Belgrave Square is fine for a young man or woman but it's not the place for a married couple.'

This tone of this was less advisory and more instructive. If Agatha hadn't looked so grave, he might have gently chided her on this.

'I imagine we'll begin looking in earnest when we return. We're not in any rush.'

Agatha nodded absently. She looked in the direction of the sea for a few moments as if building up the courage to say something. Both Kit and Mary now began to feel concern. His heart began to race. 'Is everything all right, Aunt Agatha?'

'Of course, it is. Why shouldn't it be?' replied Agatha sharply. She turned and fixed her eyes on Kit and then Mary. 'I've been giving this some thought, and I think it best if you live in Grosvenor Square.' She put her hand up to indicate that she hadn't finished. 'Don't worry, I won't be there.'

Mary was alarmed now. Agatha saw the look of concern on her face and smiled gently.

'It's nothing to worry about, my dear. I've decided to spend more time here at Cap d'Ail. I'll visit of course. I want to be nearer Agadir and Useless. But I want you to have Grosvenor Square. I've changed my will. It's yours now.'

'My word, Aunt Agatha, I hardly know what to say,' said Kit.

Agatha fixed him a steely stare and replied, 'It's not going to you.' Then she turned to Mary and her eyes softened.

Mary frowned and tears stung her eyes. She reached over and clasped Agatha's hand in hers.

25

Early evening came in Monte Carlo and not a moment too soon for four households around the Principality. The excitement in the villa at Cap d'Ail had slowly given way to nerves. Almost everyone in the household had a role to play that evening. If anything, the person with the least to do was Kit, yet a feeling of responsibility rested on his shoulders the like of which he hadn't felt for a long time. He was convinced murder was in the air and he had to prevent it happening. It almost felt like an inconvenience that they had to save the casino from being on the wrong end of a rinsing. Yet he knew it was all connected.

Mary had spent the early afternoon on a shopping trip. When she came out of the bedroom to show Kit what she'd purchased, his mouth fell open. Over the last year, Mary had become increasingly interested in the fashion designer Gabrielle 'Coco' Chanel. By the time they had reached Monte Carlo, her wardrobe had been replaced by the designer's clothes.

Dressed in black, her top was fitted to a degree that ensured the lines of her slim figure were followed with mathematical precision. This was the first time that Mary had worn yachting trousers. They were wide to allow for ease of movement but undeniably elegant too. Her look was finished off by a black beaded flapper cap. Kit stared mutely at the vision before him.

'Do you like it?' asked Mary with a smile that was probably illegal in several US states. Harry Miller appeared just then and had to stop himself staring at Mary.

'Ready?' asked Kit to Miller.

'Yes,' replied Miller.

'How were the ladies?'

Miller had just returned from the casino where he'd dropped off Agatha, Betty, and Natalie. Agatha was to resume her role as a dealer while Betty and Natalie would take on surveillance roles with the three ladies when they showed up at the casino.

'A little on edge, I think.'

'Was Aunt Agatha snapping at them?'

The answer was 'yes' so Miller said, 'I think they're clear on what must be done.'

Both Kit and Mary smiled at this likely distortion. If Agatha was on edge, it meant all her senses were in a heightened state. This would be important.

'Very well. Can you round up the others, Harry?'

-

Alessia Russo knew much depended on her man. They would all play their part in paving the way, but he was the one who would play the winning hands. Elsa too would help in this regard. Perhaps Fournier would surprise them, but it was Giuseppe Russo, the former actuary, who would have the mathematical mastery to defeat the house. She looked at him lying sleeping on the bed. His snoring would have had Beethoven smashing the ivories in frustration.

It was early evening, and he was resting following an energetic afternoon that had taken more out of him than it had taken out of the current Mme Russo. She padded over to the shutter and opened it. Overhead, the sky was a breath-taking collage of mauve, light blue, and orange. Below on the street, the town was beginning to wake up again from its late afternoon slumber. A few open-topped cars chugged past. Dashing men wearing goggles and scarves, like airmen. She sighed in anticipation. Then she left the window and returned to the bed. One particularly loud snort almost lifted Russo from the bed. She recoiled in horror. For a moment she considered shaking him awake but elected, instead, merely to lean over and kiss him gently on the cheek. Throttling him would have to wait for another occasion.

A pillow had done for her first husband.

-

Love in the afternoon was the last thing on either husband or wife's mind in the Redon household. Instead, Mme Redon read a magazine while her husband performed afternoon calisthenics. This was a daily routine and was responsible, boasted Redon, for ensuring that he was in the same shape at fifty as he had been at twenty. Mme Redon ignored the flagrant, or should that be fragrant, lie while her husband grunted through a particularly energetic set of press ups. To be fair to the old muzzler, he was in good shape. He certainly took his admiration of Ancient Greece seriously. At one point he took his old foil and began shadow fencing with an imaginary opponent. Then he was down again on the ground performing sit ups.

Finally, he leapt to his feet and beat the pit of his stomach either to indicate its geological properties or in unconscious imitation of his simian cousins. He towelled himself down and went into the bathroom to shave and then apply a liberal splash of cologne that would have made a *demi-mondaine* blanch in modesty.

This was frustrating for Mme Redon. The last thing they needed to do was draw attention to themselves. However, such nuance was beyond the prancing prig she'd married. In the bathroom she could hear a jar being unscrewed. His moustache and their dog received more attention than she did.

Mimi, meanwhile, had woken up and was happily barking on the terrace, no doubt to the ire of the other residents in the apartment block. A few other dogs replied to her and soon the rest of Monaco were involuntary eavesdroppers to a canine conversation that swept the length and breadth of the Principality.

-

Elsa Fournier stood in the entrance hallway. She knew Fournier was staring at her, but she couldn't return his gaze. She let her arms drop to permit the maid to put a coat on her. The only sound in the hallway was the echoing tick of the grandfather clock. Fournier glanced at it. Five minutes to seven. It was a little fast. After a morning and early afternoon of undisguised hostility, a crisis had been averted by the intervention of Alessia Russo and Josephine Redon.

The two ladies had begged Elsa to take something that Alessia had brought. Then they put her in a bath for an hour and chatted to her, building up her confidence for the evening ahead. Finally, she relented. It was too late to mollify Fournier. His rage was like a forest fire that was out of control. Under any other circumstances he might have paid a compliment to Elsa. If one could ignore the look of pained anxiety on her face, she looked ravishing. Desire and hatred melded in the heat of his emotions.

'You look beautiful, my love,' whispered Fournier more out of duty than feeling. He caressed Elsa's cheek with his finger. She hadn't the courage to pull her face away. Instead, all her efforts seemed to be focused on the act of not crying. She held her breath but nothing more was said. His hot breath almost scalded her skin.

Fournier nodded to the maid, and she opened the front door. He took his wife's hand and led her out of the house. She submitted to the firm grip of his hand and its pull.

'We shall see you tomorrow, Francine,' said Fournier to the maid. The door closed behind them. Neither spoke as they walked to Place de la Visitation to collect a hansom cab. The evening was thick with silence and secrets; vows and vengeance hung in the air like a dark shroud waiting to be draped over a corpse.

-

Briant and Saimbron nodded to Agatha as she arrived with Betty at the casino. They had to stand aside as a young man pushed in front of them and threw a set of car keys towards the doorman with the instruction to park the car. Betty raised an eyebrow and grabbed Agatha's arm as she threatened to do some damage with her ever-present umbrella to the rude young man.

Briant watched all this with a casual amusement. When they reached him, he motioned with his head, and she followed the policeman towards Auguste Blanc's office. Mme Cotille unlocked the office door to allow the group to enter. Briant sat down on Blanc's seat while Saimbron remained standing. Agatha and Betty both sat down facing the man from the Sûreté.

'What is your plan for this evening, Lady Frost?'

'I shall take up a position on one of the tables and wait to see if our friends join us. If they are true to their word, they will have to be along soon.'

'I see,' said Briant. 'I'm not very familiar with this game. Tell me, how long will it take for them to win a significant amount of money?'

Agatha sucked in her lips and did a rapid piece of mental arithmetic. Then she leaned forward conspiratorially forcing everyone else to do likewise as if they were passing state secrets in a Balkan bar.

'Each shoe contains six decks. Assuming we have five players including the dealer that means we have an average of just under three cards per player. So simple arithmetic tells us that if we have sat least sixteen games per shoe then we should be able to rifle through around four shoes per hour. Now if they place people at the three tables playing *vingt et un*, then we should at some point see a situation arise where the odds are tipped in favour of the player if they are counting the cards correctly. And make no mistake, this can happen on several occasions during the night. With no limits on betting, they could make a small fortune if they have the luck because they appear to have the skills.'

'Fascinating,' said Briant and meant it.

'I imagine they will circulate the ladies and gentlemen around the tables to avoid suspicion. Then, if we are correct in our assumptions, Russo will take over at the table offering the most attractive odds towards the end, when the shoe is close to being empty.'

The three policemen nodded.

'And you will be on one of the tables?'

'Yes,' replied Agatha. 'I will.'

Briant looked at the two other policemen and then returned his attention to Agatha. There was no hiding the anxiety on his face or the frustration.

'Unfortunately, Lady Frost, there is a slight problem with this plan.'

Agatha frowned and replied, 'How slight?'

-

Ferdinand Charpentier smiled benignly at his good lady wife, Claudine. Ever since he had become involved in the Blanc / Dupin double murder, he'd been promising himself that he would return to the casino. At least that's what he thought. In fact, the desire to make a social rather than a professional visit had come from Claudine. Monte Carlo was the very epitome of glamour for her, and the casino represented the optimal opportunity to rub shoulders with the very cream of Europe's elite. For a woman who hailed from the town of Bitche, on the border with Germany, this was an all too rare treat from her priggish husband.

Charpentier would have been the first to acknowledge that he probably did not treat his wife often enough. A reminder as to why came when he heard her snort with laughter when one old gentleman appeared to lose a small fortune at roulette. Claudine took rather cruel delight in the misfortune of others. This aspect of her character had not been apparent in their courtship and had only grown over the twenty plus years of wedded bliss. He reflected once more that perhaps the name of her hometown had offered a clue if he'd not been so blinded by love. Then.

The old man turned around to locate the provenance of the laughter that he, correctly, guessed was directed towards him. Charpentier quickly ushered Claudine away to a table where her unusual sense of humour would have less opportunity to manifest itself.

'Can't you keep that cackle of yours under control?' hissed Charpentier when they were out of earshot. 'You sound like the Wicked Witch of the West.'

Charpentier knew his wife well. Like any sensible woman, she would detest criticism coming from a source that was hardly objective nor immune from errors of judgement. Equally, however, her desire to blend in with people she considered the elite trumped everything. She glared at her husband, but Charpentier could see defeat in her eyes. This was a moment that he knew would be cheered by husbands the world over: the man of the house taking sole possession of the moral high ground in the ongoing war of attrition with his spouse. Of course, it wouldn't last long. This mattered not. Best to enjoy the moment while it lasted.

He smiled affectionately at his wife and said without a trace of irony, 'I'm sure you will be able to enjoy the foibles of these people just as much, if not more, if you do not let them know you are doing so.'

Unwittingly, Charpentier had stumbled across a truth so profound and so insightful that he was not intelligent enough to realise it. However, his wife certainly did. In the blink of an eye, he was forgiven, hugged, then kissed affectionately. Charpentier would not have been Charpentier if he hadn't, of course, drawn the wrong conclusion from her reaction. The next day he would try, once more, to throw his shoulders back and act with a domineering manner towards Claudine. He would be met by a volley of invective so explicit in its analysis of his shortcomings that it would have appalled the sensibilities of a Marseille trawlerman. This would force him to go for a walk in the open air and, once more, consider the mystery that was the female. But all of this was in the future…

'Why not play some *vingt et un*, my dear? You enjoy that,' said Charpentier, gently guiding Claudine away from the roulette table.

-

The Mercedes-Benz sped into Monaco. The road was clear, and the night was quiet, broken only by the sound of the German car. The sound in question was a worrying one. Every so often on their journey into Monaco, it had coughed like an old smoker clearing his lungs.

Kit was sitting in the passenger seat beside Harry Miller. He glanced towards Miller. A line of worry creased his brow. Miller shook his head. This was the first time he'd heard such a sound.

'If you have a chance, take a look and see if you can find out what's wrong, Harry,' suggested Kit. This was not the night for any mechanical failure.

'Yes, sir,' replied Miller. He reduced his speed and tried to nurse the car a little more. The sudden reduction in speed upset a car that had raced up behind them. It was a blue Bugatti, and the driver had all the patience and serenity that has not once been associated with the country that produced this beautiful vehicle.

After several toots of his horn the Bugatti picked up speed and overtook the Mercedes on a corner, causing one man in a restaurant to sit up and take note.

The young man in the restaurant who'd witnessed the daring manoeuvre was Antony Noghès. He was as full of ambition as he was full of himself. Working in the Principality's administration responsible for the management of the monopoly of procurement, manufacturing, and selling of tobacco, he was desperate to progress. The sight of the blue Bugatti overtaking the Mercedes thrilled him. A thought popped into his head; a thought so outrageous it made him laugh. He called the waiter for another glass of wine and asked for a pen, paper, and a map of the town.

Inside the car, Miller and Kit began to extol the virtues of the car that had passed them at such a rate of knots.

'Corners well,' said Miller.

'Great grip,' agreed Kit.

It took Mary to point out the obvious to the two men in the front.

'He could have killed us, himself or the person travelling on the other side of the road. Great grip my eye.'

All of which was undoubtedly true.

But still.

26

Mimi the Dobermann had been enjoying a pleasant nap. She hated it when her owners left her alone. To stave off any feeling of fear or loneliness, she used the time to catch up on her sleep. From somewhere in the middle of a nightmare where she was being chased by a tom cat with more than violence on his mind a noise awoke her.

A Dobermann is one of the few breeds of dogs bred for personal protection. Mimi took to this job description with something bordering on psychotic intensity. On more than one occasion she'd made a burglar regret the day they had ever considered the Redon household a target. In this regard she was merely saving them the misery of wasted time. There wasn't much to steal.

In Mimi's favour, indeed for most Dobermanns, her appearance was half the battle. If first impressions are important then meeting Mimi felt like a personal audience with Satan's favourite pet. Perhaps only Philippe Redon would ever have called this particular canine 'cute'. Her shiny black coat glistened malevolently like the armour of a dark knight, her cropped ears stood erect like horns and exuded diabolic intent.

Mimi was awake in split seconds. She remained seated but fully alert. Her eyes fixed on the door. It was her experience that the two other animals she shared the space with used this area as a place to enter and exit.

A slab of meat landed in front of her nose. A treat! All pretence at being a guard dog was abandoned as she gave herself up to the pleasure of the food. She wolfed it down ravenously. There was so much of it too. Bit by bit, it became more difficult to chew the food. She felt fuller and fuller. And tired. Within a few minutes she was once more asleep. This time she was chasing the dirty-minded tom cat.

Alastair Aston and Harry Miller stood outside the Redon apartment. They had been waiting for nearly two minutes since Miller had first opened the door. Neither felt particularly comfortable in doing so. It looked rather conspicuous. Each feared someone would spot them and ask them just what they were up to.

'How long must we wait?' complained Alastair.

Thankfully their wait was not long. The door clicked open, and a face appeared.

'What kept you?' snarled Alastair.

'It was a Dobermann,' pointed out Ella-Mae from inside the Redon apartment. 'I'd like to see you sneak up on one sometime.'

Alastair grimaced then said, 'Out of the way.'

Miller grinned at the exchange and said, 'I'll collect you around nine. If I don't appear by then make your own way down to the casino.'

Ella-Mae nodded and shut the door. Miller felt oddly reassured by the presence of the little maid. Alastair, meanwhile, was standing nervously beside the comatose canine.

'You're sure it's asleep?'

Mimi began to snore thus saving Ella-Mae from dispensing another withering assessment of Alastair's store of valour.

-

Rufus Watts hopped out of the Mercedes, landed lightly on his feet, and twirled around to find Miller smiling. The two men walked towards the apartment belonging to the Russos. Upon hearing of his mission that evening he had, like Mary, adopted a black ensemble he'd acquired in a hasty shopping expedition. The black shirt and trousers would soon find favour as a uniform in another country but for the moment, Rufus felt like a million dollars.

Standing near the entrance of the apartment was Lieutenant Boucher. He handed Miller a card and then both men each took an arm of a rather surprised and hopeful Rufus Watts. The night was looking up.

'Pretend to be drunk,' whispered Miller to Rufus.

Rufus Watts had been a performer all his life. The role of drunk, however, has proven to be the iceberg upon which many an actor collided with before sinking in the sea of critical scorn. The trick, as Rufus intuitively knew, was to try *not* to be drunk.

They approached the entrance of the apartment. A rather unhappy looking doorman stood there eyeing them suspiciously. Rather than stagger around, Rufus did the opposite. All at once, his movements became slower yet more precise. He saluted the doorman attempted to speak, gave up and saluted him again.

'Drunk,' said Boucher stating the obvious. He extracted his police card and Miller did likewise. Thankfully the doorman only examined Boucher's. He waved them through. They began to climb the stairs.

'This is not an official visit,' reminded Boucher to Rufus. He was clearly in the middle of a conflict about what they were about to do. However, it was for a just cause. Pragmatism defeated scruples in a close match. 'We cannot leave any trace of our presence.'

Rufus nodded and grinned. They reached the apartment door. Miller, at this point extracted the tools of his trade for lock-picking. All at once Rufus Watts felt his heart soar. This was more like it. Breaking and entering aided and abetted by a handsome young officer from the Sûreté. This was the stuff of dreams.

Miller dealt with the front door as if he already had a key. Even Boucher had to tip his hat to the efficiency displayed by the Englishman. Reluctantly. This was partly an acknowledgement that they were straying outside the bounds of legality and partly a natural aversion, deeply held by all Frenchmen worthy of the name, towards any hint of accomplishment demonstrated by their infernal cousins from across the Channel.

'We'll make our own way to the casino,' said Boucher. Miller nodded and left them to it. The doorman had wandered off as Miller reached the entrance. He jogged towards the waiting Mercedes. Kit and Mary were the sole remaining passengers.

Miller started the ignition. The car spluttered worryingly before backfiring. This sparked the engine to life. Before long they were on their way. The sound of the engine was not one to inspire confidence. The frown never left Kit's face all the way up the hill towards the 'the Rock' of Monaco. Mary, too, was quiet, sensing that the edginess in the car was a combination of what lay ahead as much as the fear that the Mercedes would conk out soon.

They parked a few streets away from the Fourniers' apartment on Rue Basse. It was a short walk to the apartment on Avenue St. Martin. The street was empty, and they arrived at the door of the apartment without arousing much suspicion. Miller dealt with the front door with the same casual efficiency as the others, impressing his two companions as much as he had the policeman earlier.

They stepped inside the empty apartment. It was pitch black inside. Miller opened one of the shutters allowing light to flood in. Mary and Miller both turned to Kit.

'Shall we each take a room?'

Kit shook his head and replied, 'No, best to work together. We'll start with the living room. I'll help in here then I'll take a taxi down to the casino to see how Aunt Agatha's faring.'

For the next twenty minutes they worked their way through the room opening every drawer, looking underneath furniture, behind cushions, behind paintings. Secret compartments in the bureau were included in the search. None were found. After they finished with the living room they went through to the kitchen. Miller found keys for a cellar in the basement of the apartment block. He went down alone while Kit and Mary searched the second bedroom. Miller returned ten minutes later empty-handed.

The three of them trooped dejectedly into the master bedroom. Mary tried to remain upbeat.

'He must have hidden it somewhere.'

The 'it' in question was assumed to be a file or a dossier or a book containing material that might have been used to blackmail the Bluebeard Club. It was a tribute to the trust that everyone had in Kit and Agatha's hypothesis that none doubted its existence. Two issues worried Kit which he had not shared. What if Dupin's murderer who, presumably, found the file had then destroyed its contents? What then? A secondary hope was that they might find a gun, but Kit felt this unlikely. Keeping the murder weapon in a convenient place to be found was the stuff of fiction. The second worry was that the murderer had hidden the material in another place. Kit had instructed all three searches to be on the lookout for any alternative storage locations like a bank or safety deposit box.

Kit sat down on the bed. Something was nagging at him. He turned to Mary and said, 'Sorry, what did you say?'

'I said, he must have hidden it somewhere,' replied Mary, her eyes narrowing in amused consternation. 'Go on. I recognise that look. What are you thinking?'

Kit remained pensive but his head shook slowly. He murmured just loud enough for Mary to hear, 'It's surprising what you miss when you're not looking for it in the first place. I can't stay. I should have joined Aunt Agatha twenty minutes ago. Here's what I suggest you do…'

27

Agatha's early warning system for the arrival of the Bluebeard Club was as unusual as it was efficient. She stationed a very willing Betty at the bar near the entrance of the casino. From this vantage point Betty was able to check on the arrivals to the casino with the very able assistance of Mister Gin and Mister Tonic.

She was midway through her second gin when the first of the couples arrived. The Redons strode through the entrance hall like they were on military manoeuvres. Redon raised and dropped his thin cane as he walked adding an additional clip to the sound of their steps. As the daughter of an army officer, Betty mentally congratulated them on their close order drill. They seemed to march in step right past her on their way to the *Salle Europe*.

Betty was on her feet in an instant. She followed them into the gaming room and then headed towards Blanc's office where Agatha had installed herself. She opened the door and held up one finger.

One down. Two to go.

Betty reached the hallway in time to see the Russos arrive. The little Italian was certainly looking very serious. Either he'd been on the wrong end of a scalding from his good lady wife, or he was preparing for battle. Betty about turned and headed back to Agatha.

Two down. One couple left.

The Fourniers arrived ten minutes later. If Giuseppe Russo had looked serious it was as nothing compared to the unpleasant, raging malevolence that was Yves Fournier as he strode forward, two or three metres ahead of his wife, into the casino. There was a look on his face and that look was murder. Elsa Fournier also had a look on her face that Betty read instantly.

Victim.

Agatha was out of her seat like a greyhound after a hare when she saw Betty appear at the door for a third time. She said nothing. Instead, she ushered Betty with her hand to follow her into the gaming room. This was rather frustrating for Betty as she'd left her drink at the bar. However, sacrifices had to be made when on the trail of a murderer.

The hunt was on. At such times, it was difficult to believe that Agatha was now in her seventies. She moved with the speed and silent stealth of a cheetah. They reached the gaming room and made contact with Natalic who was busy fending off the attentions of several young and not so young men.

'Looks like we arrived in the nick of time,' said Agatha archly although she suspected that Natalie was not entirely to blame for the attentions. Not entirely…

The three ladies formed a huddle and Agatha gave the orders.

'If my guess is correct, and it usually is, the three couples will pretend not to know one another and stay well apart. We'll need to take a couple each until Christopher arrives and releases me from surveillance. I'll take the Fourniers. Betty, you stick with the Russos and Natalie, I suggest you go to Redon. If what I hear is true, you won't have to worry about attracting his attention.'

The three ladies separated and headed immediately in the direction of their quarry. Agatha spotted Briant signalling to her. He was pointing towards a *vingt et un* table where Elsa Fournier had taken a position to the right of the dealer. But this wasn't what Briant was signalling to her about. Mme Fournier was sitting beside Claudine Charpentier. Behind her was her husband. Briant disappeared for a moment while Agatha waited for him to arrive.

A minute later, after taking a very circuitous route, Briant appeared at Agatha's shoulder. Agatha turned to him and said, 'I see what you mean. This could be a problem, all right.'

'There's nothing I can do, Lady Frost.'

Agatha stared at the little examining magistrate and the woman she assumed was his wife. Just at that moment the lady in question thumped the table in delight as she won a hand of *vingt et un*. Beside her, Elsa Fournier looked with distaste at Claudine Charpentier. Agatha couldn't blame her. It was difficult to see for sure, but it looked like the money Elsa Fournier was gambling with was particularly low. This was just as Agatha had suspected. They would not want to burn their war chest too early in the night.

The question was how to move the examining magistrate. Agatha stared at him for a moment. He was wearing the ghastly pince-nez. It made him look like a grande dame in a pantomime. Meanwhile, Claudine Charpentier appeared to be enjoying a good run of cards. She thumped the table in delight as another victory was hers. Agatha turned her attention to Mme Charpentier. She was clearly an attractive woman albeit rather garishly attired. Her makeup had been applied with a trowel rather than a light brush. Sensibly, she eschewed too much jewellery. This would have been a mismatch and even Charpentier's wife recognised this was not an area to attract attention to.

'I have an idea,' said Agatha, her eyes gleaming with a certitude that made Briant smile.

-

Betty and Natalie found themselves in a similar position across the room. The two people they were following stood near one another but pretended not to have met. Mme Russo stood next to Philippe Redon but made no attempt to converse. Instead, their attention was on two remaining *vingt et un* tables.

Natalie casually walked past Betty and whispered, 'Why aren't they sitting down?'

Betty, for once, had an answer to hand.

'They're waiting for the completion of the shoe. Then they'll join. Alternatively, they may join towards the end of this shoe just to ensure that they have a space at the table.'

As Betty predicted they joined each game a few minutes later, just before each table replaced the shoe with new decks of cards. Natalie had, by this stage, moved away from Betty and stood near to Redon's table. Of courses the chances of Natalie remaining alone to focus on her surveillance task were always likely to be negligible. Her youth, beauty and air of sentient sexuality made her seem like a beacon in coal mine. The first man to launch an attack was perhaps not at the prime stage of his life physically but there was no doubting his financial credentials. Fifty-two-year-old Comte Alphonse Trenet had the confidence that wealth and a privileged upbringing can provide. Sadly, this wealth had, in addition, provided him with a significant girth and the early onset of gout. He was dismissed with a smile just in time for the second contender, Simon Levy, an Austrian industrialist, to make his pitch.

Levy, at six feet with dark hair and piercing brown eyes, was more of a prospect and, in any other situation, would certainly have been given due consideration from Natalie. With a heavy heart she pointed to the game taking place and sat down at the table. This had always been a consideration, so Agatha and Alastair had briefed her accordingly. Unpeturbed, Levy sat down and spent an enjoyable half hour in the attractive company of the young Frenchwoman. Natalie raised no objection to this and was enjoying herself immensely. Agatha had also staked her enough money to keep her playing for several hours.

-

Agatha stood back behind a pillar and waited for her plan to be put into action. A few minutes later she saw Briant appear. He gave her a brief nod then disappeared. Saimbron appeared and swiftly disappeared again. He was dressed in a black dinner suit. There was nothing about him that did not suggest 'detective' however. Some people just were what they were.

Agatha waited.

Moments after Saimbron disappeared Agatha's heartbeat went up a notch. Mme Cotille entered the *Salle Europe* and made a beeline for the table containing the Charpentiers. She glanced briefly at Agatha and continued her way towards her target.

She approached Charpentier and tapped him on the shoulder. Mme Cotille, at forty years of age, was dressed fashionably in a black blouse and black skirt. This made her distinct from every other woman on the floor, all of whom were in a dress. She radiated quiet elegance. Her approach to Charpentier was met with a frosty reception from Claudine Charpentier. Whatever her husband lacked in masculine virility he more than made up for in charm lessness. Despite these drawbacks, he was *her* husband. Claudine was on the point of sending Mme Cotille away with more than a flea in her ear until she overheard what was being said.

'Would you like to come with me and meet the prince? He'll be on his way here soon.'

Just the mention of Prince Albert was enough to have Claudine leaping out of her seat like Charlie Paddock at the starter's pistol. Charpentier did not have the chance to say

'Yes'. Claudine had taken Mme Cotille by the arm and asked her to lead the way.

-

The next half hour gave Agatha a clue as to the strategy that would be employed. Every so often Elsa Fournier would say some things to the dealer by way of conversation. They seemed innocuous enough in themselves, but they were always made just as her husband appeared. Without knowing their counting technique, Agatha could not possibly crack the cipher. She noted that Mme Fournier kept two stacks of chips with which she gambled. Alongside them were several chips laid face down. Occasionally she would add to them or take one or two away. This may have been a code, but its nature was opaque to Agatha.

After an hour, Mme Fournier stood up and left the table to be replaced by her husband. They exchanged not a word. However, the stakes they played for remained very low. The shoe was obviously not a favourable one. Agatha watched him play out the rest of the shoe with barely contained boredom. Interestingly, Fournier positioned his chips in a similar manner to Elsa Fournier.

A similar story was playing out on the other two tables. Each table saw a switch in personnel around halfway through each shoe. Then they circulated around so that Elsa Fournier arrived at the table played by the Redons and they moved to the table played by Russo. It wasn't until around seven thirty that the first sign emerged of a table likely to yield a better opportunity for the Bluebeard Club.

Philippe Redon was in the chair. Betty heard him make a comment that it was rather hot. The instant he said this, Mme Redon made straight for Mme Russo. Betty eyed her pass the Italian lady and whisper something. Mme Russo began to wave her fan furiously to attract the attention of her husband who was sitting opposite her. Within seconds

Russo left the table he was playing on to be replaced by Mme Russo.

Betty looked over towards Natalie who nodded back to her. Then Betty walked over to Agatha's position near the table of Yves Fournier. But Agatha had already spotted the move and she passed Betty on her way to the Redon table. She arrived just in time to see Redon arrange ten chips in two neat rows of five on the table. It looked as if he was indicating the number ten. He finished off his hand and rose from the table. Russo took over. A swift glance towards the shoe told Agatha that there were less than two decks remaining.

For all the excitement, Russo played conservatively. His stakes remained relatively low on the first then the second and third hands. Agatha felt a little let down by this. Things changed on the fourth hand.

Russo was dealt a Queen face up. He turned over the card facing down to reveal another Queen. He split the two hands and threw all his chips, worth at least thousand pounds in proper money by Agatha's estimate, onto the two hands. This was noticed by several casino patrons and a crowd assembled near the table. This suited Agatha as it helped her remain incognito.

The dealer dealt an ace on the first Queen – *vingt et un*! The next card on the second Queen was a two. Russo tapped the table and increased his bet to the equivalent of two thousand pounds. The next card was a nine. *Vingt et un* once more. The crowd broke into spontaneous applause. Russo beamed in pleasure at his audience and happily collected his chips.

The next few hands managed to dissipate interest in table and patrons drifted off as Russo resumed his conservative approach. The final hand of the shoe saw him win another relatively large pot worth close to a thousand pounds. He left the table immediately it was over to be replaced by Yves Fournier.

Agatha turned around and saw Betty waving at her furiously. Elsa Fournier placed a chip down at the top of a row of four. There was another row of five alongside it. She was indicating ten, if Agatha read her right. That changed after the next hand when she added another two chips to the number. This was twelve. It was clear that the higher the number the greater the chance of beating the house. Russo was over to the table like a scalded cat. His arrival prompted Elsa Fournier to leave. Her face was white, and she seemed to be moments away from being ill.

The shoe had barely a deck remaining. If Russo was going to make any more wins, then they would happen in the next couple of hands. The first hand was a modest loss as was the second. A few patrons noticed that Russo had changed tables and they followed him over to see if his luck continued.

The third hand saw Russo with a King facing upwards. He put at least a thousand pounds in chips down and tapped the table.

He was dealt another King.

He'd lost. His face registered nothing. Then he smiled and shrugged. A few patrons patted him on the back for consolation. However, the dealer was already starting the final hand of the shoe. Russo had a nine facing up. He immediately flipped over the card facing down to reveal another nine. He split them and put another thousand pounds down on each card. A gasp went up among the people watching. One of the other players on the table immediately folded on the Queen they were holding, obviously not understanding that they were not playing Russo but the dealer instead. It was all Agatha could do stop herself snorting at such stupidity.

The next card Russo received was the Ace of spades. He now had twenty for the first hand. The next card was a Jack. This meant he was sitting on two very high hands while the dealer had a three facing up. The game was now focused on the dealer and Russo. The dealer's next card to himself was a five. He had eight showing. Perspiration was lining the forehead of the dealer. Russo looked outwardly calm. Agatha guessed his guts were churning because hers certainly were.

The dealer's next card was two. He was heading towards a five-card trick if he dealt himself another card. He did so.

A ten.

Russo leaned back and beathed out. He'd just won close to three thousand pounds once more, six thousand for the night less the one thousand he'd lost. He rose from the table and made straight for the bar. Agatha followed him at a discreet distance. He ordered tonic water with ice. He drank the glass in one go and ordered another. Alcohol would have to wait. Mme Russo appeared, and they nodded to one another but made no other attempt to communicate.

Russo was far from finished for the evening.

28

Taking a hansom cab in 1921 in a place as beautifully situated as Monte Carlo would be, for many, the very epitome of romance and a chance to connect, if only for a few minutes, with a gilded, bygone age. For Kit Aston, desperate to reach the casino to aid Agatha and the others, it was nothing short of frustrating. The clip clopping of the horse was akin to Chinese water torture, something he'd oncc experienced in a cell in India, but that's another story.

It took twenty minutes to reach the casino from the Fourniers' apartment high up on 'the Rock'. With a prosthetic lower leg, Kit was no longer able to burst onto any scene. A fast limp was the best he could manage. He met one of Saimbron's men near the entrance of the casino. He nodded to the man as he passed him. However, the man reached out and tugged on his arm. In any language, especially if the 'tug-ger' is a policeman, it means, 'come this way'. The 'please' is inferred.

Kit accompanied the policeman to Mme Cotille's office where Saimbron was waiting. Saimbron bowed briefly but his face was set to stone. Kit felt a chill suddenly. What had happened?

'Hello, Inspector Saimbron,' said Kit. 'Is something wrong?'

A raised eyebrow and a half smile appeared on Saimbron's face. Oddly this had the effect of relaxing Kit whose muscles were tensing up like traffic at rush hour on Piccadilly. He gestured with his finger to follow him outside the office. The French police were being particularly laconic this evening. Kit followed him to Blanc's office. They stood outside and listened.

-

An hour waiting in Blanc's office had slowly diluted the excitement felt by Claudine Charpentier and her husband at the prospect of meeting Prince Albert I. Notwithstanding the free champagne with which they had been liberally plied, the suspicion was growing in both their minds that the meeting was becoming less likely by the minute.

In any other circumstance, the examining magistrate might have taken great offence at such a slight. However, Charpentier had quickly begun to appreciate the benefits of sitting in a beautiful office, smoking some excellent cigars, and drinking excellent champagne. The fact that it was being served by the delectable Mme Cotille made the experience all the more exquisite. In addition, it had the decided advantage of keeping his wife well away from the well-heeled clients of the casino. A bonus such as this was not to be ignored.

Perhaps this is why Claudine Charpentier had begun to lay siege to her husband's good mood with a series of barbed comments, firstly, about Mme Cotille and now, more worryingly, about the prince. Charpentier bore these as best he could. After all, he'd had many years of practice. The vitriol had initially been confined to when they were alone, but a disturbing trend was emerging with each visit by Mme Cotille when Claudine would make a remark that was, ostensibly, innocent but with a tone that was pregnant with pique. An explosion was imminent.

Mme Cotille left the office after Claudine's latest comment about not wanting to impose on the prince *if he has better things to do*. Her air of stylish serenity was becoming distinctly ruffled. She ran her hands through her well-coiffed hair and found herself staring up into the blue eyes of the good-looking lord from England.

'I cannot keep them there much longer, Inspector,' said Mme Cotille.

Saimbron nodded and turned to Kit to explain the outline of what had occurred and Agatha's plan. This brought a smile to Kit's face although he recognised that the plan did have some flaws which were becoming all too apparent now. He turned his attention to Mme Cotille.

'Tell me, is it likely that the examining magistrate and…'

At this point Claudine Charpentier turned her suppressed anger on her husband. His obvious admiration for Mme Cotille was the subject of the initial expletive-filled salvo that could not only be heard outside the office but probably several streets away too.

'…charming wife has met the prince,' continued Kit after a short pause to take in Claudine's thoughts on her husband and the likely level of promiscuous carnality that a woman like Mme Cotille was capable of.

The ongoing diatribe from Claudine inside the office effectively answered this question as much as the dismissive look on Mme Cotille's face.

'Very well. May I suggest the following…'

A few minutes later, Mme Cotille re-appeared in the Blanc's office. She was met with a barely disguised look of venom by Claudine. She leaned over Charpentier and put her hand on his shoulder as she did so, to reach the telephone on the desk of the former casino manager. This was enough to send the temperature gauge of both Charpentiers rising albeit for entirely different reasons.

She picked up the phone and said, 'Yes, your Serene Highness, they are here.' She handed the phone to Claudine, just as Kit had suggested. This distracted her enough while Mme Cotille ran her hand along Charpentier's shoulders.

'Your Highness,' said Claudine in a voice that was barely recognisable to her husband of two score years. 'Yes, this is Claudine Charpentier. I am very well, thank you. There's no need to apologise. Mme Cotille has been a wonderful hostess.'

Even with the more refined accent she was putting on, Claudine still managed to make the word 'hostess' sound like a brothel madame in Pigalle. This stopped Mme Cotille in her tracks, and she decided to improvise on Kit's original suggestion. She stood behind Charpentier and placed a hand on each shoulder. Charpentier was dreading a few things at this point. His chief fear being the end of the phone call. It would bring to a close the delightful interlude he was experiencing just then with the ravishing Mme Cotille, and it would see the commencement of a verbal bombardment that was likely to last years, rather than seconds, if he knew his wife.

The phone was replaced just as Mme Cotille raised her hands from the willing shoulders of the examining magistrate.

'Yes, my dear?' asked Charpentier hopefully.

'Well,' said Claudine, caught somewhere between excitement and murder, 'the prince apologised for keeping us waiting. He was very nice about you, I must say. He suggested that we have dinner at the Hotel de Paris at his pleasure and he would meet us there later this evening. He says important business has kept him back from the pleasure of meeting me.'

Mme Cotille exited the office and nodded to the waiting policemen and Kit. The averting of this crisis was greeted with a sigh of relief all round. Kit abandoned the policemen and went in search of Agatha. It was now almost eight o'clock. He saw Agatha standing at the far end of the *Salle Europe* studying the table where Mme Russo was playing.

Nearer to the entrance, Natalie was sitting alongside Elsa Fournier a fact that had not gone unnoticed by half the men in the room. There seemed to be an atmosphere akin to mating season among the males of the species as they jockeyed to gain a seat at the table facing the two women. Despite giving Natalie quite a few years, there was no question that Elsa Fournier's delicate features more than held their own in the beauty stakes.

Kit caught Agatha's eye and she motioned with her head for him to come over. Avoiding the Fournier table, Kit took a roundabout route to reach Agatha. There was no greeting from his aunt.

'Look at how Madame Russo has arrayed her chips.'

Kit saw that Mme Russo had three stacks of chips and beside them were nine chips lying face down.

'If my suspicions are correct, once there are ten chips facing down, Russo will take over. He's done this a few times tonight but never when the number of chips is less than ten.'

'What do you think it means?' whispered Kit.

'I'm glad you asked this. I've been looking at them play for two hours now and I think it goes something like this. Cards between two and seven are counted as one type of card and eight and above another. Then they simply subtract one from the other. So, a five and a queen in one hand cancel each other out. If the number of chips begins to climb to ten or over then it means, there are more high value cards left in the shoe. This, as we know, favours the player against the house. Did you find anything by the way?'

'Not yet.'

There was an implicit assumption from Agatha that Harry Miller would have no problem breaking into the three apartments.

'What about the dog?'

'It seems Ella-Mae's Gurkha-like stealth remains undiminished by age.'

'Very good and she's younger than me, so less of the remarks around age, Christopher.'

Kit ignored the jibe and asked 'How are the games going? Any big wins?'

'I believe they have won around ten thousand pounds so far. I keep having to convert the amounts into proper money. Their losses are quite negligible. Russo is their main player although I gather from Betty, Elsa Fournier had a big win too at the same time. The others seem to be there just to lay the groundwork.'

Kit nodded as Agatha spoke. They were building up a tidy war chest for later when they would be able to stake greater and greater amounts. After another hand, Mme Russo reduced the number of chips lying face down from eight to seven. Kit had noted that a few of the hands at the table had royal cards. He risked a glance at Russo who was obviously disappointed with this. The shoe was now on the last deck. This probably meant there would be no attack made at this table.

Russo glanced at his wife and moved slowly across the room to look at the other tables. Kit followed at a distance and made sure to avoid being spotted by either Fournier. There was no sign of Briant or Saimbron, but Kit had no doubt they were somewhere close by.

-

In Moneghetti, Rufus Watts and Boucher had to admit defeat. It was galling for Rufus not to be the one to find the evidence that Kit and the police so desperately sought. However, he'd turned over the apartment several times without success. He trooped out the front door with a heavy heart. Rufus was not a man to deny his own destiny. This sense of destiny required that he be the one to crack the case wide open. On this occasion it was not to be, and it hurt him more than he could say.

The two men made their way dejectedly down the stairs. Rufus clicked his cane along each step. However, he was dressed to the nines and the casino awaited his arrival. This perked him up a little as he felt the night air take him in its embrace. It was pleasantly chilly. He took a deep breath and started down the hill with Boucher towards the casino.

The only thing heavier than the sense of defeat in the apartment on Boulevard de Ouest was the snores of Mimi the Dobermann.

'How much sleeping powder did you add to the meat anyway?' asked Alastair, staring at the slumbering guard dog. There was just a hint of concern in his voice. It was lying on its back, four feet in the air. Had the snores not been so deafening there would have been some cause to believe that it had passed onto the great kennel in the sky. Ella-Mae ignored the question. There was a more pertinent problem to address.

'It ain't here.'

Alastair looked around the room that they'd ransacked and then tidied. For once he had to agree with his maid. It was difficult to decide which was more galling: their failure to find anything or the prospect of acknowledging Ella-Mae was right.

He chose a middle course.

'I suppose we should join the others at the casino.'

-

Harry Miller screwed the air vent back into place and shook his head at Mary. She was sitting on the bed where Kit had sat an hour earlier. She stared into a mirror and tried to put herself in the mind of her quarry. Kit had been adamant, yet so far, his theory had turned up nothing. Her shoulders slumped. She felt a creeping emptiness in the pit of her stomach. The feeling of someone who believed they were letting the others down.

Miller flopped onto the bed and rubbed his eyes.

'Where is it, Harry? Where is it?'

Miller shook his head. They had been through everything twice now. It seemed impossible that there was something being hidden from them. Even on the second round of searches, based on Kit's suggestion, nothing had turned up. She wracked her memory for what she'd overheard between the two Fourniers. Was there anything in what had been said that might provide a clue about where they might hide a report or a book or a folder. Nothing came to mind.

What had they been talking about down at Lavrotto? She closed her eyes and tried to recall the argument. She recalled something about Mme Fournier hiding things. She had accused him of driving her mad. Mary gripped the bedclothes in frustration. What else had they said?

She felt like crying.

29

Nine o'clock saw the arrival of Rufus Watts and Boucher swiftly followed by Alastair and Ella-Mae. The latter had to be half dragged to the casino by the former. A devout Baptist, Ella-Mae had no truck with alcohol or gambling although this did not prevent her enjoying a modest income from playing bridge. One wouldn't bet against her at chess either.

More pertinently, she felt that she was not dressed appropriately for such grand surroundings. It was only an appeal by Alastair to her duty to support the others that swayed her in the end. In truth, she was more than a little curious to see what the inside of the famous casino and its aristocratic patronage looked like.

Rufus, after a rapid briefing session from Kit, gave Betty a well-earned break as he joined the Redon table. Mme Redon was sitting on a modest pile of chips but the number lying face down was an unattractive three. Her husband was resting both hands on his cane which looked suspiciously like the one Rufus was carrying.

A man of taste, thought Rufus, laughing to himself. Rufus joined the game with the casual enthusiasm of a chap who has been staked all the money and cares not a jot about the outcome.

Ella-Mae point blank refused to gamble. Instead, she accompanied Alastair, after a brief conference with Kit, to the table where Giuseppe Russo was sitting. The purpose was to distract the Italian who was making ready to engage in another strike against the bank. Alastair plonked himself down beside Russo, clapped him on the back a little more forcefully than good manners permitted and said, 'Have you missed me?'

The Italian's mouth dropped open in shock at the sight of Alastair. He tapped the table by mistake resulting in the dealer throwing an additional card his direction causing him to lose around five hundred pounds.

'Oh dear, I wouldn't have gone for another card with that ten showing. What were you thinking, old boy?' said Alastair innocently. He then placed some chips down on the table, gave the dealer a nod and smiled to the rest of table.

Ella-Mae, standing across from where Alastair and Russo were sitting, could see the fury in the Italian's eyes. She recognised that look and that feeling. Alastair could turn a Trappist into an obscenity-screaming madman in the blink of an eye. It was actually a talent when you thought about it.

Beside Russo's pile of chips were eleven chips face down. With only one deck left in the shoe, it was clear that Russo was going to strike soon. In fact, it was the next hand. He was dealt a king face up. Immediately he turned the other card over to reveal a king. He put, by Alastair's reckoning, the equivalent of five thousand pounds on each. This was enough to break Alastair's flow of inconsequential chatter for a moment. Russo was grimly silent. The dealer, Patrice Rives, was gulping in air like a man trying to avoid drowning.

Silence surrounded the table.

Kit was aware of the buzz across the room. A crowd had assembled around the table but there was silence. He was standing near a pillar watching Elsa Fournier playing for a sum of money that was close to a thousand pounds. She was white with fear. This was the last place she wanted to be. Standing at the other end of the table was Yves

Fournier glaring at her like a Svengali. His hair was matted with perspiration with hands in a knuckle-white grip.

A roar erupted from the other table followed by shouts of 'Bravo'. Russo had won again. Kit's eyes met with Ella-Mae. She made her way over to Kit.

'That man just made more money than I've made in my whole life.'

Kit shrugged but could think of nothing to say to the daughter of a slave. They turned their attention to the table that Kit was monitoring. Elsa Fournier tapped the table. She had a lot of money riding on the turn of this card. Strangely, Kit felt his heart beating fast. He was caught between siding with the prince and being drawn to the plight of the desperately sad woman before him.

A two of hearts fell beside the visible Jack of spades. Mme Fournier's eyes flicked nervously towards her husband. Kit glanced towards Fournier too. His face was red, and each eye seemed in imminent danger of popping. There was nothing he could do to help, and he was the last man in the world to hide his frustration at this.

Elsa Fournier tapped the table once more. She now had three cards that added up to, at least fourteen. She could barely look at the dealer who was dragging another card from the shoe and spun it face up beside her other cards.

The two of spades.

There was a gasp from the group of patrons watching the hand. Elsa Fournier shook her head. She would stick with what she had. All eyes turned to the dealer. He had a three showing. He pulled another card from the shoe. Nine of hearts. He turned over the face down card to reveal a seven of diamonds.

'Dix-neuf'

Elsa Fournier's face fell. Absently she turned over the card lying face down. It was a four of clubs. Eighteen. Kit turned to Fournier. The burly Frenchman spun around, stalked away from the table, and headed directly out of the gaming room. All around faces expressed sympathy. It was as if they sensed her inner wretchedness.

Elsa Fournier barely noticed either this or the arrival of the new deal. But Russo did. He had arrived at the table clutching his enormous winnings from a minute or so previously. He saw that Mme Fournier was sitting on a plus ten shoe. There was at least a deck and half still left to play. Russo caught the eye of Elsa Fournier. She played and won a modest amount on the next hand then relinquished her spot to the Italian with no little relief.

A crowd had followed him to the table. There was buzz around the room now as it became clear that the Italian was enjoying an amazing winning streak. Kit sensed Alastair joining him at the pillar.

'How much?' asked Kit simply.

'Twenty-five thousand pounds, give or take. I tried to distract him, but he didn't seem much interested in hunting in Hertfordshire.'

'Strange cove,' said Kit grimly. One thought was uppermost on his mind now.

Where was Mary?

-

The bonnet of the Mercedes Benz was up. Harry Miller and Mary stood back and looked at the engine comprising metal bolts, pipes, screws, rivets, and things neither Miller nor this chronicler knew the name of. To Mary it was as fascinating as it was frustrating.

'What do you think?'

Miller shook his head. He didn't know what to think beyond the one inescapable fact that he did not know how to fix the car. Ten minutes earlier it had shuddered to a start, backfired, and died in quick succession.

Mary looked away and felt like the little Italian she had seen in the newsreel of the Olympics staggering over the line at the Olympics only to be denied a gold medal. Underneath her arm was a thin folder containing a sheaf of papers. They'd found Dupin's report. Yet they were stuck up on 'the Rock'.

'We can't wait any longer, Harry. I think we should take one of the cabs down to the casino.'

This made sense. Miller pulled the hood down and looked at his hands. They were stained black. Mary smiled ruefully.

'I'm sure we'll find somewhere to clean you up. Let's move.'

They walked around the corner to Place de la Visitation where there were normally hansom cabs. The long rectangular 'square' was empty. Mary only just about managed to refrain from venting her frustration with a few choice, and certainly unladylike, words. They turned to one another. Resignation was etched on both their faces.

'We'll have to walk,' said Miller, stating the gloomy truth. This meant trekking from high up on one side of Monaco down the hill and across the port area before facing the prospect of a steep home straight just when they were beginning to feel most fatigued. It was with a heavy heart and an even heavier tread they set off.

The walk down the hill gave Mary an opportunity to gaze from on high at the magnificent port. Beautiful white sailing boats bobbed gently on the water. Across at the other side, the Hotel de Paris and the Opera House were lit up golden against the night sky. The rest of the town was black except for distant apartment lights that seemed like shimmering gems spread across black velvet. Had they not been so intent on reaching the casino quickly, Mary would have loved to have paused and taken in the magnificent view. Luckily her shoes were comfortable and not so raised up that they slowed her down. Miller found himself struggling to keep up.

'Perhaps we'll find a cab on our way there,' said Miller hopefully.

They didn't.

-

Inside the gloriously lit Hotel de Paris, the atmosphere was beginning to turn sour again for the examining magistrate. Claudine had long since passed the point where alcohol removed her inhibitions on speaking her mind. Sadly, the reduction in discretion was matched, conversely, by an increase in both the volume of her speech and the mean-spiritedness of its content. In short, Charpentier was weighing a number of options, the least drastic of which involved a rope, a concrete block and a Maurice Chevalier seventy-eight.

A suspicion was growing in Charpentier's mind that he had been deceived. Despite his tendency towards petty despotism, he was not a complete fool. The question bouncing around his mind was why anyone would wish to play such a joke. Who was responsible? Clearly, Mme Cotille was complicit, but it seemed a stretch to believe that such an elegant and educated lady would have conceived such a juvenile joke. With each passing drink winging its merry way down his wife's throat, Charpentier became more convinced that they had been removed from the casino for a reason.

There was only one way to find out, of course. He called a waiter over and demanded that they send the bill over to Mme Cotille. He rose from the table and said to Claudine, 'I think, my dear, it is time we left.'

'What about Prince Albert?' slurred Claudine, emptying the rest of the champagne bottle into her glass.

'I fear we have been hoodwinked,' said Charpentier, grabbing his lapels and pulling them outwards. The sight of such anger in her husband cut through the alcoholic haze that had descended over Claudine. She sat up with a start.

It was clear her husband meant business. He'd never seemed so attractive to her as at that moment. All thought of Prince Albert was forgotten. She staggered to her feet, determined to back her husband to the very hilt of something or other.

The spectacle of the glassy-eyed Claudine leaning on the table to stay upright brought mixed feelings to Charpentier. On the one hand he was delighted that she understood the gravity of what had happened and was fully supportive of his rage. On the other, the impact of his wrath would be fatally undermined by the presence of a plainly inebriated Claudine, clutching him for support.

'Perhaps you should stay here, my dear. I think I shall demand an explanation myself.'

With some relief Claudine slumped back onto the chair. The last thing Charpentier heard, as he left the restaurant, was his wife shouting to the waiter to bring another bottle of champagne.

-

The speed with which Mary and Harry Miller had embarked on their journey down the hill towards the port was in marked contrast, around half an hour later, to the speed with which they were ascending Avenue de Monte Carlo which led to Place du Casino. They finally reached the flat and saw the Opera House which adjoins the casino. The bust of Massenet which greeted patrons of the Opera House never looked so welcome as it did at that moment to Mary.

It was nearing ten in the evening and despite the chill Mary was glowing with the effort to reach their destination. They turned into the square, heading up the steps leading to the casino. Both stood back to let a little man sporting a *pince-nez* rush past them. He seemed in quite a hurry. Behind him, Miller cast an envious glance down at a car parked in front of the casino. It was the blue Bugatti that had raced past them earlier that evening.

Miller remained outside while Mary followed the little man inside but soon lost him such was his speed of movement. However, this brought out the competitive spirit in Mary. She had won many events at her school's sports day, and she was not about to be outpaced by a middle-aged Frenchman without putting up some sort of show. She broke into a jog surprising both Miller and the young Austrian, Simon Levy, who had been so entranced and then rejected by Natalie earlier in the evening. He turned tail and decided to follow the very attractive young lady dressed in black back into the gaming rooms.

30

The sudden arrival of Charpentier into the casino was both unsurprising and a shock to Mme Cotille who had just walked out into the entrance area herself. She spied Charpentier approach a waiter near the bar. She didn't need to be a lip reader to know what he was asking.

'Can you tell me where Mme Cotille is?' asked Charpentier in barely restrained irritation. The waiter glanced over Charpentier's shoulder to see Mme Cotille shaking her head furiously and making a slashing gesture with her hand.

'I don't know, sir,' said the waiter who had had, it must be said, more than enough from the Charpentiers earlier to last a lifetime. He did then what French waiters seem born to do, he turned his back on the customer and walked off without a word. To Charpentier's credit, he was used to such behaviour, especially from waiters. The rudeness was met with a shrug. He headed in the direction of the offices, narrowly missing Mme Cotille who had sprinted to Blanc's office to warn the waiting policemen of the impending arrival.

'He's here,' exclaimed Mme Cotille bursting into Blanc's office which housed Briant, Saimbron and Boucher.

'Who?' asked Saimbron, hoping it wasn't Charpentier.

'Charpentier, he's coming this way.'

Charpentier did not knock. His anger was too raw at this stage for such niceties. He opened the door to Mme Cotille's office. It was empty. He shut the door angrily and moved forward to the next office. Once more, without knocking he walked inside.

The room was empty.

The window was open, and he walked forward to gaze outside onto the Place du Casino. The square was busy with men and women sitting at outdoor cafes or walking in the gardens. Charpentier shut the window. It seemed strange to have it open at this time of night. Something felt wrong with this, in fact with the whole evening. He would head for the gaming rooms.

-

The atmosphere in the *Salle Europe* was febrile. The number of people in the room had grown as word had filtered through the casino of the success for the Italian at *vingt et un*. Every time he sat down at a table, there was a scrum to gain a view of Russo in action. A restless excitement filled the air, and no one was feeling it more than Agatha.

A moment of reckoning loomed. She knew that she had been commissioned by the prince to do something about the attacks, for they were nothing less, on the casino. Yet a part of her balked at what lay ahead. What right had she, to deny the so-called Bluebeard Club the chance at rinsing the casino methodically through the intelligent application of basic probability principles?

She had taken up a place as dealer at one of the *vingt et un* tables. Its position was in the centre of the room and allowed her a view of the entrance to the *Salle Europe*. This allowed her to observe arrivals, departures, and activity on the other *vingt et un* tables.

Then she saw Mary arrive in the gaming room. She headed directly towards Kit who had not spotted her arrival. From under her arm, she extracted a folder and showed it to Kit. She was speaking excitedly. Then Kit looked up and scanned the room.

His eyes met Agatha's.

-

Mary had spotted Kit by a pillar. He was engrossed by the game taking place before him involving Yves Fournier. It was hard to see why. They big Frenchman was playing for a paltry stake and did not seem to have won very much. A part of her would like to have stayed there for a little longer and gaze at him: his fine and refined features, the piercing intensity of his blue eyes. But another part of her recognised that what she had was just too important. It could not wait.

She jogged lightly over to Kit. He turned around as he sensed her arrival from the corner of his eye. He smiled as he saw her. Her outfit had caused many on this side of the room to stop what they were doing and gaze at her. Mary was too excited to concern herself with the attention of others but woman enough to be gratified by the reaction in Kit's eyes before the realisation dawned on him that she had delivered the goods.

Mary handed over the sheaf of papers to Kit. She extracted one and pointed to a handwritten headline.

'Good lord,' said Kit.

'That's not all,' replied Mary. 'Look at this one.' At this she took the folder from Kit while he read the first sheet. She handed him another sheet which contained explosive information about another member of the Bluebeard Club. Before Kit could take this in, Mary had given him another.

'I have to hand it to Dupin, he was good. We must find Briant and Saimbron.'

At this point both Alastair and Ella-Mae had joined Kit having also spied Mary's arrival. Kit handed Alastair the first sheet.

'Oh,' said Alastair. Then he smiled and shrugged. 'Of course, I knew. You can always tell.'

He ignored the sceptical looks from Kit and Mary. He was not beyond a bit of shamelessness when the occasion demanded. And that occasion was now. The matter was urgent tough. Kit made for a policeman who Saimbron had brought along to stand guard at the exit of the *Salle Europe*.

Gardien Jacques Dubois had jumped at the chance of a bit of plain-clothes work. His talents were, at long last, being realised. Twenty years in uniform had led the policeman to believe that nepotism, jealousy, and downright stupidity would deny him the opportunity that his intelligence and perspicacity so merited. When Saimbron had entered the mess room to look for help on this evening he had chosen Dubois. The fact that he was the only man in the room at the time was not a something that the policeman gave a second's thought to. He was the chosen one.

He saw the aristocratic Englishman approach him with his startingly attractive wife, for an Englishwoman, that is.

'Where can I find Captain Briant and Inspector Saimbron?'

The question became redundant moments later when Kit literally ran into the diminutive figure of Charpentier. Kit was on the point of apologising as Englishmen tend to do in almost any situation, especially those where none is either required or expected, when the two men realised who the other was and, just as quickly, why this was a problem.

-

Agatha saw the arrival of Charpentier, and it threw her composure sufficiently to fluff the next hand. Luckily the bank's losses were minimal. She was desperate to know what the two men were saying to one another. Charpentier looked unhappy, but then he always did. A cough nearby woke her from the reverie, and she realised that the table was waiting for her to deal the next hand. She smiled, shrugged, and began to feed cards from the shoe.

To Agatha's right was Mme Russo. She was playing conservatively which Agatha expected. Her pile of chips was stake money and no more. Of more interest was the number of chips laid out alongside the two columns. The total stood at eight even though they were barely a quarter of the way through the shoe. This suggested the arrival of her husband was likely but not imminent.

The game played out and was noteworthy insofar as Mme Russo added another chip to those laid out. They were at nine now. But just at that moment, everyone was distracted by a commotion at a table nearby.

-

'You idiot,' exploded Fournier at his wife.

The words would have been shocking enough under any circumstance in the gaming room of the casino. It was more so because no one had any idea that they were husband and wife. A few of the men tutted-tutted. Elsa Fournier looked crestfallen after another heavy loss. Her husband glared at her as a number of the patrons commiserated with the visibly upset Mme Fournier.

Watching was Simon Levy, who had quickly understood that Mary was out of reach. He had returned to the table where Natalie was sitting and had made another sally in her direction. She didn't say much but she smiled rather encouragingly at him. It was at this point Fournier had made his inappropriate comment. It occurred to Levy that there was much to gain in his quest by being seen to defend a defenceless woman. He turned to the angry Fournier and said coldly, 'I think, sir, you should apologise.'

'This is my wife,' snarled Fournier,

'You are a bully, sir. A pathetic bully. I think you should leave before the casino asks you to.'

'I think, sir, that you should mind your own business,' hissed Fournier and he turned away from the Austrian.

Levy turned to Natalie, hoping that his efforts had not gone unnoticed. The smile of admiration on her face was its own reward. Things were looking up, thought Levy. She rose from the table, glanced shyly at Levy, and went to another table which was attracting a crowd.

-

'How dare you go against my wishes,' hissed Charpentier at Kit.

Kit smiled and shrugged at the examining magistrate. A point that seemed to have been missed by the little Frenchman was that Kit was perfectly entitled to be there. He was on holiday, after all. An unusual one by any standard but a holiday all the same.

Rather than engage Charpentier he merely saluted him and walked away followed by Mary, Alastair, and Ella-Mae. Alastair added further insult to Charpentier by tipping his hat to him and chuckling as he passed. Charpentier spun around and realised he was utterly powerless to do anything. There was no doubt in his mind that he had been duped by the Englishman and his friends. This angered him immensely. There was only one thing that he could do.

Find Briant and Saimbron.

He had no power to tell the meddling aristocrat what he could or couldn't do but this was not the case with the policemen. He would make it his mission to give them a piece of his mind and that piece was anger. No one could make a fool of him and expect there to be no consequences.

Kit reached the exit of the room just as Briant entered with Saimbron. He held up the file that Mary had found.

'You need to read this,' said Kit.

Briant read Kit's face in the blink of an eye. He took the file brandished by Kit and retired to the side of the room with Saimbron and Boucher to review the contents of Dupin's report.

Meanwhile, Kit noticed that Agatha was in the middle of a growing crowd of patrons. It took a moment to understand why. Russo had just taken the place of his wife at the table. Standing nearby were the two Redons. Just behind them was Rufus Watts.

Charpentier had noted the arrival of the policemen. It did not escape his attention that they were engrossed in reading a document. This gave him a pause for thought as he considered his options. His first instinct had been to march over to Saimbron and demand an explanation. It was then that he saw Kit staring towards the middle of the gaming floor. He followed the direction of Kit's gaze and arrived at the sight of Agatha, dealing cards at a table with a large crowd surrounding it.

What on earth was going on? Curiosity got the better of him. He stepped towards the table to investigate further.

31

There was much to attract the attention of the crowd that had assembled around the *vingt et un* table that Charpentier was stalking towards. The presence of the Italian was enough to raise excitement levels. The amount of money he had won was close to fifty thousand pounds and he was proudly displaying the chips in eight neat piles.

Causing just as much interest, albeit unintentionally, was Natalie, who had just sat down. She continued to attract admirers of all ages. They were assembled around her once more like devoted followers of a female deity.

Yves Fournier joined the table, having escaped the censure resulting from his behaviour a minute or two previously. It was only when he sat down that he realised he was on the same table as Russo. A few angry women had followed him and were making their feelings known through clearly audible conversations about the decline of good manners. No one was in any doubt as to whom this exchange of views was directed. Russo certainly wasn't and he glared at the Frenchman for bringing such unwanted attention to himself, the table, and their activities.

This was enough for the Fournier. He stood up abruptly from the table and left it moments after sitting down. The crowd parted for him, and he strode over towards Elsa Fournier who was being consoled by Betty and another woman.

Charpentier's eyes were fixed, however, on the other reason why the table had become the apex of attention in the room. Agatha was the dealer. She noted the arrival of Charpentier by raising her eyebrows and smiling. If anything was designed to set a seal on the growing paranoia of the examining magistrate, it was this. However, once more, he was powerless to act. This was doubly apparent as his attention was taken by the size of the winnings in front of one of the patrons. He glanced from it then back to Agatha.

'This is what the prince feared,' said a voice beside Charpentier. He turned to find Kit Aston and then Mary standing beside him.

'You deliberately ignored my instructions,' snarled Charpentier. A rage burned within like an inferno. He needed someone to shout at. Twirling round he returned his gaze to the three policemen engrossed in reading sheaves of paper arrayed in their laps. Ignoring Kit, he headed towards them.

Which is a pity because matters were reaching a head on the table he'd just left. There were just three players in addition to Agatha: Russo, Natalie and Simon Levy who decided to enjoy a better view of the young Frenchwoman from the vantage point of the seat beside her. Natalie smiled at him as he sat alongside her.

Agatha dealt out the cards from the shoe. To a man and woman, everyone leaned in. From Kit's vantage point, it was clear there were not many hands left in this shoe. Agatha dealt herself a six. A five went to Natalie, a king to Levy and a four to Russo. Kit suspected this would put him off making any big bids.

As the game played out, Kit saw Alastair appear. He took a seat beside Russo, across from Natalie and Levy. There was low murmur around the table as the hand petered out with everyone losing out to Agatha's three card eighteen. Alastair chuckled at the result and pointed out to Russo, 'Not much in there for you, old friend.'

Russo tried to ignore him, but Alastair kept up a commentary on the proceedings.

'An eight for me. Very good. A bit of a chance here. I don't fancy your six much,' said Alastair. Nor did Russo, suspected Kit.

The hand played out with both Alastair and Natalie winning. The next hand followed swiftly. Agatha was not hanging around. Mary gripped Kit's hand when she saw Russo given a King of hearts, face up. Kit looked at her and raised his eyebrows. Moments later, Russo turned over his other card. It was a King of spades. He split them. Agatha threw two more cards face down.

Russo glanced swiftly at the cards and then placed the equivalent of thirty thousand pounds worth of chips on one of the hands. The watching patrons gasped at the amount being wagered.

Agatha was showing a six. Her heart was beating like a drunk drummer in a Parisian jazz club. She glanced at the face down card. It was an Ace of clubs. This meant she might have either a seventeen or seven depending on how she deployed the ace. Both Natalie and Levy were sticking with two cards. Attention turned to Alastair. He tapped the table.

A ten of hearts. He chuckled and shrugged.

'Oh well.'

This left Russo. He tapped the table and Agatha dealt him a seven of clubs. This was added to the hand with the low wager. Agatha held her breath now. She wasn't the only one. The rest of the watching audience held their breath too. Russo put his hand over the other two cards. No more cards. All attention turned towards Agatha. Mary's grip on Kit's hand tightened. Agatha's hand reached down slowly to the shoe.

-

With all the attention in the room centred on the *vingt et un* table, only Betty saw Fournier striding towards them with murder in his eyes. Elsa Fournier looked up fearfully and shrank away from him. Betty stepped in between Fournier and his wife.

'What do you think you are doing, sir?' snarled Betty in a manner that indicated that she was a woman who meant business. 'You leave this poor woman alone, you bully.'

Betty backed this up by putting her hand out which stopped the big Frenchman in his tracks. He hadn't been expecting this. His normal form would have been to face down such a woman. They always gave in. Something in him correctly guessed that this may not be the case with the Englishwoman facing him. She was barely five feet tall. Despite her height he would have put her at middleweight. There was a pugnaciousness to her eyes that suggested that if things got physical, she would give as good as she got.

Betty felt a tap on her shoulder. It was Mme Fournier. She shook her head. It was the look of submission that Fournier knew so well, that once had attracted him but was now so repugnant.

'Out of my way, madame,' demanded Fournier.

The look on Elsa Fournier's face was neither fear nor submission. It was acceptance. Had it been anything else Betty would not have relented. Betty had no choice but to give way. She watched helplessly as Fournier grabbed the hand of his wife. Without a backward look, she was led away towards the exit of the gaming room. Anger burned within Betty. There had to be something she could do. She looked around the room and saw the policemen sitting at the other side of the room. She started out towards them. Just then she saw a small man wearing a pince-nez approach them. He didn't sound very happy.

Betty turned away from the policemen and headed towards Kit who was standing with Mary at Agatha's table.

-

Boucher was the first to see the little examining magistrate approach them. He nudged Briant who glanced up from the document that had transfixed him for the last few minutes. He smiled up at Charpentier. This was always meant to anger Charpentier. To be fair, it did.

'What is the meaning of this?' demanded Charpentier. A wild frenzy of frustration brought on by alcohol, by the behaviour of his wife and by the flagrant disregard for his orders by all and sundry was frying his blood. He shouted at the sitting policeman, 'How dare you ignore my instructions, Saimbron. Saimbron? Aren't you listening to me?'

Saimbron hadn't looked up yet and continued to read the paper on his lap. He held his hand up. This was maddening enough but then Saimbron slowly extended his index finger. Moments later, he wagged it.

Vesuvius erupted.

However, the sound of Charpentier's passionate denunciation of the policeman was drowned out by a roar emanating from the table in the middle of the room.

-

An odd calm descended on Agatha. Her heart which had been racing madly resumed its more genteel rhythm. She fixed Russo a steely stare. The Italian's face was like an erupting geyser. Beads of sweat ran down his face. One hand was tapping the table. His other hand was at the back of his head. He ran a finger around the inside of his collar. Agatha slowly dragged the card from the shoe. She lifted it up and glanced at it. Then she threw it down.

A Queen of spades.

Russo looked at her hopefully. Agatha shook her head. She stood at seventeen now, but Russo could only guess this was the case. He glanced down again at his hidden card for the thirtieth time in the space of the last few seconds. It was a Jack of hearts. He was sitting on twenty. He suspected the dealer knew this and was going for bust.

Russo felt his wife's hand on his shoulder. Across the table, Philippe and Josephine Redon were staring hungrily at the chips on the table. The light of expectation shone from their eyes. But a shadow passed over the Italian's just for a moment. A dark, worrying thought that would simply not go away. Had he been too greedy? The cards were surely against the bank. They were sitting on a few million francs. All this old woman had to do was turn her cards over and admit defeat. He watched Agatha slowly move her hand down towards the shoe. All around the table was silent but there seemed to be a commotion going on behind them. Russo closed his mind to the noise. All he could hear was the sound of his heart beating.

Agatha made a show of rolling the card along the green table as slowly as possible. She glanced at Alastair. Her brother was biting on a panetela cigar holding some matches. He nodded to his sister and raised his eyebrows.

Kit didn't know whether to laugh or faint. The tension was unbearable as was the aching in his hand from Mary's grip. She was feeling it too, but less painfully perhaps than her husband at that moment. Agatha picked the card up and looked at it.

A Jack of diamonds. Her hand was a bust.

The sound of silence was broken by Alastair striking a match loudly. A flame erupted and died on his cigar.

'Sorry,' said Alastair unapologetically.

Agatha threw down a card onto the table.

The card she threw down was a four of hearts. She turned over her other three cards. They added up to twenty-one.

The crowd erupted in a roar. Giuseppe Russo stared at his two cards. They lay like poisoned fish thrown up by the sea. He put his head in his hands. Mme Russo fainted.

Kit had no time to celebrate. Betty grabbed him by the arm. She shouted into his ear.

'Fournier has dragged his wife away. They've left the room.'

Kit's eyes widened. He turned to the exit, but no one was there. Dubois had abandoned his post and strolled over to see what was happening on Agatha's table. Kit turned to where Briant and Saimbron were sitting. Charpentier was standing over them reading the document that Mary had found earlier. However, the commotion had distracted Briant. He saw Kit gesticulating to him. He flew out of his seat, accompanied by Boucher. He was with Kit and Mary within seconds.

'Arrest Russo and Redon,' said Kit. From the corner of his eye, he saw two policemen enter the room.

'I know,' said Briant. 'Where are the Fourniers?'

'They've left. Two minutes ago.'

Briant's reply was lost as suddenly screams erupted from the other side of the *vingt et un* table.

-

Rufus Watts had been riveted by the battle taking place on the table between Agatha and Russo. However, when the game finished, he was quick to observe Redon's reaction. After the initial shock he glanced towards his wife and they both edged backwards out of the scrum at the table. Then their eyes widened in shock. Rufus followed their eyes towards the arriving policemen.

Redon, ignoring his wife, started to move quickly towards the door. The policemen switched direction and went towards Briant. However, *Gardien* Jacques Dubois had seen Redon's intention. Rufus Watts watched him stand in the way of the escaping former soldier. Redon was momentarily shocked by the impertinence of the policeman. But only briefly. Seconds later he withdrew from his cane a thin sword. He held it up to the throat of Dubois.

This struck Rufus as un-sportsmanlike. In a few light steps he was behind Redon. He tapped him on the shoulder. Redon turned around. There was a frown on his forehead as he took in the sight of the little artist. Redon knew he was looking at a man very much like himself. And then Rufus showed Redon his cane. Seconds later Redon was looking at a sword very much like his own. Rufus adopted a fencing pose.

A few of the patrons were now aware of what was happening. Screams came from some of the more faint-hearted onlookers. However, a few the men turned away from the excitement of the green table to what looked like a very well-matched contest between two gay blades.

The blades in question clashed and Rufus knew he was in a fight. His reaction to Redon's threat to Dubois had been instinctive. The reality of the cold steel he was facing woke him to the danger he faced. A martinet he may have been, but Redon was no slouch with a sword. The first few thrusts demonstrated he had balance and speed. Rufus parried them easily, but he needed to do something quickly to avoid being skewered.

He chose to attack.

The sudden leap forward by Rufus coincided with a feeling within Redon that while he could almost certainly defeat the strange little man facing him, the police were suddenly taking an interest in the proceedings.

The thrust by Rufus missed its mark but convinced Redon that it was time to exit stage left. He turned and ran towards the unguarded exit. Moments later he was lying on the ground alongside a very drunk woman.

Claudine Charpentier rubbed her nose and looked at the prone man she'd just banged into.

'Call yourself a gentleman?' hissed Claudine angrily.

32

Harry Miller patrolled the outside of the casino. After the excitement of the previous hour when he and Mary had found the hidden file, the cold night air had begun to act on Miller's satisfaction their find. Once more he was being asked to stay outside while the real business of the evening was transacted inside by his betters. It felt like a metaphor for his position in life. A situation that would once have represented a dream come true was becoming a source of disenchantment. Did it have to be this way? The war had changed everything. Old ways, feudal acceptance of rank had been crushed into the mud of Flanders. The world was changing. Harry Miller was changing, too.

His thoughts were broken by the sight of the Fournier couple emerging from the casino. Miller watched Fournier half drag his wife into the square. They hailed a taxi and, before Miller had collected his senses, a car drew up. Elsa Fournier seemed reluctant to enter but her husband all but bundled her in.

Just then a woman distracted Miller. She had long since passed the point of sobriety and was probably minutes away from insensibility. She staggered up the steps towards the casino just as the taxi set off.

Miller had an idea. He ran towards the woman and said, 'Let me help you.'

The woman looked at Miller through the one eye that was managing to stay open. She nodded her thanks as speech was now almost beyond her. Miller half carried her up the steps and into the casino. Once inside he felt a trifle un-gallant as he abandoned her to her fate.

Meanwhile he sprinted in the direction of the loud cheer. He reached the entrance just in time to see the gaming room in uproar. On one side Rufus Watts was facing Redon with a sword in his hand. Two policemen were approaching Russo who was crying into the green beige table. Miller started forward towards Kit. Just then he felt a hand grab his arm.

-

Agatha had been one of the first to see the Fourniers leave. While the onlookers had reacted to Russo and his mammoth loss, Agatha immediately left her position. She went past Alastair and handed him a playing card. It was the Jack of diamonds that she had originally picked up from the shoe.

Alastair looked at the card and chuckled.

'Well played,' he said, but Agatha was already on the move, heading towards the exit when the screams erupted nearby. She ignored them. Her eyes were fixed on the unguarded exit and the arrival of Harry Miller. Oil covered his face and shirt. This was not a good omen. He hadn't seen her, so she reached out and grabbed his arm.

Miller turned around and was about to shrug the hand off when he saw who it was.

'The Fourniers are escaping,' said Miller. The situation in the gaming room was the strangest he'd seen, and he'd been witness to a fair few strange ones in his time. To his right, Rufus Watts was fencing with Redon. To his left the examining magistrate was screaming at the police, demanding to be heard. Up ahead, two policemen were now in the process of manhandling Giuseppe Russo, who was in tears. His wife was hitting one of the policemen with a clutch bag.

'I know,' replied Agatha. 'Tell Christopher.'

Just then they were aware of Redon turning tail from his bout with Rufus Watts. They watched him run straight into the woman Miller had helped earlier.

'On second thoughts, restrain Redon,' said Agatha looking at the former army officer sprawled on the floor. She left Miller and headed in Kit's direction. He turned around just as she reached him.

'I know,' said Kit, glancing towards Miller who was now sitting on top of Redon. He turned to Briant, 'The Fourniers have escaped.'

As the situation appeared to be under control. Kit, Mary, and Agatha along with Briant and Boucher raced towards the exit. As they moved towards the entrance hall, Mary felt now was the time to drop the bombshell.

'We don't have a car,' said Mary. Kit and Agatha stopped in their tracks and stared back at Mary. 'It broke down.'

Just then Natalie arrived, followed swiftly by her latest admirer, Simon Levy. There was a reason why the Austrian had made a large fortune in share trading. He was exceptionally quick on the uptake. He shot Natalie a glance.

'Are these friends of yours?' asked Levy.

Natalie nodded. Levy turned to Kit and took a car key from his pocket.

'If you need a car, take mine,' said Levy. 'It's the blue Bugatti. It's parked just outside.'

Kit looked from Levy to the key and back again. He nodded a thanks and took the key. Levy, meanwhile, looked hopefully at the young Frenchwoman. Natalie smiled, stood on tiptoe, and pecked him on the cheek.

'While we're waiting for them, perhaps I can buy you a drink now,' suggested Levy.

Natalie looked at the tall, good-looking Austrian and decided it would have been churlish to refuse. Furthermore, it was only good manners that she should allow him to take her hand. Anything else would have seemed ungrateful.

Outside, the blue Bugatti gleamed like a giant sapphire deposited on the street. Kit threw the keys to Agatha. It was not done without the moment of misgiving most men feel when they hand car keys to a woman. This is one of the more remarkable examples of male delusion as they are, in fact, much likelier to cause accidents than the more sensible sex.

Briant and Boucher were already in a police car and driving away. The Bugatti was an updated Type 13 which was an excellent racing machine but had not been built with touring in mind. Kit, Agatha, and Mary found it a tight squeeze. Mary perched on Kit's knee while Agatha occupied the driving seat, which was technically, the only seat.

'I hope you know what you're doing,' said Kit.

'Nonsense, I was driving cars while you were still at school,' replied Agatha huffily.

Mary nodded to Kit in a 'that's-told-you' manner which is always appropriate at any time of the day when a man has been deservedly put in his place. Agatha started the engine and within seconds they were all thrown back as the Bugatti raced off in pursuit of the police car and their quarry.

A quick word about the Bugatti, and that word is 'velocity'. The 1.4 Litre engine was capable of up to one hundred and twenty-five kilometres per hour in the hands of a racing driver. If the Type 13 lacked a little in raw power, it made up for it elsewhere in handling, steering, and braking. Agatha did not quite reach such exalted speeds but, given the additional weight she was carrying with the passengers, the car made a brave effort and came close to the one eighty kilometres per hour as they tore along Avenue de Monte Carlo which led down to the port from the casino.

Walking down by the port to take in the fresh night air was Antony Noghès. He heard the police car first before seeing it race past him along Boulevard de la Condamine. This was followed moments later by the extraordinary sight of the blue Bugatti he'd seen earlier. This time at the wheel was, if he was not mistaken, an old woman. Crowded in beside her were two young people. They speeded past him. The young woman seemed to have a smile on her face as she clung to the black beaded flapper cap.

It was either a tribute to Italian car design or Agatha's driving, but the Bugatti soon gained ground on the police car carrying Briant and Boucher up ahead. Certainly, Kit at no point felt the need to urge his aunt to greater feats of speed. She was doing an exceptional job on her own, thank you very much.

The two cars raced up Avenue de la Porte Neuve which led to the Rock and the likely destination of the Fourniers. As they drove, Kit updated Agatha on the contents of the dossier compiled by Dupin. When he'd finished Agatha let out a sigh of relief.

'I feel a little better,' said Agatha, which is more than could be said for Kit as they took at high speed the sharp corner which led to Place de la Visitation.

'Corners well,' observed Agatha as two of the wheels lifted slightly off the ground.

'Great grip,' added Mary, casting a mischievous glance in Kit's direction.

'Very funny,' replied Kit but even he had to smile. But it was just for a moment. His heart was pounding, and it was not solely because of the high speed they were driving. With one hand gripping his hat and the other holding Mary, Kit knew a showdown was looming. Up ahead the police car had pulled up and so too had the Fourniers.

Agatha brought the car to a halt just inches away from the back of the police car. Briant and Boucher poured out of the back of the car along with one uniformed officer. The next few moments seemed to take an eternity. Kit and Mary were out of the car just in time to see Briant shouting something at Yves Fournier. The big Frenchman had his back to the policemen. He was obviously hustling his wife from the cab because she fell to the ground. Elsa Fournier was white with terror. She rose slowly but she was shouting, 'Please don't.'

'Stop, Fournier,' shouted Briant.

Fournier glanced around. Moments later all could see the gun he was holding. It was pointed at his wife. She screamed in terror.

A shot rang out around Place de la Visitation. A body fell to the ground.

Dead.

33

Although the goodbyes had been said, Agatha, along with Betty, accompanied her brother to the train station. It was the morning after the tragic events of the previous evening. There was no sign yet of the train, so they stood on the platform in a companiable silence. All that needed to be said had been said. And that was just Agatha. To say anything else would have been to reveal too much of the aching emptiness she felt at seeing her brother depart on the train that would ultimately lead to Cherbourg and a liner back home to the United States.

An announcement said that the train would be late.

'Typical,' said Agatha.

They were silent for a few moments. The weight of their collective sadness was unbearable. Agatha felt her chest tighten and breathing became more difficult. Even the usually effervescent Betty was taking her cue from the gloomy atmosphere surrounding them. Finally, the silence became too much. Alastair spoke.

'Don't leave things so long next time.'

Agatha smiled and replied, 'I suppose not.'

No one wanted to admit what was on all their minds. There would be fewer and fewer such partings in the future. They were all at an age where long distance travel would become impossible. Agatha fought back the tears. An announcement said the train would arrive in five minutes.

'They're becoming worse every year,' said Betty.

There was no disagreement from her two companions. They stared into the black tunnel waiting for something to come. It seemed like a portent.

'Do you ever find yourself forgetting things?' asked Agatha, out of the blue.

Alastair giggled and replied, 'All the time. Age, I suppose.'

Betty could say nothing. She glanced at her friend. An acrid sadness swept over her; tears stung her eyes. The thought of Agatha being anything other than indestructible was unimaginable and too painful to bear. She turned away.

The train arrived. Alastair hugged his sister and then Betty. With a shrug and a smile, he climbed up onto the train. Pausing for a moment to say something, no words came. He stepped inside and disappeared into the corridor. He reappeared moments later at a window a little further down the train.

'Is Harry loading his cases?' asked Agatha.

'Yes, I can see him down at the far end. He's on his way back now. Does he know which car to find her?'

'Yes, I told him.'

Miller was fifty yards away on the platform. He climbed up onto the train. Moments later he reappeared and took a wheelchair down and put it on the platform. Having done this, he hopped back onto the train. A minute or two later he reappeared, helping a woman of a similar vintage to Agatha and Betty down from the train onto the platform and into the wheelchair.

'Here they come,' said Betty.

Miller and the woman in the wheelchair approached Agatha and Betty. The woman smiled revealing a row of teeth that resembled a well-maintained piano.

'I say,' said the woman brightly.

Betty bent down and hugged the woman, 'You've missed all the excitement, Sausage.'

Jocelyn 'Sausage' Gossage looked crestfallen, 'I say, I haven't missed another case, have I?'

'I'm afraid so, dear,' replied Agatha.

'Oh, chaps. Couldn't you have waited?'

-

The arrival of Sausage brought a lift to the household following the departure of Alastair. The mood was very much your standard morning-after-the-killing-gambling-highspeed-chase the night before. Her arrival was an opportunity for Kit to obtain an update on an issue close to his heart.

'How's Reggie?'

Sausage rolled her eyes and replied, 'That fat-headed grandson of mine is well on the road to recovery. His cast is off, but he refuses, point blank, to tell me what happened.'

Thank heavens, thought Kit. However, at this point he became aware of several pairs of eyes trained on him. Even Sam had woken up from his slumber at this point.

'Well, you know how it is, ladies,' said Kit, spreading his arms and attempting what he hoped was a disarming grin. In fact, this effort appeared only to add a hard glint to the stares coming back at him. Sam sat up in his basket. This was interesting. His ears pricked up.

An explanation was expected. If the determination on the faces of the ladies arrayed in front of Kit was any guide, an explanation would be forthcoming.

-

Six weeks earlier:

'...ger,' screamed Reggie falling backwards. His descent to the jagged rocks below was arrested by the foot which had fortuitously lodged itself under a rock. On the plus side, Reggie realised, this had almost certainly saved him from being dashed against the rocks. However, the spearing pain and the loud cracking sound suggested that it had not been without cost.

Reggie screamed in agony.

'I say,' said Spunky, 'Reggie sounds a bit off.'

Chubby leaned over the side of the cliff once more.

'What on earth are you doing, old boy? Stop messing around.'

Reggie somehow regained his balance on the narrow ledge. His concerns about hypothermia, drowning and being attacked by giant incontinent birds had diminished in the face of the excruciating pain he was feeling in his ankle. It was enough to make a chap cry. And Reggie was just that chap.

'Hurry up,' sobbed Reggie to his friends up above.

'Hold on,' suggested Spunky, which was a stout, if rather obvious, piece of advice.

The rain, which had been threatening for a while, began to fall in sheets now. The situation was moving from highly dangerous to the ultimate level of challenge any Englishman can face. It was becoming a bloody nuisance.

-

'What happened then?' asked Sausage. Her hands were gripping the arms of her wheelchair as if she, too, was hanging for dear life on the edge of a precipice just like her grandson.

'Oh, we just tied our coats together and pulled him up,' said Kit, rather airily.

'What?' exclaimed Mary. 'Is that it?'

Kit frowned and shrugged his shoulders.

'What did you expect?'

'Did no one climb down to rescue him heroically?' asked Mary in a voice that betrayed her disappointment at the rather prosaic conclusion.

'It was a bit wet,' pointed out Kit defensively.

'So are you,' replied Mary, stiffly. Then she broke into a grin and shook her head. 'Men'

'Don't start me,' replied Agatha.

'Children the lot of you,' admonished Betty, effectively closing the topic for now.

-

The special guests that evening for dinner were Captain Briant, Inspector Saimbron and Lieutenant Boucher. Much to the chagrin of Sausage, Kit and Agatha held back from revealing too much of their new case until the policemen arrived. The finer details of what had transpired the previous evening would be handled by the man from the Sûreté.

The three policemen were surprised that Alastair had left so suddenly as, technically, he was a witness but there was an acceptance that the evidence Dupin had accumulated was impressive and comprehensive enough to send at least four of the Bluebeard Club to prison or an appointment with a Madame Guillotine.

'I must confess, Inspector,' said Kit, who paused for a moment as he realised that this was not the best way to start a conversation with a policeman, 'I would like to have met this chap Dupin. This was exceptional detective work.'

Saimbron shook his head sadly.

'He was good. Too good, perhaps. And he knew it. The police force was never enough for him. He wanted more.'

The inspector rubbed his fingers together to indicate what motivated his former colleague.

'I see,' said Kit. He recognised the sadness felt by Saimbron for a man that would probably have been his friend once upon a time. 'So, what of our Bluebeard Club now?'

'Thanks to your Monsieur Miller we have Redon and who can forget the heroic actions of Monsieur Watts,' said Briant.

Rufus Watts gave a brief nod to the captain. Anything else would have been vulgar. He wanted it to seem like it was all in a day's work for him. Of course, the more modest the reaction, the greater will be the acclaim forthcoming. Everyone around the table took a moment to congratulate Rufus on his astonishing bravery in taking on a former soldier. The extent of this folly was something Rufus hardly needed reminding of, so he waved away the praise.

'You should not be so modest,' said Briant. 'Redon was a dangerous man for all his pomposity. Not just a dangerous man. A cruel one too. The dossier from Dupin makes clear that he was thrown out of the army for blackmailing a fellow officer. The young officer in question chose to commit suicide. I think we can all guess the nature of the hold that Redon had over him. Dupin managed to obtain evidence of the transfer of money to Redon from this poor officer. I can imagine Dupin was not above using illegal methods to obtain such evidence. The transfer of money, the suicide of the young man and communications by Redon to the young man will be enough to have him tried as a blackmailer.'

Briant looked at Kit as he said this. Kit raised his glass in a mock toast to illicit acquisition of evidence.

'Of course, the army tried to cover this up,' suggested Kit.

'They did. Shameful,' agreed Briant.

'Even if I cannot officially condone how Dupin obtained this evidence, nor indeed the actions of Lady Mary and Mr Miller, there is no question they have ensured that justice will be served. Speaking of which, Lady Mary, where exactly did you find the dossier?'

'Well, I have my husband partly to thank for suggesting where I should be looking. Initially we were having a tough time of it, but then I recalled an argument between the Fourniers. The dossier was hidden behind a painting, wedged into the back of the canvas. It had been taken down and placed between the wall and the sideboard. Quite ingenious.'

'Well done,' said Kit proudly. 'No doubt the intention was to use it to blackmail the other members of the Bluebeard Club. There's certainly no honour among thieves. Now perhaps we can hear more about this rather ghastly collection of individuals. Perhaps we can start with Russo, or should I say, Ravenelli?'

Briant took this as his cue to takeover.

'The police in the United States will be very interested in Russo. He was known, as you say, as Ravenelli over there. Thanks to the dossier we were able to discover that there is a warrant for his arrest in New York for the murder of his first wife. Aside from this there is also a charge of conspiracy to defraud his insurance company both here and in the United States.'

'Yes, I saw that Yves Fournier, or Foucault as I believe he was also called, and Russo had an interesting relationship. I wonder how they met?' asked Kit.

'Dupin assumes, correctly I think, that Russo investigated the unusually large insurance policy that Foucault claimed upon the death of his first wife. This was a man after his own heart. He showed him how he could repeat the trick by changing his name to someone, probably a child, that had been orphaned and then died while still quite young. We've seen this before,' said Saimbron. 'I'm sure when we investigate further, we'll find out that the real Giuseppe Russo and Yves Foucault died many years ago.'

Briant took over from Saimbron at this point as the detective took a generous mouthful of the excellent wine that Agatha had served.

'I think there can be no doubt that Fournier had always intended murdering Elsa Fournier as he had his first wife. How many others would have followed had Blanc, through the efforts of Dupin, not stumbled across him?'

'How did Blanc find out about these people and start blackmailing them in to working for him?' asked Mary.

'We can never be certain,' replied Saimbron, dabbing his mouth delicately and taking over like a relay runner from Briant who now picked up his glass of wine. 'My guess is that Russo came up with the plan to take on the casino at the *vingt et un* table. As a mathematician, Russo would have been just the person to devise a system to beat the house. Why, we can only venture to guess at this moment, but I would imagine it was easier than marriage.'

Kit burst out laughing at Saimbron's rather droll comment. He quickly regretted this as both Mary and Agatha gave a look that suggested a trip to the doghouse would be on his travel itinerary imminently. Briant caught Kit's eye and he smiled the smile of an old hand at the marriage game. That smile read: you'll learn…

Saimbron was modestly pleased with his comment but decided to press on lest he get wounded by friendly fire.

'We shall certainly find out more in the coming weeks. My hypothesis is that they both realised too late that the women they had married were not as rich as they'd first hoped. After their first success at the casino the previous summer, Blanc set Dupin on them to investigate. When he saw what my old colleague came back with, it is probable that Blanc decided to use Fournier and Russo for his own ends. Blackmail was out of the question as neither were rich enough, despite appearances. Instead, he decided to make use of Russo's plan only he would be the one to profit, not them.'

'How did Redon become involved?'

'Blanc had Dupin create a dossier on everyone of note who came to visit the casino. I believe Captain Briant mentioned this to you,' replied Saimbron. 'Blanc was a very visible and welcoming host. Everyone knew him and he knew everyone. In fact, the dossier he kept suggests that his true purpose was to find out as much about the casino patrons as possible with a view to blackmailing them.

Interestingly, none of the Bluebeard Club was included in the dossier which suggests that they were the ones he had selected to blackmail. But you can imagine the scale of the opportunity in such a place where fortunes were lost more often than won. He could pay Dupin from the profits of the casino to investigate bad debts, yet his true purpose was much more malign. I can only speculate but Redon and his wife were probably useful additions to the team he had built for draining the casino from time to time.'

Kit nodded at this and added, 'Truly a nest of vipers. But I saw nothing about Mme Redon.'

Briant glanced at Boucher who reddened slightly.

'I think that Mme Redon is guilty of nothing more than having a very modern and enthusiastic approach to *amour*. As you may have gathered, it was a marriage in name only.'

'But Redon was not a Bluebeard?' asked Mary.

'Dupin was searching for evidence of this. But clearly, he had not been able to find any. Redon's first wife died a long time ago. The circumstances were not investigated. I think we should keep an open mind on this, however,' said Briant.

Agatha had been unusually quiet throughout all this. Despite her extraordinary stamina, the events of the previous evening and the departure of Alastair had taken their toll which even the arrival of her old friend could not offset. Her fingers drummed on the table, and she seemed particularly interested in the swimming pool. She stared at the seat where Alastair often sat and smoked his panatela cigars.

Although she had not admitted as much, her relief at hearing of Russo's guilt was an enormous weight from her mind. The moment when she had palmed the card to deprive Russo of the win had played on her conscience. The trick had been taught to her by a gleeful Alastair the night before. Her brother was always going to feel no remorse about putting one over his former friends. But then again, he wasn't the one who had cheated. For Agatha the dilemma had been as great as any she could remember.

When Briant had finished discussing Redon, Agatha appeared to awake from her reverie. In moments such as this, there is a sense that something needs to be raised, to be spoken out loud so that all could join in the collective absolution needed following the death of the previous evening. It was to Agatha that this moment fell. She spoke the question that was uppermost on all their minds. As she did this, her eyes flicked towards Boucher who, like Agatha, had been silent throughout.

'We haven't spoken of Elsa Fournier yet.'

Epilogue

Two weeks later:

Versailles Men's Prison: late April 1921

Henri Landru stopped in the doorway and looked around the room he'd been moved to. It was very different from his cell. Bright light flooded through the thick glass. Grey paint was peeling off the walls; the temperature was too hot even for the rats. This was strange though. Why had they moved him? The trial was still ongoing so it couldn't be a sudden trip to meet his executioner. That would happen of course. He could see it in their eyes. The blood lust they accused him of having was in their eyes too. Hypocrites!

He waited.

This was deliberate. Sweat gushed like a waterfall from his face and body. He could barely breathe in the hot, stultifying atmosphere. He waited some more. At least half an hour. Every moment sizzling in the fiery furnace-like heat of the cell increased his hatred for his captors. His hair was matted on his head as if he'd just taken a shower. The back of his shirt was wet all the way round to his armpits. Afterwards, they would throw him into a cold cell buried somewhere in the bowels of the building to join his rodent cellmates in catching a chill.

He stared down at the heavy iron handcuffs and the chain that led down to his manacled legs. They weren't taking any chances, were they? Even to move his feet hurt as the iron manacles cut into his shins and the tops of his feet. The sweat ran like tears down his face now.

Just then he heard activity outside the cell door. More clanking like a ghost in a haunted house. The door opened and a ghost from his past appeared. It took a few moments for Landru to understand what was happening. His stomach lurched in sadness at seeing his old friend.

'Pipsqueak'

'Henri.'

Landru looked at the handcuffs and the manacles around the feet of the new arrival.

'You, too, Pipsqueak,' said Landru. There was genuine sadness in his tone, and he watched Pipsqueak move forward slowly and sit down facing Landru across the table. The cell door closed behind them.

'What happened?' asked Landru.

What was there to say to this? Pipsqueak glanced towards an air vent. Landru turned and looked down towards the air vent and understood. They were not alone. The air vent led to another room next door. In the room sat two men: Captain Briant and Lieutenant Boucher. They were listening to every word.

Briant listened for a few seconds and then shook his head.

'Landru knows we're listening,' he whispered.

Landru did know they were listening. He smiled at his friend and shrugged. Pipsqueak was thinking of the events two weeks ago.

-

The cab drew up to Place de la Visitation. Nothing had been said during the journey. Elsa Fournier sank into the seat opposite her husband. She could barely look at him. The angry silence filled the interior of the cab. But from her position in the cab, she could see through the window behind her husband's head. She saw the police car arrive swiftly followed by a blue car. Her luck was in. She sat up in her seat as if pulled by an invisible hand

'What are you going to do?' demanded Mme Fournier tearfully. 'More humiliation, Yves?'

Anger surged through Fournier. At that moment he doubted he hated anyone as much as the woman before him. She had promised so much and given him nothing but weakness. What money she had she'd kept hidden. It was as if she'd read his motives from the start.

He would never do this again. The risk was too great. The debilitating daily strain of marriage to someone you despised was like living in a prison. But what was the alternative? Russo's plan to win pots of money from a casino seemed no less risky but at least it was over in an evening.

'I don't want to hear a word from you,' snarled Fournier. 'How much have you cost us this evening?'

Elsa Fournier shrank before the sheer intensity of the revulsion in her husband's eyes. She threw open the doors of the cab and launched herself out. She fell to the ground. Fournier looked at her in disgust. She couldn't even descend from a cab without humiliating herself. She was shouting as he got out.

'Please don't'

Fournier glared at her in confusion. She was rising now. Her hand was inside her clutch bag. She threw something towards him. Fournier caught it.

It was a gun.

'No, please don't,' screamed Elsa Fournier.

Fournier heard a shout from behind. He half turned to see some men. They were familiar. His wife screamed.

-

Henri Landru took Pipsqueak's hand and squeezed. He could see the faraway look in her eyes. His little Pipsqueak had grown up. So beautiful. So dangerous. Should he have married her? Perhaps things would have been so different.

But she was more like a sister to him. It would have been inconceivable. Marriage changes things. He couldn't have accepted the idea of the two of them ever arguing over children, over money, over every little pointless thing that married couples' bicker about. Not Pipsqueak.

'How many?' asked Landru.

Elsa Fournier held up three fingers.

Landru raise his eyebrows and smiled. He looked at her more sternly, like a parent pretending to scold a child they are secretly proud of. The look had enough scepticism in it to make Elsa Fournier smile. She shrugged and held up another two fingers.

'Six,' mouthed Landru. Not bad all things considered. It was easier for men, of course. 'How did they find out?'

Elsa Fournier thought of the dossier. She should have destroyed it. Oh, what a fool she'd been. Greed had overcome her. The chance to stop making risky marriages. Blackmail was so much easier than murder. Dupin and Blanc had taught her that.

Yet here she was. Facing her old friend. Facing the Bluebeard who had inspired her. In those long conversations where they discussed everything.

Everything.

And now all was lost. Tears formed in her eyes. For once they were genuine. She looked at her old friend. The boy she had loved like a brother. His eyes spoke of the sadness he felt.

'How could you let yourself be caught?' he whispered.

Indeed. How? Was it agreeing to be part of Russo's ridiculous plan to win money from the casino? Perhaps. It exposed her to the devil incarnate, Blanc. And the devious Dupin. A part of her regretted Dupin's murder. There was much to admire in someone like him. Certainly, more than the big oaf she'd married. Dupin never trusted her, never believed her act. He *knew* just like he knew the minute he opened the door to her. It was in his eyes. He made no appeal. No, he turned his back, walked back inside, and sat down. He'd picked up the photograph and held it to his breast. The two young soldiers. Then he'd looked at her in the eye. He wasn't just daring her to pull the trigger. He wanted her to. Yes, it was in his eyes.

He'd died a long time ago.

Blanc was an idiot. Pretending to fall in love with him, making him feel like he was the one had been easy. Poisoning him was even easier while her fool of husband waited in the cab not knowing what his 'weak' wife had done to protect him, protect them all, not just the Bluebeard Club. Poisoning him had been a mercy killing for everyone who had come into contact with that vile man.

Rat poison for the biggest rat of all.

The cell door opened. Lieutenant Boucher appeared, framed in the doorway. Landru and Pipsqueak looked at one another for what they knew would be the last time. A tear ran down her pale cheek and she clutched his hand. Then she felt Boucher's hand on her shoulder. It was a gentle reminder that she had to go. A lifetime spent pretending to be submissive had trained her to react instinctively. She stood up and walked out of the cell with only a brief backward glance.

She passed Briant and continued along the corridor. Briant watched her walk away. He nodded to the policeman standing guard. The cell door closed leaving Landru to sour in the heat.

But Landru didn't care. The moisture on his face was no longer just sweat. He cried for his friend. He cried for what they would both face. The cards of fate had been dealt.

The bank always wins in the end.

-

Four weeks later:

London: Early June 1921

Kit and Mary Aston strolled along the street oblivious to the rain as only lovers can be. Around them London glistened and shimmered. A dazzling array of small suns reflected on the puddles on the pavement. Cars splashed along the road. Pedestrians skipped away from as whiskers of water were thrown up by the traffic. Rainwater overflowed from a gutter overhead forcing Kit and Mary to take a sudden diversion to avoid a soaking.

They were outside a Moving Picture House. Posters proclaimed the latest film to be shown. Mary took no notice. She was so happy and too in love to notice anything other than the man she was with.

Men, of course, over hundreds of thousands of years of hunting mammoth and the like have evolved to take more in from their surroundings, even when they are as blindly in love as Kit Aston.

'Oh, look, Mary,' said Kit. 'The poster has Alfred's name on it.'

'Alfred?'

'Alfred. You know, Aunt Agatha's Alfred who went into moving pictures.'

'Oh, that Alfred,' asked Mary in the tone of voice women reserve for a subject that is of no interest and the male needs to move on quickly.

'Yes, it's called *Dangerous Lies*.'

The name of the film woke Mary with a start.

'Let's go, darling, I think the rain has lessened.'

It was coming down in sheets. Kit glanced toward Mary. A slight frown on his face. This, accepted Mary, was a problem when you are married to an amateur detective. They suspect motive in *everything*. Not without reason in this case. Mary tugged Kit's arm. He wasn't moving. Instead, he'd turned to study the publicity photographs beside the rather lurid poster that had attracted his attention originally. In this case, the highly tuned antennae originally developed for the detection of sabre-tooth tigers had spotted an attractive female in the poster.

"Always the Haunting Fear" read the tag line to the film. But Kit had moved on and his attention was engrossed by the stills.

'I say, Mary, this actress Mary Glynn looks awfully like you. Come and look. In fact, the older lady bears a very good likeness to Aunt Agatha.'

Mary's mouth went dry, and she gave a cursory glance at the pictures before turning away and saying, 'Nonsense.'

'Fear that the man she loved and had married would learn the truth she had deliberately evaded,' read Kit from the poster. Kit glanced from Mary and back to the publicity still.

'Let's go, darling,' said Mary more slowly, curling her hand up behind his head. An unspoken promise in her eyes.

It was tempting.

But she was hiding something.

'I think we should go in and watch the film. It'll be starting any minute.'

'Let's not, Kit,' said Mary. There was more than a hint of appeal in her voice.

'No, let's,' laughed Kit, taking her hand, and pulling her gently towards the box office.

Mary was laughing, 'Kit, honestly, it looks dreadful.'

'Right now, darling, it looks fascinating,' replied Kit, giving her a tug. Mary had to jog a little to keep in step with Kit. She began to giggle.

'There's something I forgot to mention, darling,' said Mary.

'Apparently,' laughed Kit.

-

Four weeks later:

A cemetery in Agadir, Morocco: 1st July 1921

'I say, it's rather hot, isn't it?' said Sausage Gossage.

Betty stared down at her friend unsympathetically and pointed out, 'You should try pushing the wheelchair.' A wave of guilt immediately engulfed her. Sausage laughed however which made her feel better. She hated to be unkind, but it was rather hot, and she was becoming fatigued by the effort. Agatha was walking a few steps ahead of them.

'It's somewhere around here,' said Agatha pointing her umbrella in the direction of the sea. Between the umbrella and the sea lay several hundred, if not thousand, graves. 'I don't remember having such trouble last time.'

They marched on and then Agatha spotted a landmark that she recognised. She waved her hand like a general at a battle and her 'men' followed her forward. They reached a white marble stone. It was small and simple, in stark contrast to the extraordinary constructions all around.

The top of the headstone read: 'I'm sleeping. Please be quiet.'

Beneath it read: 'Lord Eustace Leonard Frost – Born 23rd April 1844 – Died 1st July 1911'.

Agatha stared at the headstone barely able to breathe. A part of her life had ended on that dreadful day ten years previously when the German gunboat had entered the port at Agadir, witnessed by Eustace. His last words were, 'There's going to be a war.'

It had taken three years, but his prophesy had come terrifyingly true. The war had almost claimed the life of her favourite nephew. It had claimed the life of Betty's only son. Agatha stared at the headstone through her tears and willed Eustace to appear one last time to her. She'd still have told him off, but he would have laughed and shrugged as he always did.

The trip to Agadir had taken almost twenty hours by boat. They stayed at the grave less than twenty minutes. The heat was just too much for all of them.

'We should return to the car,' said Agatha at last.

They turned and began to walk away slowly. Two cars appeared fifty yards away. One of the cars was a police car. The cars stopped and several men appeared. Two of the men were in uniform. One older man lit a cigarette. A younger man stood near him. He was tall and erect, wearing a straw panama.

'I say,' said Sausage.

'I wonder what's going on,' asked Betty. The men seemed to be looking and pointing in their direction.

'The young man looks familiar,' said Sausage. 'Where have I seen him before?'

But Agatha's attention was not on the young man. It was on the older man. He was without a hat. His bald head shone in the sunlight. His bushy handlebar moustache crossed his face like weeds in a garden. He sat on the bonnet of his car like a hunter waiting for his prey.

'That's Inspector Berrada,' said Agatha as they drew closer. Betty gasped as she, too, recognised the old man sitting on the car smoking.

'Who's he?' asked Sausage.

'My nemesis,' replied Agatha.

The young man turned away and climbed into the second car before Agatha could see his face. But her attention was always taken by the smile on Berrada's face and the malevolent triumph in his eyes.

'What does he want?' asked Sausage.

'I think he wants to arrest me,' replied Agatha, quickly. 'Perhaps we should go.'

Betty was already on the move.

'I say, chaps,' asked Sausage in that familiar plaintive voice. 'Do tell me what's going on.'

One hand on her hat, and the other on her umbrella, Agatha led the way back to the waiting car. The sight of the ladies rushing his direction had emboldened the driver, Ahmed, to step out of the car and come towards them. Without a word he took over from Betty helped Sausage into the back. Shouts in the distance suggested that Inspector Berrada and the other policemen were somewhat dismayed by the turn of events.

'What is happening your ladyship? asked Ahmed.

'No time,' gasped Agatha. 'Drive.'

In a matter of seconds, Agatha and Betty had joined Sausage in the back. Ahmed rushed around to the driver's seat. Agatha turned and looked through the back window at Berrada. The detective had stopped, turned, and was running back to his car.

'He'll have a stroke if he's not careful,' said Agatha unkindly.

'But why is he after you?' exclaimed Sausage. Their car was now moving and quickly towards the gates of the cemetery.

'For some reason he thinks I killed Gabrielle Fish. Complete nonsense of course. Anyway, this is a bit of a problem. Ahmed, you'll need to take us somewhere safe.'

'Of course, your ladyship,' grinned the old driver.

'And we'll need to send a telegram as soon as possible.'

Agatha turned to Betty and Sausage. She nodded to them that everything would be all right. Whether she was feeling this particularly herself was not for discussion. She sat back in her seat and took in a few deep breaths.

'Who must I send the telegram to?' asked Ahmed.

'Kit and Mary Aston. They live in Grosvenor Square in London. I need their help.'

The End

Research Notes

This is a work of fiction. However, it references real-life individuals. Gore Vidal, in his introduction to Lincoln, writes that placing history in fiction or fiction in history has been unfashionable since Tolstoy and that the result can be accused of being neither. He defends the practice, pointing out that writers from Aeschylus to Shakespeare to Tolstoy have done so with not inconsiderable success and merit.

I have mentioned a number of key real-life individuals and events in this novel. My intention, in the following section, is to explain a little more about their connection to this period and this story.

For further reading on this period and the specific topics within this work of fiction I would recommend the following: The Riviera Set – Mary S. Lovell, Bringing Down the House – Ben Mezrich. As a long-time fan of Charlie Chaplin, I can recommend without hesitation one of his greatest Films – Monsieur Verdoux. The subject was suggested to him by Orson Welles who had taken an interest in the case of the famous French Bluebeard, Henri Landru.

Henri Landru (1869 - 1922)

Henri Désiré Landru was a French serial killer who is believed to have murdered at least ten women and perhaps one young man in 1915 – 19. The true number of his victims may never be known and is almost certainly higher.

He was nicknamed 'Bluebeard' after the folktale adapted by Charles Perrault.

After his capture he continued to maintain his innocence. The prosecution claimed that Landru met his victims through personal advertisements in the newspapers. The evidence has often been questioned but the result was a verdict of guilty and he was executed in 1922.

One final note: Police stated that around 283 women were contacted by or contacted Landru, but in the archives they admit there were 72 still missing.

Prince Albert I(1848 – 1922)

Prince Albert was the ruling Prince of Monaco between 1889 and his death in 1922. A fascinating man, he devoted much of his life to exploration and had a deep interest in oceanography and science. Alongside his expeditions, Albert I made substantive political, economic, and social reforms and bestowed a constitution on the principality in 1911.

Alfred Hitchcock (1899 - 1980)

Alfred Hitchcock was born and educated in London. After studying art at the University of London he took on/he did various jobs. In 1920, Hitchcock entered the film industry with a full-time position at the Famous Players-Lasky Company designing title cards for silent films. Within a few years, he was working as an assistant director. There is no evidence that he directed any part of '*Dangerous Lies*' of course. He did begin to direct his own films from the mid-twenties and had notable success from the thirties with films such as *The Man Who Knew Too Much* (1934) and *39 Steps* (1939). He went to Hollywood in 1939. One of his most popular films was about a retired cat Burglar, John "The Cat" Robie, starring Cary Grant with Grace Kelly, one of her last films before her marriage to Prince Rainer.

Dangerous Lies (1921)

This film is now lost. As indicated in the book, it was directed by Paul Powell hot from his success with Pollyanna featuring Mary Pickford. It was released in September 1921, so I have employed a degree of artistic license in bringing this forward.

Mary O'Connor (1872 – 1959)

Mary O'Connor came into films via journalism. A period spent in Hollywood writing scripts was followed by a stint on London working on 'Dangerous Lies' and 'The Mystery Road'. She retired from films soon after this to concentrate on fiction.

Antony Noghès (1890 – 1978)

The world-famous Monaco Grand Prix was the brainchild of Antony Noghès. I am not sure if the idea was borne from witnessing a high-speed chase through the streets of Monaco but allow me this whimsy!

About the Author

Jack Murray lives just outside London with his family. Born in Ireland he has spent most of his adult life in the England. His first novel, 'The Affair of the Christmas Card Killer' has been a global success. Four further Kit Aston novels have followed: 'The Chess Board Murders', 'The French Diplomat Affair', 'The Phantom', 'The Frisco Falcon' and 'The Medium Murders'. The Bluebeard Club is the sixth in the Kit Aston series.

Jack has also published a couple of novels in a spin off series featuring a young Agatha Aston. More recently, Jack has started a new series featuring the grandson of Chief Inspector Jellicoe. The DI Nick Jellicoe series is set in 1959.

In 2022, a new series will commence set in the period leading up to and during World War II. This series will be published by Lume Books and will include some of the minor characters from the Kit Aston series.

Acknowledgements

It is not possible to write a book on your own. There are contributions from so many people either directly or indirectly over many years. Listing them all would be an impossible task.

Special mention therefore should be made to my wife and family who have been patient and put up with my occasional grumpiness when working on this project.

My brother, Edward, helped in proofing and made supportive comments that helped me tremendously. I have been very lucky to receive badly needed editing from Kathy Lance who has helped tighten up some of the grammatical issues that, frankly, plagued my earlier books. A word of thanks to Charles Gray and Brian Rice who have provided legal and accounting support. A word also for one of my usual readers – TBJ. Get well soon!

My late father and mother both loved books. They encouraged a love of reading in me. In particular, they liked detective books, so I must tip my hat to the two greatest writers of this genre, Sir Arthur and Dame Agatha.

Following writing, comes the business of marketing. My thanks to Mark Hodgson and Sophia Kyriacou for their advice on this important area. Additionally, a shout out to the wonderful folk on 20Booksto50k.

Finally, my thanks to the teachers who taught and nurtured a love of writing.

A TIME TO KILL – NICK JELLICOE BOOK ONE - TASTER

9th January 1959

'Not exactly Agatha Christie, is it?'

Detective Inspector Nick Jellicoe swung around to the person speaking. His gaze fell on a rotund male somewhere between fifty and sixty. The man in question had a ruddy face and a beaming smile which seemed somewhat at odds with the grisly scene before them. The look on Jellicoe's face quickly wiped the smile from the other man's face.

'Sir?' said Jellicoe, one eyebrow cocked like a duellist's pistol.

The man shrugged, 'Dead body, in a library. Bloody candlestick.'

Jellicoe knew exactly what his boss had meant.

'You're thinking of that game, sir,' pointed out Jellicoe, coldly.

'Ah yes. Good point, Jellicoe.'

They both turned their attention to the dead body. It was lying face down on the floor, with arms splayed out as if he'd completed an inelegant belly flop in a pool. There was a candlestick by the dead body.

The head was a bloody mess. Jellicoe forced himself to take in the sight of the horrific injury that had been inflicted, almost certainly, by the heavy gilt candlestick. The murder weapon was at least two feet long with a wide, square base that had, at some point in the last six hours or so, met with the skull of the dead man. A single, fatal blow.

Just a single blow. It was not a mad frenzied attack. It felt pre-meditated. Jellicoe logged this away before switching his attention away from the candlestick. He crouched down to get a better look. The body was near the French window, facing away. Jellicoe studied the floor between the man and the window. There was no sign of any footsteps. No such luck that the murderer had stepped in the blood and left convenient footprints. A sixth sense told Jellicoe that Chief Inspector Burnett was more interested in what he was doing than the crime scene itself. He sighed.

'Thoughts?' asked Burnett.

Jellicoe rose up and looked out of the French window.

'Murderer came in through the window and either surprised Colonel Masterson or, at least, was known to him. It could have been spur of the moment, but this feels planned. He knew what he wanted to do. The choice of weapon was, perhaps, the only aspect of this that feels spontaneous. Obviously, we need to know if anything was stolen but everything looks to be in order.'

The two men looked around the library. It was tidier than a spinster's cottage.

Jellicoe continued a moment later, 'He struck the colonel once and left him to die.'

'You don't think he died instantly?' asked Burnett.

'There's a lot of blood.'

There was certainly a lot of blood, like someone had decided to douse a fire on the Persian carpet with red paint.

'What a way to go,' said Burnett. There was sadness in his voice. 'Survives two world wars. Gets beaned in a library by a coward sneaking up behind.'

'Yes, sir,' agreed Jellicoe. He stood back from the dead body to allow a photographer to capture the scene. Someone opened the French window and a blast of icy air rushed in. Burnett glanced up irritably at the new arrival. Jellicoe pulled his Burberry raincoat around him more tightly. The weather had taken a turn for the worse over the hour they'd been at the manor. The snow was falling thick and fast. If this kept up it would become more like an Agatha Christie after all.

The new arrival was younger than Jellicoe by half a dozen years. Detective Sergeant Yates saw the face on Burnett and quickly surmised his arrival had brought with it an ill wind. He quickly shut the window. Jellicoe smiled at this. At least he'd had the wit to realise why Burnett was so irritated. Although this was close to a permanent state.

It was Jellicoe's first week with this police force. The relative tranquillity of the first week had been brutally interrupted by the slaying of Masterson. Perhaps his transfer to 'the sticks' was not going to prove the break it was meant to be.

'Sorry, sir,' said Yates, aware he had incurred the displeasure of the chief inspector. He didn't seem too perturbed though. Jellicoe could see there was cockiness to the young man that might not sit well with an older man like Burnett. He waited to see how Burnett would react.

He didn't. This wasn't entirely a surprise. Although only his first week, it was apparent to him that Burnett was not a martinet. Jellicoe had encountered enough of them at the Met to know what they looked like. Instead, Burnett preferred sarcasm over censure and derision to dressing-downs. Jellicoe, oddly, quite liked him for it.

'Don't worry, son,' said Burnett nodding towards the open window, 'You can carry my coffin at the funeral when I die of hypothermia.'

'Will do, sir.'

'So?' asked Burnett, a hint of impatience was never very far away from his voice. Jellicoe suspected this was put on. A bit of show for the young whippersnappers. Keeps 'em honest, don't you know.

'No sign of forced entry. No footprints in the snow.'

Jellicoe looked out of the window. The wind was blowing snowflakes this way and that. This was a problem. The weather was busily erasing any trace of the murderer's arrival. This was assuming, of course, that he had come through the

French windows. Jellicoe had not reached a conclusion on that point yet. Outside, in the distant field, a woman was walking a dog. She wore a headscarf and a dark tweed overcoat. She could have been sixteen or sixty. In this part of the world, dress codes were functional. The opposite was increasingly the case in London. Your dress was your tribe.

A man with grey whiskers appeared in the library, distracting Jellicoe from his reflections on fashion. Jellicoe assumed this was Dr Taylor. Old doctors always had whiskers, or so he'd been told once. The doctor was one of the few people he hadn't met in his first week. A murder scene seemed as good a place as any for introductions to be made.

'Hilary,' said Burnett warmly.

Hilary? Jellicoe suppressed a smile. Why do parents do that? Did they hate their child so much that they would impose a name on him that was guaranteed to draw attention? May as well stick a target on his back and print 'bully me' on it. Taylor looked suitably serious.

The doctor shuffled into the library smoking a pipe. He wore a grey homburg which he removed and threw onto a nearby table. He and Burnett could have been brothers. They'd worked alongside one another for decades. Both were of a similar vintage which seemed an appropriate metaphor as Jellicoe suspected a friendship based on alcohol and mutual support against the true enemy, not criminals, but their wives.

'Without rupturing your imagination too much, what do we have here Reg?' asked Dr Taylor, crouching down to study the dead body.

Reg? It all seemed very bowls club to Jellicoe. He could just imagine what his former boss, Detective Superintendent Lane, would have thought of all this. He still remembered the curl of his mouth when he told Jellicoe that a spell away from London would do him good. Help him forget.

Now *there* was a martinet.

'Body was discovered this morning by the maid. I don't think it's suicide.'

Taylor glanced up at Burnett, a ghost of a smile on his face. There was obviously a history of gallows humour here, realised Jellicoe. Once more, Jellicoe found this strangely reassuring. No disrespect was intended. It was a way of dealing with the often-sickening reality, an unimaginable horror that most people never had to face. If the price of this protection was the occasional catharsis granted by humour, then so be it.

'No, I suspect death was as a result of this implement,' commented Taylor nodding towards the candlestick. 'We'll do the needful though and confirm this. Don't ask me time of death until you tell me if the French windows were open or not.'

'They were closed when the maid found the body,' said Yates, a little too keenly.

Burnett looked a little relieved at hearing this, which amused Jellicoe. He'd clearly forgotten to ask. Or perhaps he was at a point in his career where he managed cases rather than taking an overtly investigative role.

'If the window was closed then it will have slowed down the process of rigor mortis so we should have a better understanding of when he died. My estimate would be in the last eight hours to twelve hours.'

It was nearly nine in the morning now so the intruder or gang would have come after the staff had gone to bed.

'What time do the staff usually retire?' asked Jellicoe to Yates.

'Around ten or eleven,' came the immediate reply, 'but the colonel would often stay up later. He was listening to the third test in Sydney.'

'How did it finish?' asked Burnett, suddenly animated.

'Two hundred and nineteen all out,' said Taylor sourly. Burnett didn't need to ask if it was Australia or England who'd been batting. 'Benaud took five. Then we dropped McDonald first over.'

Burnett shook his head and muttered an oath under his breath. For the first time since seeing the dead body, Burnett seemed genuinely put out. Such was the importance of cricket.

Jellicoe wondered for a moment if Gilbert and Sullivan had been alive now how they would have written about the life-and-death importance of cricket for Englishmen. As if aware their conversation might be considered somewhat inappropriate by the newcomer, Burnett and Taylor resumed a more professional mien.

'When can you have the body with me?' asked Taylor.

Burnett glanced around. The photographer had just left. He looked at Jellicoe who nodded. Burnett turned to Yates.

'I'll see to it, sir,' said Yates, anticipating the order about to come his direction.

'I'm sure you will,' replied Burnett giving the impression that he was displeased with Yates' efficiency. Yates ignored him; no doubt inured to the chief inspector's permanent state of curmudgeon. Burnett turned to Jellicoe; eyebrow raised. A question hung in the air, or perhaps an order.

'I'll take statements from the staff, sir,' said Jellicoe.

Burnett made a show of rolling his eyes causing Taylor to chuckle.

'Looks like you're not needed here, Reg,' said Taylor.

The four men paused for a moment and looked at one another. There was one thought on each of their minds. The elephant in the room was not lying at their feet. Finally, Burnett asked the question on all their minds.

'There's no sign of the boy, I take it?'

'No, sir,' replied Yates.

'How old is he?' asked Burnett although he knew the answer already.

'Sixteen, sir.'

Burnett nodded and turned to Jellicoe.

'So, Jellicoe, do we think he is a murderer or…?'

Jellicoe glanced down at the bashed in head of the colonel. The case was barely an hour old and his new boss was publicly putting him on the spot. The new boy from London. From Scotland Yard, no less. Jellicoe could see the look in Burnett's eyes. It was somewhere between curiosity and envy. Curiosity because of his background; he was born to be a policeman. Envy because of his background and, perhaps, youth.

Let's see what you're made of sonny boy.

Jellicoe's mouth shaped into a half-smile; the gauntlet was accepted.

'Kidnapped. The boy's been kidnapped.'

Printed in Great Britain
by Amazon

71660084R00184